Lies AND Deception

BOOK FOUR OF THE SYDNEY LEGAL SERIES

CHRIS TAYLOR

LCT Productions Pty Ltd
18364 Kamilaroi Highway, Narrabri NSW 2390

ISBN. 978-1-925119-52-7 (Paperback)

Lies and Deception is a work of fiction. Names, characters, places, brands, media and incidents either are the product of the author's imagination or are used fictitiously. Any resemblance to actual persons, living or dead, events, or locales, is entirely coincidental.

Published in the United States of America.

BOOKS BY CHRIS TAYLOR

THE MUNRO FAMILY SERIES
(In order)

The Profiler
The Investigator
The Predator
The Betrayal
The Deception
The Negotiator
The Christmas Vigil
The Ransom
The Defendant
The Shooting
The Maker
(Available in Audio)

THE SYDNEY HARBOUR HOSPITAL SERIES
(in order)

The Perfect Husband
The Body Thief
The Baby Snatchers
The Final Bullet
The Debt Collector
The Lab Test
The Stolen Identity
The Cliff-top Killer
The Likeable Fraudster

THE SYDNEY LEGAL SERIES
(in order)

An Accidental Murderer
At the Hand of Her Father
A Woman Scorned
Lies and Deception
Ordinary Evil
The Ties That Bind
The Perfect Crime
Malicious Love
Toxic Inheritance

THE BARRINGTON FAMILY SERIES
(in order)

Broken Lives
Broken Promises
Broken Bonds
Broken Spirits
Broken Vows
Broken Minds
Broken Dreams
Broken Hearts
Broken Homes

THE CRAIGDON FAMILY SERIES
(in order)

Callum
Joel
Isabella
Nicholas
Sophia
Flynn
Noah
Logan
Elizabeth

Get a FREE book when you sign up for Chris Taylor's
newsletter at: www.christaylorauthor.com.au

Love Audiobooks? Check out Chris Taylor Books on audio
on Audible.com, Amazon.com and the iBooks store.

Join Chris Taylor's Facebook reader group/fan page and be
among the first to receive news of book releases, read and
review books prior to release and other amazing offers. Join
Now at: www.facebook.com/groups/1758023621144744/

Find out more about all of Chris Taylor's books, by visiting her
website at: www.christaylorauthor.com.au/about/books

DEDICATION

This book is dedicated to my children:
Angus, Imogen, Rory, Millie and Madeleine

And as always, to my very own sexy hero: my husband, Linden.
I love you to the moon and back.

Acknowledgments

As usual, no book comes into being without a lot of help and support by my friends and family. A world of thanks must go to my wonderful editor, Pat Thomas. Thank you for everything that you do to make my stories even more amazing than I could ever dare to dream. To former Detective Superintendent Michael Kilfoyle, thank you for lending my story credibility. Any mistakes are wholly my own.

To Damon Freeman, Alisha Moore and all of the staff at damonza.com, thank you for yet another fantastic cover. To my sister, Nicole Guihot and to my friend, Ally Thomson, thank you for your excellent editorial comments, proof reading skills and suggestions. I hope you like the final result.

To Amy Atwell and her dedicated staff at Author E.M.S. who are so much more than book formatters. Amy, once again, thank you for your magic.

To the fantastic writer organizations such as Romance Writers of Australia, Romance Writers of

America and Romance Writers of New Zealand for all the help, support and encouragement they offer new and aspiring writers, including me.

To my readers, thank you for your support and love for my stories. Your encouragement and enjoyment make this journey all worthwhile.

And lastly, to my friends and family, especially my husband and children. Thank you for putting up with late dinners and even later conversations as I've emerged day after day from the sometimes scary but always enthralling world I've created on my computer.

CHAPTER 1

Colby Shearer picked up his scotch glass and drew it to his lips. Ice clinked as he took a sip, relishing the slow warm burn as the whisky glided down his throat. He settled against the back of the steel-and-rattan bar stool and surveyed the wedding guests who filled the pool area of the glitzy Fijian resort.

The wedding was almost over. Most of the guests had partied into the night and were now a little worse for wear. With his bow tie loosened and his hair askew, he included himself in that assessment. His little sister, Katie, gorgeous in her white satin dress, had danced what could be loosely described as the bridal waltz with her new husband. A small wooden platform had been set up in front of the band for that purpose. The musicians had been part of the wedding package supplied by the hotel and had been playing soft, slow love songs most of the evening, interspersed with the occasional hit of rock.

It had been a nice ceremony, as far as

weddings went. At weddings past, Colby hadn't bothered to take much notice of all the details, but this was Katie's special day and he could only guess how much time and effort and organization had gone into the event, right down to the thick round candles that smelled like vanilla and spice and the delicate frangipani decorations that graced the white linen-clad tables.

So what was he doing sitting all alone at the bar, feeling introspective and morose and downing his third scotch? He should be out on the dance floor—what there was of it—kicking up his heels with one of the bridesmaids. The three girls had been friends with his sister since kindergarten. He knew them almost as well as he knew Katie. And therein lay the problem.

All three of them were smart, funny and attractive, but he looked upon them as he did his sister. The thought of getting romantic with one of them just seemed plain wrong. It was too bad. At thirty-three, he was feeling the need to settle down. He guessed it had something to do with the fact he was at a wedding. Such events seemed to highlight the fact he was still single and all those gooey words of love and the look of adoration on the happy couple's faces made him yearn to have that for himself.

What would it feel like to be so in love with someone that you couldn't imagine wanting to spend a second of time apart? On days like this, he wished he knew.

"Colby! What are you doing over here all by yourself?"

He turned slightly on his stool and offered his mother a lopsided grin. "Feeling sorry for myself?"

She *tut tutted* and pulled up the stool beside him. "What are you talking about? Surely you're not unhappy about Katie and Jason? I've never met a couple more in love."

He hurried to assure her. "Of course not. I think they're great together."

She tilted her head and looked at him. "Then what?"

Colby sighed and emptied the contents of his glass. The bartender materialized and asked if he wanted another. He shrugged. *Why not?*

"Would you like a drink, Mom?"

"No, I'm fine, thanks. I've already had two glasses of champagne." She giggled and he grinned. His mother had never been a drinker.

The bartender collected his empty glass and set a fresh drink in front of him. Colby murmured his thanks and handed over a few bills. The bartender moved away.

"Talk to me, Colby," she said softly. "Tell me what's wrong. It's your sister's wedding. You should be celebrating, not sitting here alone looking all forlorn."

He lifted his glass and sipped at his drink. "I *am* celebrating, Mom."

She shook her head and rolled her eyes. His grin widened. She held his gaze, her dark brown eyes, the exact same shade as his, remained serious. He looked down at his drink and cleared his throat.

"I'm happy for Katie and Jason. I really am. It's

just the whole wedding thing. Sometimes it gets me down."

"How come?"

"I'm thirty-three, Mom. I'm not exactly young. I want to get married, have a family. What if I never meet the right girl?"

"Colby Albert Shearer! Stop talking such nonsense! You're sweet and kind and sinfully good looking. You have a great job, a nice apartment. What are you talking about! Any girl would fall over herself in order to call you hers."

"Thanks for the pep talk, Mom, but it's not necessary. My self-esteem's still intact. I'm not feeling unloved, just... I want to love and *be* loved. I want to know what it's like to be so totally in love that there will never be anyone else. Like Katie and Jason. I want to have a girl look at me the same way Katie looks at Jason and I want to feel the same way."

He stopped, a little embarrassed by his revelations. He'd had way too much to drink. He ought to stop talking right now, kiss his mother goodnight and retire to his room before he said anything more. Intent on putting that thought into action, he set his glass down on the bar and pushed back his stool. His mother's hand on his arm stilled him.

"I understand, Colby, truly I do. But you don't need to worry. You're going to make someone a fine husband and father one day. I know it."

He grimaced. "You have to say that. You're my mom."

She looked affronted. "Of course I'm not just

saying that because I'm your mom! Yes, I might be a little bit biased in your favor, but let me assure you, there are plenty of young female guests who've been watching you all night. Any one of them would welcome an invitation to dance."

She looked toward a table where a group of guests were gathered. At least four of them were young, attractive females who appeared to be unattached. Colby thought about what his mother had said and wondered if he should try a little harder to socialize with them. As if reading his mind, she patted his arm.

"See? All you have to do is go over there and speak with them. Don't you remember the way Katie met Jason? If he hadn't found the courage to ask her out after she discharged him from the emergency department, they'd have never gotten together! Imagine that!"

She laughed and Colby gave her a reluctant grin. He'd heard the story of how Jason had been brought in by ambulance after he'd collided with a teammate on the football field. Katie had been one of the doctors on duty and had attended to him, providing treatment in the form of five stitches across is forehead. The two of them had hit it off right away and as he was leaving, he asked for her number. The rest was history.

He had to admit, it was a nice story and now, a year down the track, the two of them had made it permanent. He was glad the breakdown of their parents' marriage hadn't put him or his sister off matrimony. Katie looked deliriously happy with her new husband and Colby still believed in forever love. With that thought in mind, he smiled with tenderness at his mother.

"Okay, Mom! You win! I'll make an effort to speak to at least one of them. There. Are you happy?"

She leaned over and pecked Colby on the cheek. "That's my boy! Just because things didn't work out between me and your father doesn't mean they won't work out for you. Now, head over there to that table. I'm sure you won't be disappointed. I look forward to meeting her!"

She gave him a cheeky grin and he shook his head and smiled. "Mom, you're incorrigible."

"Have a good night, Colby," she replied unrepentantly. She turned away and disappeared into the crowd.

Colby finished his drink and then stood and left the bar. The tableful of girls beckoned. Before he was completely aware of what he was doing, he was making his way toward them through the crowd of wedding guests. He took a step forward just as one of the women pushed back her chair to stand. The chair came into contact with his hip and he stumbled, along with the blonde who wobbled precariously on a pair of outrageously tall high heels.

"Oh! Oh! Oh!" she squealed in alarm.

Colby reached out to steady her. Her arms were slim and tanned and toned in her sleeveless black dress. Her skin was warm beneath his hands. She turned and looked at him and his breath caught in his throat.

"I-I'm sorry. Are you all right?" he stammered

and silently cursed the blush that crept up his neck and spread across his cheeks.

The woman laughed, her blue eyes twinkling with good humor. "Of course. I'm fine. And please, *I'm* the one who should be apologizing. I should have looked before I pushed back my chair."

Colby smiled down at her and tried to steady his heartbeat. Her golden hair was swept upwards in a sophisticated style. Gold hoop earrings matched an expensive looking necklace. Her lips were perfect and full and shimmered with glossy pink lipstick. When she smiled, he caught a glimpse of even white teeth. His gaze drifted lower, across the firm tanned skin of her exposed neck, and lower still, to the impressive bust line that strained against the bodice of her dress.

His body hardened in response. He couldn't remember ever seeing a more beautiful woman and wondered if her outer beauty matched the beauty in her heart. All of a sudden, he wanted to find out.

Releasing her arms, he stepped back and offered her a bow. It was embarrassing and corny and no doubt he looked ridiculous, but for some reason, it felt right.

"Colby Shearer, at your service, ma'am. And you are?"

"Monica," she replied and graciously shook his proffered hand.

Her skin was soft against his. Her nails were long and well-manicured, gleaming with polish that matched the color of her lips. She smiled and his heart skipped another beat.

"It's nice to meet you, Monica. Are you a friend of the bride or the groom?"

"The groom. Jason Georgetown and I work together. I'm his PA."

Colby nodded. "That's why we've never met before. I'm pretty confident I know all of Katie's friends. At least, the ones she invited here."

The woman who'd identified herself as Monica raised a single brow. "So, you're a friend of the bride."

"You could say that. I'm her brother."

Monica smiled in acknowledgement. "Did you have anything to do with the wedding preparations?"

Colby gaped in mock horror. "No way! I managed to stay well clear of anything remotely connected with the event."

She laughed and looked around her. "Well, someone did a great job. It's such a beautiful place. I've never been to Fiji. I can understand why people have their weddings in places like this. The island is absolutely amazing. I've never seen water so clear. It's just like the photos in all those glossy tourist brochures, isn't it?"

Colby grinned, delighted by her enthusiasm and lack of artifice. And then she blushed and he was absolutely certain he was in love.

"I-I'm sorry," she stammered, averting her gaze. "I sound like a wide-eyed school girl. You must think me terribly unsophisticated."

He shook his head. "To the contrary. I find you refreshingly honest." His gaze roved over her from head to toe. He took his time, liking everything he saw. "And very, *very* sophisticated."

Her blush deepened and he was even more intrigued. She looked like a million dollars and yet she blushed like a young woman who felt awkward and uncertain in her skin. A rush of curiosity went through him. *Who was this woman who worked with his new brother-in-law?* He very much wanted to find out.

"Would you like to dance?" he asked.

Her eyes widened in surprise, but to his relief, she nodded. "Yes. That would be lovely."

"Great."

After sliding her chair back beneath the table, he took her hand and led her to the makeshift dance floor. The tiny square of faux wood flooring was already occupied by two other couples. Colby moved them into the only space available and took her in his arms.

She danced well.

The thought was only one of about a million others that flooded through his mind. She was tall for a woman, but she still fit snugly beneath his chin. His hand rested on the small of her back, pulling her close but not too close. He didn't want to scare her off. The band was playing another slow love song and it was just as well. Anything faster and his scotch-soaked brain might not have been able to keep up.

He closed his eyes and enjoyed the feel of the beautiful woman in his arms. The music flowed over them. A gentle breeze lifted his hair and brought with it the tang of salt and the sweet scent of frangipani. The pleasant smells mingled with the scent of her perfume that wafted toward him every now and then.

"So, the bride's your sister? Katie often drops into Jason's office. She's a lovely girl."

He opened his eyes and blinked her back into focus. "Yes. She takes after her older brother."

She smiled. "I didn't notice you at the head table."

"Well, there wasn't really a head table. My parents are divorced and both of them remarried years ago. Mom and Dad are civil toward one another, but apparently there haven't been enough years pass yet for them to share a table at their daughter's wedding. Katie and Jason and their attendants sat at one table and Mom and Dad each hosted a table of their own. I sat over there, with my brother, Eamon, and a group of our friends."

She looked in the direction he pointed and nodded. "I heard you laughing through the speeches. You sounded like you were having fun. Are you and your brother married?"

"Nope. Katie's the youngest and the first one down the aisle. Go figure."

She looked up at him from beneath impossibly long lashes. "Where do you fit in?"

"I'm the oldest. Eamon is three years younger. Katie's another four years younger than that."

"Ouch." She laughed. "I bet you've been getting sidelong looks from the elderly relatives all evening. They'll be wondering what's going on with you and when it will be your turn."

Colby grinned. "Oh, yes, don't worry, Eamon and I have already had an earful from old Aunty

Mavis and I was tied up with Aunty Nellie for more than an hour while she quizzed me about why I wasn't married. It almost made me wish I'd brought along a pretend fiancé, maybe even a couple of kids. At least I would have warded off the well-intentioned but nevertheless irritating lectures from my relatives about being on the shelf."

She laughed again and the musical sound of it sent ripples of desire shivering along his veins.

"Do you *want* to get married?" she asked lightly.

He stared down at her and all of a sudden, people, the music, the whole damn island disappeared. It was just the two of them: him and Monica.

"Of course I do," he answered softly. "But I was old enough when my parents' marriage fell apart to realize it isn't something I want to rush into. I don't intend to become another statistic, like them. I want to make sure that the woman I choose is prepared to be in it for the long haul. She'll be my partner for life."

"What about kids?" she asked and her voice was a little breathless.

"Kids are great. I love kids. Two, three, four. The more, the merrier."

The woman gazed at him, her eyes a deep cobalt. A soft, sexy smile played around her lips. "You sound like every woman's dream man. Are you *sure* you're still single?"

Monica Radford stared at the man whose hand was still pressed firmly against the small of her back and wondered if he would answer. She'd posed the question teasingly, but waited on tenterhooks for his reply. From their earlier conversation, she guessed that he probably was, but she didn't know for sure and one thing was certain: She needed to be sure.

After all, she might be desperate for a baby and to find the man who could make that dream come true, but she drew the line at married men or men involved in serious relationships. She hoped Colby Shearer was neither.

He'd attracted her from the moment she'd set eyes on him and that initial attraction hadn't waned while they'd been dancing. He was tall and dark and handsome—very dark and handsome. His hair was midnight black and his eyes were a shade of brown that could only be described as dark chocolate. He was smart and pleasant and polite and it was obvious he was part of a caring family.

His parents might be divorced, but they'd both seen fit to attend the wedding and support their only daughter, albeit from separate tables. She'd seen the identical expressions of love and pride on their faces as they'd walked Katie down the aisle and the way the bride talked and laughed as she danced with her father. Divorce or not, this was a family that was close and who cared about each other—an important attribute in the father of her yet-to-be-born child, although not an essential one. If she had her way, the father of her baby would never be part of the baby's life—or even know about it, for that matter.

Oblivious to her thoughts, Colby's arm tightened around her and he pulled her up close until her breasts were crushed against his chest. He bent his head and his lips grazed the soft skin of her ear. "Let me assure you, I am *very* much single."

His voice was a low and husky drawl that sent heat flooding to her core. His hand moved from the small of her back to her ass and curved around her butt cheek. He pressed her forward and her belly brushed against the unmistakable feel of his erection.

She swallowed a gasp of excitement and desire rushed through her veins. Her nipples tightened from the delicious friction caused by his tuxedo jacket. She ought to be shocked at his forwardness, at the unspoken invitation in his eyes. But the truth was, he was the epitome of what she'd been searching for and she couldn't believe her dreams of having a baby had just taken a huge leap forward.

"I'm glad to hear it," she replied. Her voice was soft and breathy, foreign to her ears. Her pulse beat a fast tempo in the side of her neck.

He spun her around and then dipped her low. She gasped in surprise and clung to him. His strong arms held her easily and then he drew her back up. She draped her arms around his neck and laughed at the sheer fun of it. If she were ever looking for a husband, Colby Shearer would be at the top of the list. But she wasn't in the market for a life partner. No, a baby was all she needed. And he was the best darn baby daddy she'd found.

CHAPTER 2

Colby slid his keycard into the slot on the hotel room door and waited for the beep. Turning the handle, he pushed the door open with his shoulder, all the time maintaining contact with the woman he'd met downstairs. *Monica.* His arm was around her shoulder and hers was around his waist. They'd shared their first kiss in the elevator. It had blown his mind.

He couldn't believe he'd asked her up to his room. They'd met barely sixty minutes earlier. But there was something about her that he couldn't resist—or rather, many somethings. There were the long tanned legs that went on forever, the cloud of golden blond hair. The wide blue eyes, the perfect lips. He wanted to touch the bountiful breasts that almost spilled out of her dress.

He was rock hard and aching. He burned with need and anticipation. When she'd agreed to his suggestion she might like to join him upstairs, he'd almost thrown back his head and roared with excitement. The scotch had left him feeling warm and fuzzy, but he had no fear it would impede his performance. He prided himself on his skills in the bedroom. He couldn't wait to taste, to lick, to touch.

The door closed behind them and she came into his arms like she'd been born there. He cupped her ass in his hands and pressed her close. She draped her arms around his neck. His head came down and her lips parted in silent invitation. She tasted as good as she looked.

He groaned as the kiss deepened. Tongues ventured out and tangled in wild need. Releasing her, he reached behind her and fumbled with the knot of fabric that was tied around her neck. At last, he got it free and the front of her dress fell forward. The golden glow from the lamp he'd left on beside the nightstand, illuminated her skin. She wore a strapless lacy black bra. He glimpsed part of one pale pink nipple.

Without conscious thought, his hands went out and he cupped her luscious breasts and squeezed. They filled his hands to overflowing. His cock strained against his pants.

"You're so beautiful," he breathed, his voice husky with need. She merely stood in silence and let him look his fill.

Unable to help himself, he pushed her dress down further and was pleased when she stepped away and shimmied out of it altogether. The black lace bra was matched with equally sexy panties. Within moments, she stood naked except for her underwear.

Another rush of desire surged through him and

he shucked off his jacket and loosened his bow tie. He fumbled with the tiny buttons on his pleated shirt and cursed when they resisted his efforts. Finally, he got them free. The shirt went the same way as his tie and jacket. His pants quickly followed. At last, he was also naked, but for his silk Homer Simpson boxers.

Her eyes widened in surprise at the sight of them and her lips curved upwards in delight. "Homer Simpson? Really?"

"Hey! What's wrong with Homer Simpson?"

She laughed. "There's nothing wrong with Homer Simpson. I'm one of his biggest fans."

"Then we have more in common than we realized," he replied and drew her hard against him.

Once again, their lips met and opened in a rush of need. His hands stroked her back, her hips, the sweet curve of her ass. His cock throbbed almost painfully, but he wanted her to set the pace. Thankfully, she appeared to be every bit as eager as he was for their coupling and when she pulled away and took his hand and led him to the bed, he almost sighed in relief.

They sank down together on the soft mattress and immediately resumed their kiss. She tasted of wine and chocolate. He smiled inwardly. She must have indulged in his sister's wedding cake. Katie had turned her nose up at the traditional fruit and marzipan concoction and had insisted on a chocolate mud cake with lashings of chocolate frosting. He could taste remnants of it on Monica's lips. She tasted delicious.

Finding the clasp of her bra, he released the hooks and tugged gently at the fabric. Her breasts sprang free and he sighed in wonder. They were even larger than he imagined. He buried his face between their softness and couldn't hold back a groan. There were some men who were intimidated by large breasts. He sure as hell wasn't one of them.

He kneaded them, squeezed them, flicked his tongue across her nipples. He licked them, sucked them, loved them. He couldn't get enough.

"*Mm*, that feels good," she murmured and he thought he might explode.

He moved lower and kissed his way down her sternum, paused at her belly button and then buried his face between her legs. Breathing in her unique scent, he pressed his hand against her mound. Not satisfied with feeling her through the black lace, he tugged at her panties. She lifted her hips to assist him and he slid the underwear down. She kicked them off and he returned to his position between her legs. As much as he wanted to linger, this was going to be quick.

He licked her soft folds up and down and tasted her musky need. Dipping his tongue inside her, he relished the small sounds of her excitement. Her breathing had quickened, her hands had tightened into fists. Her eyes were closed and her head moved slowly from side to side.

"Please, Colby. I need you."

And he needed her. Though his scotch-soaked brain was a little slow to react, his body suffered no such limitations. His cock was painfully erect.

He came up on his knees and her legs fell open, encouraging his approach. And then, as if from a distance away, he thought about protection.

"Shit," he cursed.

In the dimness, he saw her frown. "What is it?"

"I don't have a condom."

She struggled to a sitting position and smiled. "Then I guess it's lucky I do."

Monica swung her legs over the side of the bed and hunted for her abandoned purse. Her fingers closed around the foil packets she'd tossed in their earlier on the off-chance she might have the opportunity to use them. She pulled one out and then paused, remembering how she'd sabotaged them with pin pricks in her first deliberate attempt to increase her chances of getting pregnant.

She was beset with a sudden attack of conscience. Colby Shearer was a good man who looked forward to marriage and kids. She had no intention of playing happy families with anyone. *Was it fair to deceive him? And was it possible to steal something he was freely willing to give?* Then again, he thought the condom would protect him. He wasn't offering to father her a child. Not only would she be a liar, she'd also be a thief. The thought troubled her.

"Monica? Did you find one?"

Colby's husky question intruded on her sober thoughts. *What should she do?* She was desperate for a baby, but was this the way to do it? What would he think if he found out? She was almost certain he'd be furious, and quite rightly so. She would be deceiving him, plain and simple and that wasn't who she was. Decision made, she dropped the condom back into her purse and turned back to him with a shrug.

"I'm sorry, I thought I had one. It turns out I don't."

Colby groaned and ran his hands through his hair. His breath came hard. Monica understood his frustration. She'd been looking forward to it as much as he and not just because she'd instantly recognized him as father material. The time they'd spent together on the dance floor and afterwards, at the bar, she'd gotten to know him as a person and what she saw, she liked. It was the reason she'd suddenly had an attack of conscience. He was much too nice a guy to deceive in that way. In fact, the more she thought about it, the more she couldn't believe she'd given it any consideration at all.

"Come here."

His quiet order penetrated her thoughts and her heart skipped a beat. The look of need in his eyes sent adrenaline rushing through her. She dropped her purse and climbed onto the bed. He pulled her up beside him, his gaze intent on hers.

"I want you," he said.

Excitement accelerated her heartbeat. Her lips parted on a sharp intake of breath. She stared down at him.

"W-what are you saying?" she stammered.

His gaze remained glued to hers. In silence, he reached up and traced the shape of her mouth. The pad of his thumb scraped over her bottom lip and with infinite slowness and moved lower, down the column of her throat. When he reached her sternum, his hand cupped the fullness of her breast. Her nipple instantly hardened. Her heart took off at a gallop.

"I'm saying, I'm clean and disease free and I'm trusting you're the same. I'm up for this if you are."

His words sent a rush of need pulsing straight to her core. She burned for his touch, for the feel of him long and thick and hard inside her. As if reading her thoughts, he pressed his cock against her entrance. It was all she could do to hold back a moan.

"What about the risk of pregnancy?" she managed.

"It's a one-off. What are the odds? Besides, I'll pull out before I come."

She nodded, satisfied. A tiny bubble of hope rose within her. Perhaps she'd be blessed with her much-longed-for baby, after all? She smiled and reached for him...

Colby shuddered at the feel of Monica's soft hands on his heated flesh. She circled his cock and squeezed. At the same time, she pressed her breasts against him. He reached down between them and stroked her slick flesh and blood surged hot and hard inside him. It was madness taking her without the protection of a condom, but he was drunk enough not to care. Besides, he was so turned on, he had to have her or he'd explode. It was now or never.

Forcing any doubt away, he gently removed her hand. Any more of that and he'd disgrace himself and that was one thing he had no intention of doing this night. For whatever reason, this angel had stumbled into his path. Who knew if she was looking for forever? He intended to spend whatever time he could with her. He hoped like hell she was staying on the island for a few more days...

Easing her backwards, he positioned himself between her legs. His cock probed her entrance and with a single thrust of his hips, he pushed all the way inside. She was warm and moist and wonderful. She felt like heaven on earth. A couple of hours earlier, they were strangers. Now he wanted her for all time.

The force of his feelings took him aback, but then she tightened her legs around his hips and her arms clung to his shoulders. He stroked in and out and held on to his control, despite the urgings of his body. She groaned in ecstasy and called his name and all of a sudden he was lost. Faster and harder, he pounded into her. Together, they reached for the stars.

It didn't last anywhere near as long as he wanted it to, but it was magical just the same. She cried out her release moments before he found his. Just in time he remembered his promise to withdraw. He pulled out and spurted jets of warm fluid all over her belly.

Drawing her close, he relaxed against her and promptly fell asleep.

———

Monica spooned against Colby's body and did her best to get her heart rate back under control. His arm was slung comfortably over her side, his fingers splayed against her ribs. When she'd set out on her plan to find a baby father, she had no idea it would feel so good.

From the moment they kissed in the elevator, she'd struggled to keep her hands off him. She'd burned with a need so great, it was like she'd die if she didn't have him. His tux only emphasized the fact he was tall and broad and muscular—and naked, he hadn't disappointed.

She'd run her hands over the taut hard planes of his stomach and the well-defined pecs. The scattering of dark hair across his chest had intrigued her as she'd flicked her tongue across his nipples and even though he'd pulled out like he'd promised, he'd waited for her to climax first. It was a generous act from a man she not only liked, but respected.

It was weird. She hardly knew the man who now lay curled up against her side and yet, it felt like she'd known him forever. Once again, she felt a stab of regret that her future didn't include a husband.

No, there wasn't any room for a husband in her neat and ordered life. She liked the independence that came from being single, having no one to answer to, no one to pretend to care for. She knew all about divorced parents and hers had been a hell of a lot nastier than the situation Colby had described.

No. She didn't need a husband, and her unborn child didn't need a dad. After all, *she'd* grown up without one. The last time she'd seen her father, she was three and she'd grown up okay, hadn't she?

She'd graduated from college with honors and had secured a good job that she enjoyed. She owned a condo in a nice suburb and was financially secure enough that she could give a child all that it might need. And the bottom line was, she was thirty-two. The alarm on her biological clock was clanging. Time was running out. There was no way she wanted to risk losing her ability to be a mother. It was the most important thing she could do.

Thirty-two wasn't ancient, but it wasn't young, either. Health risks to both mother and baby increased exponentially when one skipped over the other side of thirty-six and that was a mere four years away. Besides, she didn't want to be an old mom. As much as she loved her own mother, she could still remember how embarrassed she was whenever her mom visited at her school. Audrey Radford was a striking woman with a cloud of beautiful hair, but she'd gone gray way before her friends' moms and Monica had wanted to run and hide rather than admit to her young friends that the woman with the gray hair was her mother.

It was immature and silly, but that's the way she'd felt and she didn't want her child embarrassed either, by a mom who was older than most of the mothers of the kids who shared the classroom. She only hoped that what Colby and she had just done together had resulted in the baby she yearned for. Otherwise, she was back to square one.

CHAPTER 3

Two months later

"Police! Open up!"

Tommy Radford came awake with a start and squinted through the dark. His eyes felt like they were glued together with sandpaper. He wasn't sure what time he'd finally fallen asleep on the couch, but it had been way past late. The banging on the front door came again and the shouting voices suddenly registered.

"Police! Open up!"

He frowned in bewilderment and the faintest feeling of dread stirred in his gut. Blinking hard, he stared at the clock above the mantelpiece. It was barely six o'clock. An urgent visit from the police at that hour couldn't signal anything good. His thoughts went straight to his younger sister and he sent a silent prayer heavenward that everything was all right.

Stumbling out of the den, he made his way down the hall and across the foyer, the marble tiles cold under his bare feet. He shivered as he opened the door. Two uniformed police officers stood on the stoop. One held a flashlight in Tommy's face.

"Mr Thomas Radford?"

He held up his hand to shade his eyes from the glare of the light. "Yes?"

"Mr Radford, I'm Detective James Shepherd."

Tommy turned at the voice that came out of the darkness and noticed two more men standing at the bottom of the steps. Both of them wore suits. The one who'd spoken came up the stairs, his expression somber.

"Detective Shepherd," Tommy acknowledged. "What can I do for you?"

The detective indicated the other suit. "This is my partner, Detective Joel Craigdon. We'd like to ask you a few questions about Sara Nakamura."

Tommy's heart skipped a beat and his chest tightened with fear. Dear God, not Sara...

"W-what would you like to know?"

"She was found murdered in her apartment an hour ago. We understand she was a student of yours," Shepherd said.

A roar filled Tommy's ears until it blocked out most of the detective's words. He stared at the men in horror and disbelief.

"No, no, it can't be! You must be mistaken. Not Sara. It can't be Sara!" As if from a distance, he heard the panic in his voice and did his best to try and contain it, but despite his efforts, the enormity of what had happened hit him and he doubled over with a gasp.

"Mr Radford? Are you all right?"

Tommy heard the detective's concerned question, but was beyond responding. Sara was dead. Murdered. No, it couldn't be. Not Sara, not his beautiful Sara...

"What the hell is going on here, officers?"

At the sound of his wife's strident tones, Tommy froze. Oh, God. Not here. Not now. He couldn't deal with Pamela now. And not when he'd just learned the woman he loved with all his heart was dead.

By way of reply, Detective Shepherd pulled out his police badge. "I'm Detective Shepherd. This here is Detective Craigdon. Are you Mrs Radford?"

Pamela drew her housecoat around her and stood up tall. Despite the early hour, her hair was brushed into a neat ponytail and she'd taken the time to apply lip gloss. Trust his wife to ensure she looked good at every opportunity, even when the police made an unexpected early morning house call.

"Yes, I'm Pamela Radford. I'm Tommy's wife. What seems to be the matter, Detective?"

"I'm afraid we have some bad news. One of your husband's students has been murdered. We've come to ask him some questions."

Shock and disbelief widened Pamela's eyes and left her mouth gaping. "Why, that's terrible, Detective! Do you have any idea who did it?"

"No, but we'd like to ask your husband some questions."

"Surely you can't think he's involved?" she asked.

The detective's gaze remained steady on hers.

"We don't know anything for certain, yet. We're investigating a homicide, Mrs Radford. We have reason to believe your husband can assist us in our investigation."

Pamela turned her wide-eyed gaze in Tommy's direction. He cringed and looked away from the accusation he saw there.

"Tommy? What are they talking about?" she demanded, her voice strident.

"I'm not sure, Pamela. Don't worry about it. I had nothing to do with anyone's murder."

She smiled sweetly, her face flooding with relief. "Of course you didn't." She turned the smile on the detective. "See, Detective? Tommy knows nothing about this girl's unfortunate death. I suggest you take your enquires elsewhere."

To Tommy's consternation, the detective's gaze hardened. "I'm sorry, Mrs Radford. There's no easy way to tell you this. We have reason to believe Sara Nakamura was having an affair with your husband. Because of this connection, he is very much at the forefront of our enquires."

Pamela gasped and turned to Tommy. He could hardly bear to look at her, even though the detective's announcement couldn't have come as a surprise. "Pam, I'm sorry…"

"We'd like you to accompany us down to the station," Detective Shepherd said, ignoring the exchange.

The second detective stepped forward, a piece of paper in his hand. "In the meantime, we have a warrant to search the premises." He thrust the paper in Tommy's hand.

Feeling like his world was caving in, Tommy slowly sank to his knees. With his head in his hands, he cried out his shock and his pain...

Another surge of hot, sour vomit filled Monica's mouth and spewed out into the toilet bowl. Down on her knees, she clung to the sides of the cold porcelain and prayed for the bout of morning sickness to be over. She was eight weeks into her pregnancy. All the books she'd read told her that for most women, the nausea and vomiting was more common during the first trimester. Another four more weeks of hell, and that's if they were right. Occasionally, it went for longer.

She wondered fleetingly if she would have been so eager to have a baby if she'd known how awful the morning sickness would be. In fact, to call it morning sickness was totally misleading. She felt ill *all* the time. But despite the agony, she realized the answer was still yes. She wanted this baby more than she wanted anything and if it meant she had to empty her stomach contents into the toilet bowl morning, noon and night then she would do it.

With the latest bout of retching over, she staggered to her feet and wiped her mouth. Flushing away the evidence of her distress, she opened the stall and went over to the sink. She was startled to discover she wasn't alone.

Her best friend and work colleague, Natalie

Johnson, stood with her back to the sink, her arms folded across her chest, her eyes filled with accusation. Her lips were taut and there was a no-nonsense look on her face.

"Is there something you want to tell me?"

Monica swallowed a sigh. She'd known she'd have to tell people at some stage. She could hardly go through an entire pregnancy working in a busy office without someone noticing, and in particular, her best friend. Natalie had been preoccupied lately with the murder trial of her ex-husband and finding love with his lawyer, but she was still her friend and would definitely want to share in Monica's news.

Still, she would have preferred to wait until after she was through the first trimester. She'd read a ton of books on the subject. Too much could still go wrong. Buying time, she turned on the faucet and bent over the sink. She rinsed her mouth, she reached for some paper towel and patted her face dry before replying.

"What makes you think I have anything to tell you?"

Natalie's gaze narrowed and she shot Monica a warning look. "Really? I've just caught you hanging over the toilet bowl for the third time this week and you're going to pretend there's nothing going on?"

Her friend's tone was filled with exasperation. Natalie stared at her, as if willing her to speak the words she expected to hear. Monica bit her lip in indecision and then sighed. *What did it matter if Natalie knew?* She was her best friend. If she miscarried, Natalie would probably be the only person she told. With her mind made up, she nodded.

"You're right. I'm pregnant."

Natalie smiled. "I guessed as much. It sounded like you were tossing the entire contents of your stomach into the toilet bowl two times over. You either ate some really bad Chinese three nights in a row, or...?"

"Yes. I was going to tell you, but I wanted to wait, at least until after the first trimester. You know how things often go wrong during those first twelve weeks."

Natalie nodded in understanding. "Of course. I made the same decision with my three. How far along are you?"

"Eight weeks."

Natalie's eyes widened in surprise. "Eight weeks?"

"Yes. I... I wanted to tell you. I just didn't know how."

Her friend laughed and shook her head. "What are you talking about? Why wouldn't you know how to tell me? I didn't even know you'd met someone! My goodness! I've been such a terrible friend, lately. What with the trial and Blake and...everything."

"You've had a lot going on," Monica agreed.

"Still, it's no excuse. I can't believe you've met someone and now you're having a baby! That's amazing!" Natalie smiled and Monica forced herself to respond in kind.

"Yes, it is, isn't it?"

She rested a protective hand against her stomach. She liked to think there was the slightest rounding of her belly, but she was probably imagining it. When she looked at herself side on naked in the bathroom mirror, her belly looked as flat and toned as it usually did. She still found it hard to believe her much-longed-for child nestled within.

"Well…congratulations!" Natalie offered belatedly and engulfed Monica in a hug. "So, who's the lucky guy?"

Monica pulled slowly away and busied herself hunting for her lipstick in her handbag.

"Um, you don't know him."

"Okay, so what's his name?"

"Um… It's Colby."

"Colby. That's a nice name. When do I get to meet him?"

A blush crept up Monica's neck and spread across her cheeks. "It's… It's complicated."

Natalie frowned. "What do you mean?"

"I mean… We met in Fiji. It was a holiday fling. We're…not together."

"Oh, honey! Please don't tell me he's married."

"No, nothing like that. We just decided… Listen, we had a magical five days together on a tropical island, but all good things come to an end. Life isn't a fairytale and I'm totally fine with that. I wasn't looking for a husband, anyway. A baby is everything I need."

Natalie's eyes widened in shock. "Monica Radford, please don't tell me you deliberately set out to get pregnant?"

She shrugged uncomfortably. "No, not exactly. He asked if I had a condom and I told him no. I had some in my purse, but..."

Natalie frowned. "You lied about not having condoms?"

"Yes."

"Why?"

"Come on, Natalie. Don't judge me! You know how much I've wanted a baby! I love your boys to bits, but at the end of the day, they're yours. I... I wanted a baby of my own. My biological clock's been ticking louder and louder. For a long time now, I've been feeling that my time is almost up. If I didn't do something about having a child soon, it might be too late. I've been tossing up the pros and cons about going it alone for months, and finally the stars aligned and it happened." She smiled softly and held her palm against her belly. "I still can't believe it."

"So you and some stranger decided to go for it without protection and just leave it in the hands of the gods?" Natalie's tone was laden with sarcasm.

Monica blushed, embarrassed. "Yes."

"Very mature. And of course, you were more than happy to take the risk of catching an STD. You had the chance to get pregnant. Nothing else mattered."

"Please, Nat. It wasn't like that. He told me he was clean. I believed him."

Natalie shook her head. "What about him? Is he still in the picture at all?"

"No."

"So he's happy for you to go it alone? I assume

he's at least going to offer financial support."

Monica shook her head. "No, he's not going to have anything to do with the baby."

Natalie gasped in shock. "What are you talking about? What kind of man gets a woman pregnant and then turns his back on her?"

"It wasn't like that, Nat." Once again, embarrassment heated Monica's cheeks. She kept her gaze fixed on the zipper of her handbag as she continued. "He... He doesn't know about the baby."

Natalie's eyes were huge and horrified in her face. "Do you mean to say you haven't *told* him?"

Guilt burned on Monica's cheeks, but she bravely lifted her head and met her friend's gaze. "Yes, that's right."

Okay, she wasn't proud of her actions, but in this case the end justified the means. She was pregnant with the baby she'd wanted for so long and she was prepared to be a single mother. She didn't expect anything from the father other than what he'd already freely given. After all, he'd been the one to suggest they have sex without protection, and even though it had only happened like that the first time and they'd used condoms thereafter, he had to know there had been a chance, albeit a very slight one, that she'd get pregnant. They'd even talked about it and he'd been willing to play the odds. It was his fault as much as hers. She refused to take all the blame.

"So, just so we're clear, this man has no idea you're having his child?" Natalie stated, interrupting Monica's thoughts.

Monica stared at her defiantly. "Right. And that's the way it's going to stay."

Natalie's face filled with disbelief. "Who *are* you? What happened to my beautiful friend who couldn't lie to save her soul? How and when was she replaced by this deceitful stranger?"

Monica lowered her gaze. "I'm sorry you feel that way, Nat. I don't think I've done anything wrong. He knew the risk he was taking. He hasn't once called since that week to ask if I was okay or to check if...you know, if I were pregnant." She paused and then looked at her friend beseechingly. "I was hoping you'd understand."

"Understand? You're pregnant with this man's child. Okay, so he loses points for not being in contact, but Monica, he deserves to know."

"I'm sorry you don't approve." Monica's chest went tight. A tear ran down her cheek. "You have no idea what it's like! You're lucky! You're already a mom! I'm thirty-two without a single prospect in sight! I've wanted a baby for so long...

"Then, Jason invited me to his wedding. It was held in this beautiful resort on a gorgeous tropical island in the Pacific. It was a perfect setting for romance. The day went off without a hitch. Jason looked great in his custom made tux and—"

"I'm glad Jason's wedding day went well, but cut to the chase," Natalie interrupted. "My break's almost up."

Monica picked at a loose thread on the cuff of her silk blouse. "Somewhere along the way, I got the idea of hooking up with a stranger, a wedding guest. Someone who at least was there because they knew the bride or groom, which meant that they weren't just anyone, if you know what I mean."

Natalie was already shaking her head slowly back and forth. "No, Monica. I don't know what you mean. I've never met anyone who sought out a man they didn't even know to father their child."

Monica compressed her lips and accepted the criticism. She'd hoped, but really didn't expect, that Natalie would understand. But after all, Nat was already a mom. She didn't feel the indescribable panic that Monica did at the thought she might never have a child.

She pouted. "Do you want to hear about this, or not?"

Natalie sighed and held up her hands in a sign of surrender. "Okay. I'm sorry. Finish the story. I promise I'll keep my mouth shut."

"Colby was at the wedding. We kind of collided with each other at the reception. He asked me to dance and we got to know each other."

"Right. Did you even swap names before you took him up to your room?" Natalie asked dryly.

Monica narrowed her gaze at her and once again, Nat held up her hands. "Okay, I'm sorry! I'll zip it, all right? Keep talking."

"We got chatting on the dance floor and we went for a drink afterwards. He's a great dancer, by the way. Anyway, he came from a good family and told me he loved kids and... Things just went from there. Not only was he sinfully good looking, smart and funny, he has Italian heritage. His hair is black as midnight and his eyes are almost as dark." She paused for breath and then continued, hoping to make her friend see.

"You of all people know how much I hate being labeled a dumb blonde. It's happened all my life. People take one look at me and assume I have nothing going on up here." She tapped the side of her head and continued. "They judge me purely on my looks and it totally pisses me off. There's nothing I can do about my coloring, short of dyeing my hair black and I can only imagine how that would look with my fair skin, but I can try not to pass it on to my offspring. This guy's so dark, I'm sure his genes will dominate mine—and that's another bonus."

Natalie continued to stare at her, shaking her head slowly from side to side. "Do I even *know* you anymore? You look like the Monica Radford I know and love, but you're talking like a stranger. Let me get this right: Months ago, you decided you wanted to be a single mom. You set out to find a baby daddy, but not just anyone. You wanted someone who had a higher probability of spawning a dark-eyed, dark-haired child. So you handpicked some Italian guy, lied about not having any condoms and had a wild fling with him on a tropical island paradise. Now you've come back pregnant and he doesn't even know about it. Did I leave anything out?"

Monica tried to keep the embarrassment from her face. "No. That's about it."

"What's going to happen when he finds out? You're going to have to tell him eventually."

"Why? Why am I going to have to tell him? I'm hoping I never see him again. In fact, I don't even know where he lives."

"He sleeps with you over the course of a week and you don't even exchange personal details? Did he even give you his number?"

"Yes, of course."

"Did you give him yours?"

Monica was filled with another surge of guilt. She offered a reluctant nod.

"Well, what if he calls you and wants to take up where you left off? What are you going to do if he turns up on your doorstep?"

"It's been almost two months. He won't," she mumbled.

"How do you know? This holiday romance might have meant more to him than you think. What's to stop him from calling you and asking to see you again?"

"I'm telling you, he won't call me."

"How can you be so sure?" Natalie persisted. "Does he live overseas?"

"No, he's Australian. But I know he won't call me because he can't. I gave him a false cell phone number."

Natalie's horrified gasp bounced off the bathroom walls. "*What?*"

Monica shrugged and kept her face averted. "He asked me for my number. Several times. In the end, I gave it to him. Only, it wasn't my number. I just made it up."

"Monica! How *could* you?"

Monica squirmed under the accusation in her

friend's eyes. She already felt bad enough about deceiving Colby about the condoms and for not telling him they'd conceived a child. She didn't need her friend making her feel even worse.

"What else could I do?" she replied defensively. "Whether I was pregnant or not, it was never my intention to take on a husband, or even a boyfriend. Men complicate things. I like being on my own, answering to no one. My life's just fine without a man, regardless of whether there's a child or not."

Natalie shook her head. "But there *will be* a child! How can you still think like that?"

"Hey!" she protested. "It's not like my decision to deceive him was easy! I liked him a lot! We really connected. We had a good time. Just... I want to do this on my own."

"You're having his baby. He has a right to know!"

"Why do you keep saying that? Why does he have a right to know?"

Natalie threw her hands up in the air in disbelief. "Are you even *listening* to yourself?"

Monica made an impatient sound in the back of her throat. "Look, I grew up without a father. The man who contributed the biological material necessary to give me life walked out on his family when I was three. My brother was eight. The only memories I have of my father are those I have collected from the few photos Mom kept for us. I don't know why she bothered. The love between them died long ago and I never had any interest in getting to know him. It was obvious he hadn't wanted to stick around long enough to get to know us."

Natalie's expression softened. "That's awful. You poor thing. I understand how you might have felt as a child, being abandoned like that. But what about later? As you grew up? Didn't you want to get to know him?"

"It was too late. He was killed in a car accident the year I turned thirteen."

"Oh."

The sound of Monica's phone ringing broke the silence. She pulled it out of her handbag. The number was blocked. Natalie made a move to go.

"I'll leave you to take that call. I have to get back to work, anyway. Listen"—she reached out and squeezed Monica's arm—"we'll talk soon, okay?"

"Sure," Monica replied and managed a smile. Natalie exited the restroom and Monica returned her attention to the phone. With a sigh, she answered the incoming call.

"Monica Radford."

"Mon, thank God you picked up!"

Monica frowned at the urgency in her brother's voice. "Tommy? Are you all right? What's going on?"

"No, Mon. I'm not all right. I... I'm calling from the police station downtown. I've been arrested and charged with murder. I need you to post bail."

CHAPTER 4

If Monica's older brother had said he'd woken up that day and decided to become a woman, she couldn't have been more surprised. Her jaw fell open in shock and as the muddled thoughts flew around her brain, she struggled to speak.

"W-what are you talking about? Murder? You can't be serious!"

"I'm afraid I am. Look, the whole thing is ridiculous, but it's true. The police charged me earlier this morning. Bail has been set at fifty thousand. I was hoping you might be able to help me out."

Monica gasped, still in shock. "I don't have that kind of money, Tommy!"

"If it makes things any easier, they don't need to have it in cash. You can put up your condo as collateral. I know it's a lot to ask, little sis, but I really need your help."

"What about *your* assets? Surely you and Pamela could come up with that kind of cash?"

"Yeah, well, it's complicated. Most of our money's tied up in trusts and the share market hasn't been so kind to us lately. At the moment, we don't have access to that kind of cash. Besides, this is only for the duration of the case. Once it's thrown out, the bail conditions are null and void. The only risk you're taking is if I don't show up in court—and we both know that's not going to happen."

Monica shook her head in an effort to clear it of her frantic thoughts. She was still trying to get her head around what he'd told her. *How could her brother have been charged with murder?* It seemed inconceivable and yet, apparently it was true.

She thought of the home she'd made for herself and winced. She'd worked so hard to save the deposit. The thought of losing it filled her with panic. Then there was her baby to think about... But this was her brother. Her only sibling. The one person who always had her back. *How could she say no to him?*

"Okay, I'll do it."

His sigh of relief was audible. "Great! Thanks so much, Mon. You don't know how much I appreciate it. Now, you have to get yourself down to the court house and fill out some paperwork. You'll need to register a copy of your house deed. Can you do it as soon as possible? They won't let me out of here until bail's been posted."

"Sure. I'm at work, but I'll try and get away."

"Thanks, sis. You're the best. I owe you one."

"Don't worry about it. What's family for?" She paused and then added, "Who is it, anyway?"

"What do you mean?"

"The person you're supposed to have murdered. Who is it?"

"Just a girl. No one you know."

She frowned. His voice sounded hollow, like he held something back. He'd been charged with murder. Of course she was curious about the details. "What's her name?"

"Sara Nakamura. What does it matter? I didn't do it. That's all that's important now."

"Of course you didn't. You couldn't hurt a fly. Remember when we were little kids and that mean Bradley Fairfield kept stealing my lunch and I wanted you to beat him up?"

"Yeah, I remember."

"But you couldn't do it, even when I begged you to."

Tommy sighed. "I was never one for fighting, but I got him back for you, didn't I?"

"Yes, you did. Instead of one, you packed two lunches. You filled the one he usually stole with dirt sandwiches disguised in vegemite. He took a huge bite and then his face went all red and he started choking and sputtering and ended up spitting it all out. It was so funny! He never stole my lunch again."

Silence fell between them as they were lost in their memories. Monica was the one to break it. "Did you know her? The girl who died?"

"Yes, she was one of my students. It's very sad."

"Oh, my goodness! How's Pamela taking the news?"

He took a moment to answer. "Not so good."

"Poor thing. I'm sure it came as a shock."

"Yes, and to make matters worse... Pam and I had a fight last night. I stormed out. The police arrested me early this morning. I haven't had a chance to explain anything to her."

"Well, you need to talk to her. She deserves to hear what happened directly from you, before the media get wind of it."

"Yes, you're right. I'll try her after this call."

"She rang me last night, way past late," Monica said quietly. "It was going on for three. She wasn't in a good way. At the time I guessed you two must have argued."

Monica heard him sigh heavily on the other end of the phone. "Yeah."

"What's going on, Tommy?"

He sighed again and took so long to reply she wasn't sure he was going to. "She's unhappy, Mon. She has been for a long time."

"Do you still love her?"

"I think so. It's hard to know. Lately, all we seem to do is fight."

"About what?"

"Everything. Work, money, starting a family."

Monica sighed. She hadn't yet told her brother about the baby. In fact, apart from Natalie, nobody knew.

"Oh, Tommy. If you want this marriage to work, you're going to have to sort this stuff out and fewer late nights working back wouldn't hurt, either."

"What did Pamela tell you?" He sounded wary.

"Nothing," Monica hastened to reassure him. "But she was really upset last night. She said something about you spending so much time with your students, or maybe it was just one student? I'm not sure. She woke me from a deep sleep. I was still trying to work out what she was going on about. She was shouting and crying—something about a baby, but I wasn't sure if I'd heard right. It's so sad that she's still mourning the loss of your child. You should try and get her to see another therapist. I think she'd been drinking. You guys must have had a really bad fight. She told me... She told me she wished you were dead."

Monica suddenly realized what she'd said. The reference to death probably wasn't the best thing to share under the circumstances. Still, she was only repeating what Pamela had told her.

"Did she really say that?" Tommy asked.

"Yes."

"Oh, hell, Mon. I've been such a shit to her. It's true, I've been spending a lot of time at work. I've got my eye on a professorship and I'll never get there if I don't impress the board with my willingness to put in the long hours and go the extra mile. But I'm sorry it's caused Pamela grief. She deserves to be happy. Everyone does."

He sighed. "The truth is, we probably wouldn't have gotten married if it hadn't been for the baby. And then, when she lost it, it seemed like our reason for being together dissolved, too. I'm not sure I can make her happy, sis."

"Oh, Tommy!"

"Yeah, well, it's the truth."

"What about another baby? You could always try again."

"It's not that easy, even if I wanted to. Pamela's left fallopian tube was irreparably damaged from the ectopic pregnancy and the ovary on the right doesn't work properly. Our chances of a natural conception are next to nil."

"What about IVF? Surrogacy?"

He was silent for a moment and then quietly admitted, "I just don't think I care enough about her to go through all that stuff."

"Oh, Tommy, that's so sad!" Monica cried.

"Yeah."

"What are you going to do?"

"I don't know. Right now, I have a murder charge hanging over my head. Pamela will probably run for the hills if things get tough. I guess that will solve one problem."

"Don't joke about this, Tommy!" Monica remonstrated. "I know you couldn't have murdered this girl, but you'll still have to prove it."

"No, Mon. I don't have to prove anything. That's one of the benefits of our criminal justice system. I'm entitled to a presumption of innocence. It's the police who have to prove I did it."

"I don't understand why they charged you! What do they have on you?"

"I don't know. I haven't spoken to my lawyer, yet. He should be on his way down."

"I hope you called someone reputable."

"Of course. Blake Harton Junior. He's the best, right?"

"Yes, he's a good lawyer. I wonder if Natalie knows," she mused.

"Probably not. I only got connected to the guy right before I called you."

"Well, I'm glad he's representing you. Hopefully he'll get this thing thrown out of court before it goes any further."

"Let's hope so."

Monica sighed. "I'll come down to the court house as soon as I can, okay?"

"Okay. And thanks, sis. I mean it."

"Anytime, big brother." She paused and then added, "I love you, Tommy."

"I love you, too."

———

Monica stepped through the automatic doors of the New South Wales Supreme Court and headed toward the registry. She'd stopped by her place and collected a copy of the deeds to her house before making the journey across town. She'd completed a mountain of paperwork, the end result being that she agreed to put her house up as surety for her brother's bail. Then she was done.

"When will he be released?" she asked the clerk behind the counter.

The man scratched at his scruffy salt-and-pepper beard and eyed her balefully over his glasses.

"I'll telephone the jail, let them know his bail's been posted. It depends how busy they are over there, but usually they're released within an hour or two."

Monica nodded in relief, glad Tommy would soon have his liberty restored. He'd been arrested early that morning. It was now going on for noon. Any time in prison was too much time, as far as she was concerned. She was relieved she'd been able to come to his aid.

She'd suffered the slightest hint of nerves as she'd signed on the bottom line, but she ignored the faint disquiet as she committed her home in return for her brother's freedom. Her surety would only be called upon in the event he failed to appear in court and, like he said, there wasn't a chance in hell that was going to happen. She still couldn't believe he'd been charged with murder. He was the most law-abiding citizen she knew. He'd never even had a parking ticket. She was confident he wouldn't skip out on his bail.

With a murmur of thanks to the registry clerk, she shouldered her handbag and headed for the exit. She wished she could call Tommy and let him know he wouldn't have to wait much longer, but she assumed the registry clerk would do his job and notify the jail. It was the best she could do.

Exiting into the midday sunshine, she debated whether or not to return to work. She had a huge pile of things on her "to do" list and she hadn't told Jason the reason she needed to duck out for a while. She'd purposefully remained vague on how long she might be, but she couldn't be gone for hours. Still, things hadn't taken as long as she'd anticipated at the registry. She could probably swing by the jail and offer Tommy a ride home.

With that thought in mind, she headed toward the parking garage.

The gloomy gray brick two-story building that housed the City of Sydney Police Station rose up from the warm asphalt. She climbed the wide steps to the front doors, her high heels clacking on the concrete. A fresh-faced, uniformed officer sporting a military buzz cut stood behind a high counter. His name badge identified him as Constable Burlington. He spied Monica and nodded in greeting.

"Good afternoon, ma'am. How can I help you?"

"Hello. I'm looking for Thomas Radford. He… He's incarcerated." The word sounded so harsh and foreign in her mouth. She forced away a fresh wave of shock.

The constable nodded and tapped away on his keyboard. "Thomas James Radford. Yes, we've been holding him on a charge of murder. He's waiting to post bail."

"I'm his sister. I've just posted bail."

The constable returned his attention to the screen and tapped on the keyboard again. "Yes, you're right. A call has just been logged. Bail's been posted. He's free to go."

Monica managed a shaky smile, filled with relief. "Great. I'm here to take him home."

"Take a seat. I'll call down to the cells and let them know he's good to go."

"Thank you."

The officer picked up the phone near his elbow and spoke quietly into the receiver. A moment later, he hung up the hand piece.

"They're short staffed down there at the moment. A couple of them are on their lunch break. It might be twenty minutes or so before they can bring him up."

Monica tried hard to hide her dismay. It would take at least half an hour to get Tommy to his place and she'd already been gone a few hours. She'd have to call Jason and let him know she'd been caught up. Turning away, she pulled out her phone and dialed her boss' number. The call went through to voicemail and she was guiltily relieved.

"Oh, hi, Jason. It's me. Look, the appointment I mentioned has run overtime. I'm afraid I'll be another hour. I'm really sorry. I'll get back as soon as I can."

She ended the call and tossed the phone into her handbag, grateful once again that she'd managed to avoid his questions. She and Jason had worked together for years and had a healthy respect for one another and though he was her boss, he'd always treated her as an equal. She appreciated that. Still, she never took advantage of their relationship and she wasn't about to do so now.

On the other hand, she had to be there for Tommy. He was her big brother and only sibling and since he and his wife couldn't come up with the surety themselves, Monica was his only option. She had no choice but to wait it out.

With a quiet sigh, she took a seat on one of the hard plastic chairs that lined the back wall of the reception area. Taking her phone out, she opened her mail and scanned the items in her inbox. A door to her left opened and male voices raised in conversation, filled the room. Curious, she looked up at the new arrivals. And froze.

Both men wore tailored suits. One wore navy-blue, the other was in dark gray. Both were tall and broad shouldered. One was blond, the other had hair as black as midnight. He was partially turned away from her and his hair was longer than she remembered, but she'd spent enough time with him that she'd know him anywhere.

Colby Shearer.

Of all the men in Sydney she could have run into... The thought rushed through her mind at the same time she looked around for somewhere to hide. She was seated in the waiting area of the reception room. Other than the constable and Colby and his companion, she was alone. Four walls covered in various crime-related posters and an automatic glass door surrounded her. That was it. There was nowhere to hide, and short of getting to her feet and making a quick exit, no way to disappear.

Quickly averting her gaze, she kept her attention focused fiercely on her phone and prayed silently that the men would pass without noticing her. Unless they approached the counter, it was possible. Unwilling to look in their direction again, she stared unseeingly at her emails and then heard the slide of the automatic doors.

Unable to help herself, she glanced in that direction. Without hesitation, the men continued their conversation, all the way out the door. Neither of them noticed her. When they disappeared down the stairs that led to the street, Monica blew out her breath on a sigh of relief.

Drawing in a lungful of air, she worked to get her heart rate back under control. She pressed a protective hand to her belly and hoped the baby hadn't sensed her alarm. The last thing she wanted was to upset the child growing inside her. She drew in another breath, easing the panic that still lingered in her veins.

Colby Shearer.

She couldn't believe she'd almost run into him. She knew he lived in Sydney, of course and he'd also shared with her the fact that he was a lawyer. She supposed it wasn't too much of a stretch to accept that he'd spend some of his time at police stations, but still, she hadn't considered that possibility when she made the decision to come and collect her brother. In fact, given that they lived in a city of more than two million people, she'd been hopeful they might never run into each other again. She couldn't believe how wrong she'd been.

Still, he hadn't seen her and she was totally grateful for that. When she'd set out to find a baby daddy, she'd never given any thought to how hard it might be to keep the news of the conception from the man who'd made it possible. Prior to meeting Colby, the father of her baby had been a vague male figure in her head—someone to contribute the necessary genetic material and who would then fade away from sight. He didn't have a face or a name or any other significant feature—and she'd been fine with that.

Now that she'd met him and the deed was done, she was alarmed to discover she felt a little differently. Natalie's attitude toward Monica's baby plan had contributed to that. Her friend had made it clear she disapproved of the decision to keep the father in the dark and Monica was filled with another wave of guilt as the unknowing father of her baby walked down the steps of the police station, away from her, oblivious.

"Dammit!" she muttered. This was supposed to be the easy part, keeping her baby secret. She hadn't thought about the moral right or wrong of keeping the news from the baby's father. She just knew that's the way she'd wanted it, the way it was going to be. But now, the baby daddy was real, a real man with a real name and real emotions, with real wants and needs. He was flesh and blood and a moment ago he'd been right there, a few yards away. A word from her and he would have noticed her... And then what would she have done?

There was no way she was going to tell him. It was like she'd told Natalie. She didn't want a man in her life. Not now, not ever. It was selfish and wrong and so much more, but it was the way it was, and would be. Period.

CHAPTER 5

"Monica!" At the sound of her name, Monica looked up and smiled in relief. She stood and walked toward her brother. He wore a rumpled T-shirt and sweatpants and looked like he'd just rolled out of bed. His sandy-colored hair was askew and his cheeks were roughened with a five o'clock shadow. His eyes were red, like he'd been crying. That startled her. He'd always been so brave and strong, the protector.

They'd both been young when their father walked out. Her only memory of a male role model was her brother. Rightly or wrongly, she'd relied on him for everything and so did their mother. He'd borne the extra responsibility without complaint and had never let them down. He'd stood up to schoolyard bullies and to debt collectors who'd come knocking on their door and he'd done it all with a smile.

He'd always been good with words. Most people walked away from him feeling dazed and confused, not sure if they'd gotten the upper hand or if they'd been played. Monica had been surprised when he went into teaching—and economics of all things. It just didn't seem to suit her sensitive, thoughtful brother. Still, he'd made a success of his career and was well on the way to promotion.

Now he looked weary, like the worries of the world weighed him down and he looked much older than his thirty-seven years. It broke her heart to see him looking so sad and forlorn. She couldn't imagine what it had been like to spend time inside a jail cell. To have your liberty taken from you. To be behind bars.

"Tommy! Thank God! How are you? Have they been treating you all right?" She threw her arms around him and hugged him tight.

He returned the hug and then gently set her aside. "I'm fine. Thanks so much for bailing me out—literally—and for hanging around. I owe you big time."

She waved his words away. "Don't be silly. You owe me nothing and it's not like you wouldn't do the same for me. We're family. There's no need to say anything more."

He smiled his gratitude and threw an arm across her shoulders. "Come on, let's get out of here."

Together, they walked through the automatic doors of the City of Sydney Police Station and headed down the steps. A barrage of reporters and cameramen met them on the street. Microphones were shoved in their faces from every direction and questions shouted amidst the din. Monica gasped in surprise. *Where did they come from?*

"Mr Radford, did you murder Sara Nakamura?"

"Mr Radford, she was your student, wasn't she?"

"Mr Radford, were you having an affair with Sara Nakamura?"

"Mr Radford, will you be pleading guilty?"

The questions came thick and fast and the noise was loud and confusing. Monica held her hand up to shield her face from the flash of cameras and Tommy did the same. He pushed his way through the crowd of reporters, with Monica in tow. She clung to his hand and stumbled along behind him as he found a way through the throng.

The questions continued to follow them and a few reporters jogged along beside them, keeping pace. Tommy ignored their increasingly demanding questions. Monica did the same.

"Where did you leave your car?" Tommy shouted.

"In the parking garage on George Street."

Tommy cursed and Monica understood his reaction. They were three blocks away. A cab drew even and Tommy flagged it down. Almost simultaneously, he turned to her. "Got any money?"

She nodded. "Yes, of course."

"Good. Get in."

He opened the door of the cab and bundled her inside before climbing in beside her. He shut the door and turned to the driver. "Take us to the George Street parking garage."

The cabbie nodded and pulled away from the curb. Tommy threw himself back against the seat. Monica sighed quietly in relief.

"Tommy... What just happened out there?" she asked, dazed.

Tommy's lips compressed and his expression grew dark. "Someone tipped off the media. Probably the clerk at the court registry. They got here fast."

She shook her head and suppressed a shudder, remembering the horde of reporters chasing them, intent on getting answers.

"What were they talking about? They asked if you'd had an affair with someone by the name of Sara Nakamura. Isn't that the name of the girl who was killed?"

He stared at her a moment and then looked away. "Yes."

Monica thought about what else had been put to her brother and barely dared to ask him the question. "Was she... Was she your lover?"

She waited for him to issue a swift denial and when it wasn't forthcoming, dread spread its icy tentacles through her belly. "Tommy?"

He remained silent, but a guilty flush crept up his neck and stained his pale cheeks. Her dread morphed into shock and disbelief.

"Tommy? Don't tell me you were sleeping with her!"

He offered her a shrug. Anger rushed through her, flooding her with heat. "You told me she was no one!"

He looked at her, his eyes pleading with her to understand. "What did you want me to say? I didn't know how to tell you!"

She stared at him like she'd never seen him before. It was exactly the way she felt. All her life, she'd looked up to her brother and now... It was like staring into the eyes of a stranger.

"How *could* you?" she asked, her voice breaking with emotion. "How could you do something like that to Pamela?"

Once again, he offered her a shrug. "I don't know. It just happened. I married Pam because she was pregnant; to do the right thing. I'd never known real love, Monica. And then Sara came along. She kept leaving me little notes, telling me how attractive I was and how much she'd like to get to know me. At first, I ignored it, but she was persistent. She sent me a couple of photos. She was...naked."

Monica slowly shook her head, appalled. She wanted to block her ears, to tell the cab driver to pull over, to run away until the brother she knew and loved returned.

Tommy took her hands in his and stared at her beseechingly. "I didn't mean for it to happen, to fall in love with her, Mon. I swear, I didn't. She was young and beautiful and she wanted me. She's almost half my age. I was flattered by the attention. Who wouldn't be? And I loved her. God, I loved her so much." His voice hitched on emotion. His eyes pleaded with her to understand.

Monica made a sound of disgust and her hands tightened into fists. She couldn't believe this was her brother, her hero. Life would never be the same again.

"How long did it go on?" she asked, though forming the words was difficult.

"Six months."

"Does Pamela know?"

"Yes."

"Oh, my God! Who *are* you? I can't believe you tried to make me think she was unhappy because you wouldn't give her a child! She's been mad at you about this affair, hasn't she?"

"Yes, but the baby thing's been the real issue. I swear! She only found out about the affair a few months ago. That was probably the catalyst for our recent arguments, but the baby or lack of one has been driving a wedge between us for a long time." Tears glinted in his eyes. "It's one of the reasons I turned to Sara. I was lonely."

Anger seared through Monica's veins. Her breath came fast. "Don't you *dare* blame this on Pamela!" she hissed. "You did this all on your own! If you're having marriage problems, you go and see a therapist. You *don't* have an affair with one of your students!"

Tommy held his hands up in a sign of surrender. "Okay, okay! I'm sorry. You're right. This was all on me. I shouldn't have done it. I know that now and as much as I'm torn apart about what happened to Sara, I will try to make things right with my wife."

"I can't believe she still lets you in the house! I would have thrown you out onto the street! You broke your wedding vows in the most horrible of ways. I can't fathom the level of your deceit! I've never been particularly close to your wife, but my goodness, she deserves better than that!"

"You're right, Mon. She does. And if I could do it all over again, I'd make better choices. But no one can turn back time and now I have to live with the consequences. Including facing a murder charge because my lover was stabbed fourteen times in her bed."

The enormity of all that had happened suddenly overwhelmed her. She gasped for breath, trying hard to stem her panic. Her brother had been having an affair with his student and now that girl had turned up dead. The police were obviously aware of the connection. *Why else would they arrest and charge him with her death?*

It was too much to take in, not the least the lies Tommy had told his wife. Monica didn't believe for an instant that he'd committed murder, but she couldn't help but wonder what other untruths he might have told.

And then she was beset with another surge of guilt and it had nothing to do with her brother. Unconsciously, her hand went to her belly. She was also guilty of deceit. *Was hers in the same category as Tommy's?* She had a horrible suspicion the answer might be yes.

Colby Shearer pushed back a hank of thick hair that had fallen across his forehead and into his eyes and thought about getting a haircut. He'd been so busy at work, he couldn't remember the last time he'd been to the barber. He normally favored a short back and sides. It fit with his image of a young and successful crown prosecutor, but only recently his secretary had joked that with his hair longer, he looked more like the kind of male model used on the front covers of a Harlequin romance—one depicting a billionaire Italian tycoon—than a city lawyer.

He'd never read a romance book in his life and he didn't care too much if he resembled one of the men on their covers, but the fact was, he needed to make time for himself, and that included a haircut. He hadn't had a day off since returning from his sister's wedding.

The memory of the week he'd spent on the tropical island in the middle of the Pacific hit him without warning. He'd spent five glorious days in the arms of a beautiful woman, almost certain he'd found "the one," only to discover that she'd given him a fake phone number.

He'd thought they felt the same way about each other and experienced that indefinable, magnetic pull. But he'd been wrong. The realization that for her, their week together had been nothing more than a holiday fling had been gut wrenching, but through a sheer act of will and by throwing himself into his work, he'd almost managed to remove the memory of her from his mind. *Almost.*

He could still remember the bright blue of her eyes and the perfect golden tan of her skin. Her luxurious waves of golden hair that he'd sifted through his fingers like fine silk. Her generous mouth that laughed and teased and kissed him all over. The way she straddled his hips and rode him with wild abandon. The way she stared into his eyes and silently promised him forever...

Yep. There really wasn't much at all that he remembered about her or their time together. He grimaced at the lie, annoyed with the direction of his thoughts. Their week of magic had come to an end—and with her giving him a fake number, she'd made it clear she didn't want to see him again. He didn't even know her last name.

He guessed he could try and track her down through his new brother-in-law. She'd told him she was Jason's PA. Still, why would he bother? It was clear she didn't feel the same way he did. No need to get his heart trampled a second time. Besides, he didn't really have the time to put into a new relationship. Only that morning, he'd been buried for hours going over the witness statements in his current trial with the lead detective at the City of Sydney Police Station and they'd barely made any headway.

A knock on his office door snagged his attention. Pushing his thoughts aside, he bade the person to enter. Christian Grayson's dark head appeared in the opening. Colby smiled in greeting at the sight of one of his fellow prosecutors—a man he also counted as a good friend.

"Christian! It's good to see you! To what do I owe this pleasure?"

"Cut the crap, Shearer. I'm here to give you a case."

"Hey!" Colby protested. "I'm being serious. It seems like forever since I saw you. Where have you been hiding yourself?"

"Well, I've been knee-deep in a drug matter, if you really must know. It's the reason I have to offload this. One of the co-accused has just applied for a separate trial. It means we have to dismiss the jury and start again."

Colby groaned in commiseration. "Sorry to hear that, buddy." He nodded toward the file Christian held in his hand. "What have you got?"

"It's the matter of Thomas James Radford. He's been charged with first degree murder. He's currently out on bail. The matter will be mentioned tomorrow with a view to entering a plea and assuming the plea is 'not guilty,' setting a committal date. There's enough evidence to send it to trial, so it would be best to prepare for that eventuality."

"Look, I'd love to help you out, but I'm kind of snowed under at the moment. Can't you find someone else to do it?"

"I've already asked Greg Villa and Luke Walker. Neither of them are able. I thought of you next because I know you love this kind of stuff and you're very good at it."

Despite himself, Colby was intrigued. "What kind of stuff?"

Christian threw himself down in the chair that stood opposite Colby's desk. "Thirty-seven-year-old Thomas Radford is employed by Sydney University. He teaches economics and business. The victim is his nineteen-year-old student, Sara Nakamura.

She's an international student, so a couple of suits from the Department of Foreign Affairs are also poking around."

Colby grimaced. "Great."

"Yeah. Should make good TV. Lucky you have the face for it. Anyway, Nakamura was found dead in her apartment. Stabbed fourteen times."

"Overkill. Sounds personal."

"Yes. That's what the police thought. They went through her phone and emails and talked to her friends. They discovered she was having an affair with Radford. Fresh semen was found at the scene. We're still waiting for the DNA results. When Radford was interviewed, his only alibi was that he was at home, asleep. Apparently his wife was also home at the time. She backed him up. Notwithstanding, he was arrested and charged with murder."

Colby nodded thoughtfully. "So what's the police take on it?"

"That Radford and Nakamura had a fight after having sex. Young lovers can sometimes be so demanding."

Colby grinned. "I wouldn't know."

Christian winked. "You need to get out more, Shearer."

Colby chuckled and then sobered. "Perhaps little Miss Nakamura asked him to leave his marriage," he said thoughtfully. "They fought about it and it ended with her dead. It wouldn't be the first time. What's Radford got to say about it?"

"He denied killing her, but he lawyered up

pretty early. Blake Harton Junior from Sydney legal is representing him."

Colby grimaced. "Sounds like Radford's not short of funds."

"Yeah, and that he means business. He's engaged the best criminal defense lawyer in the city. You have your work cut out for you." Christian slapped the file down on Colby's desk and pushed back his chair. "I've got to go. Thanks for doing this, mate. I owe you one."

"Yeah, yeah, yeah," Colby muttered around a grin. Christian threw him a wave and left the room.

Colby dragged the file toward him and opened it. He scanned the police facts and then looked over the autopsy report. It was gruesome reading. Along with the fourteen stab wounds, the victim had suffered deep cuts to her hands—defensive wounds sustained while she'd been frantically trying to save her life. Colby couldn't help but wonder what kind of person could do such a thing to another human being.

He skimmed over the next couple of paragraphs which dealt with the size and weight of the victim's organs. All were healthy and were within normal limits. And then his gaze snagged on something else. He read the sentence twice and dread centered in his gut. Sara Nakamura had been six weeks pregnant. It was stated in black and white. Like the semen found at the scene, DNA tests on the fetus had been ordered. They were awaiting those results.

Colby flipped over the next page and found a stack of 8 x10 colored photographs. Most were taken at the crime scene. The murder had occurred in the victim's bedroom. He could see the cheap yellow-and-orange curtains that covered the only window in the room and the wall adjacent to the bed, decorated with posters of rock stars and other celebrities. A hairbrush and hair ornaments lay in a pile on the nightstand, along with an economics textbook.

Apart from the bloodbath on the bed, he could have been looking at pictures of any typical teenager's room. The senselessness of the murder tugged at his heart. *Had it been a lover's quarrel that had ended in the loss of a young girl's life, like the police seemed to think?*

Colby turned to the witness statements that were contained in the file. The first one was the defendant's record of interview. Thomas James Radford had confirmed his full name, date of birth, occupation and address. He'd also confirmed he knew the deceased. And then he'd lawyered up and the interview came to an abrupt end.

Colby found statements by some of Nakamura's college friends. It was her girlfriends who'd alerted the police to the fact the defendant was more to the dead girl than what he led on. According to Nakamura's friends, she'd been having an affair with her teacher for almost six months. She'd been the one to instigate it, but once Radford had been persuaded, he'd embraced the affair with enthusiasm.

Nakamura's friends had stated that Mr Radford often asked Nakamura to stay back after class and they knew he had visited her apartment on several occasions. Only a week before her murder, Sara had bragged to them that he was in love with her, even though so far he'd refused to leave his wife.

The theory that a lover's quarrel had resulted in her death certainly had merit. It wouldn't be the first time tempers had flared in a relationship to the point that things turned deadly. Still, the evidence at this point was circumstantial. Colby would almost bet on Radford pleading not guilty. Murder carried with it a sentence of twelve to fifteen years. Serving that wasn't for the faint hearted. But Colby was in the business of putting murderers behind bars and Radford was no different. If the evidence pointed to his guilt, Colby would do everything in his power to convince the jury of that fact. And that was that.

CHAPTER 6

Six weeks later

Monica paced the industrial strength gray-and-black checked carpet that lined the foyer outside the courtroom and tried to contain her nerves. Being so overwrought wasn't good for her baby and she sent a silent apology in the direction of her bump, but it was the morning of the first day of her brother's trial and she could hardly bear to sit still. She couldn't believe things had gone so far... That she was waiting for his case to begin—a case that would determine his guilt or innocence on the charge of murder.

She'd been shaken to the core when she discovered Tommy had been having an affair, but still, infidelity was a long way from murder. It was ludicrous to contemplate, for even a millisecond, the possibility he could be guilty of killing his mistress. And Monica had told Blake Harton Junior exactly that on several occasions. But, despite her unshakable belief in her brother's innocence, here they were. She only hoped Blake lived up to his reputation and would convince the twelve men and women who would make up the jury that they had no choice but to set Tommy free.

The elevator *dinged* and she turned in time to see the doors slide open. To her surprise and relief, her sister-in-law emerged, dressed from head to toe in Versace. Pamela's eyes were hidden behind a pair of huge black sunglasses that remained fixed in place as she came to a halt beside Monica, who gave her sister-in-law a hug.

"Pamela, you made it. Thank you for coming."

"Of course I came. Despite everything, I *am* his wife. It's my duty to remain by his side."

Monica remained silent. It would do no one any good to remind Pamela that until that moment, Monica had had no idea if her sister-in-law would show. If relations between her brother and his wife had been strained prior to Tommy being charged with murder, they'd deteriorated even more since.

Though he was out on bail and back living at home, she knew he and Pamela were merely keeping up appearances for the sake of the media who'd been camped outside their door in the weeks leading up to the trial. Monica had taken to visiting discreetly by parking more than a block away and making her way into their back garden via a laneway and little-used gate. She'd picked her way through the overgrowth and long grass, grateful for the fact that winter had arrived and would keep the snakes away.

She'd sit at their table and do her best to make conversation, to lift the spirits in the room. Tommy would answer in monosyllables. Pamela wouldn't answer at all. Even as late as the night before, Monica hadn't been sure Pamela would support her husband by attending the trial, but Monica was terribly relieved she did. The jury would see Tommy's wife seated behind him, looking spectacular in her designer clothes and it would be obvious to them that she supported him and believed in his innocence. Why else would she be there? Surely for the same reason Monica was there.

Once again, the elevator *dinged* and Monica's gaze was drawn to the sliding doors. Blake Harton Junior filled the opening and behind him was his wife.

"Natalie!" Monica cried, engulfing her friend in a hug. "I didn't realize you were coming."

"Of course I came," Natalie replied. "I'm here to support you and Tommy. From what Blake says, he needs all the support he can get."

Monica bit her lip as Natalie voiced the very same fears that had kept her sleepless for much of the last six weeks. It was no secret Blake had his work cut out for him. Still, it made her feel better to have her best friend by her side, helping her through it. She introduced Natalie to Pamela.

Her sister-in-law gave the slightest inclination of her head in Natalie's direction and then returned her attention to her manicure. Monica bit down on her irritation. At least Pamela was here. It was all Monica could ask.

"How are you feeling?" Natalie asked, her voice pitched low.

Monica put a hand on her stomach. There was a barely noticeable bump. "I'm fourteen weeks along and still sick as a dog. Morning, noon and night. All the books I've read tell me the worst of it is usually over by the end of the first trimester. And yet, here I am, still puking."

Natalie nodded sympathetically. "Does anyone else know?"

Monica shook her head. "No. With everything going on in Tommy's life, I figured I could keep this news quiet for a bit longer. Mom's not well and I worry about him so."

Natalie gave her a quick hug. "Honey, there's nothing you can do to help Tommy but be here and you're already doing that. All we can hope is that Blake works his magic and convinces the jury to let your brother off."

Monica sighed quietly. "Yes, you're right and I need to think about the baby. My stress levels have been way higher since this happened. I don't know what I'd do if I endangered it in any way. It's already become such a part of my life. I can't imagine it any other way. For both of our sakes, I need to try and distance myself from everything."

"Good luck with that," Natalie replied and squeezed her arm comfortingly.

"You're right. I'm kidding myself. I can't wait for all of this to be over."

Natalie nodded in agreement. She looked around the foyer. "Where's Tommy?"

"He went outside for a cigarette."

Natalie looked at her in surprise. "I thought he'd given up?"

"Yes, he did. But ever since he was charged, he's been smoking again." Monica sighed again. "Just another side effect of this nightmare."

They fell silent, lost in their thoughts. Monica saw Blake check his watch. It was nearly time to go in. She looked toward the elevators and prayed that her brother would appear soon. The elevator *dinged* a third time and she sent up a silent prayer of thanks.

The doors slid open. A tall broad-shouldered man, carrying a leather briefcase, strode out followed by a young woman dragging a trolley laden with files. As a matter of curiosity, Monica's gaze glided over the man's features and her belly somersaulted in shock.

Colby Shearer's gaze slid in her direction. He recognized her in almost the same instant. His step faltered and his eyes went wide. The woman behind him frowned and stepped around him. It had been six weeks since Monica had seen him at the police station. Six long weeks where she'd second-guessed her decision to keep the news of their baby from him. She kept justifying it by reminding herself how common it was for women to miscarry in the first twelve weeks and later, when she'd passed that milestone, she clung to her original reasoning that she didn't want her baby daddy in her life. She still felt that way.

Hastily, and with her heart pounding so hard she feared it might explode in her chest, Monica turned her back on him and busied herself, frantically looking through her handbag.

Natalie shot her a curious look. "Are you all

right? You look pale. What are you looking for?"

Before Monica could respond, a low drawl sounded far too close to her ear. "Well, well, well. It's Monica the mystery woman from Fantasy Island—or should I say, Fiji. Fancy seeing you here."

Monica froze. With no choice, she forced herself to turn and face him. His tone had been nonchalant, but it belied the icy steel in his dark eyes. Instinctively, her hands came to rest on her stomach and then she quickly lowered them. There was no sense drawing his attention to her belly. With a bit of luck, even in her form-fitting dress, he wouldn't realize she was pregnant. After all, she was barely showing.

Belatedly, she wondered what he was doing there. She recalled him mentioning he was a lawyer. With a sinking feeling, she took in his black robes, the expensive tie, the ivory-colored wig.

"C-Colby. What are you doing here?" she managed.

With a sardonic expression on his face his gaze raked over her. "I see you remember my name. I guess that's a start. And, I could ask you the same thing. What are you doing here?"

"I... My brother, Thomas Radford, is appearing in court this morning. I'm here to show my support."

His dark eyes flared wide with surprise. "I'm appearing in court this morning, too. I represent the Crown."

"What case are you involved with?" she asked.

"The murder trial involving Thomas Radford."

Her hand came up to her mouth at the same

time she gasped in shock. She tried to breathe through the tightness in her chest, but it was difficult.

"Monica? Are you all right?"

Natalie's worried face materialized beside her. Monica opened her mouth and tried to speak, but at that moment, words were beyond her. She clutched at her friend and silently pleaded for help.

Natalie's frown deepened. "Here, let's go and sit down. You don't look so good."

To Monica's relief, Colby turned away from them. Natalie took her elbow and guided her over to a seat situated along the far wall. Her friend touched the back of her hand to Monica's forehead.

"You look flushed, Mon, but you don't feel hot. Are you feeling okay?"

Monica forced air back into her lungs and nodded weakly. "I-I'm fine. I just... I just had a bit of a shock." Unable to help herself, her gaze was drawn back to Colby. He stood talking to the woman who'd accompanied him, his expression dark. Nat followed the line of her gaze.

"Why are you looking at Colby Shearer like you've seen a ghost?"

Monica started in surprise. "How do you know who he is?"

"He assisted the Crown prosecutor during my ex-husband's trial. He was there for me in more ways than I can count. He really helped me through that terrible ordeal. He must be involved in another case."

"He is."

Just two words, but something in her tone must have alerted her friend. Natalie's eyes widened in shock. "Oh, no! Don't tell me he's here for Tommy's trial?"

"Yes."

"Oh, Mon! I'm so sorry. I wish I could say he's a terrible prosecutor, but I'd be lying."

"Thanks," Monica managed. She considered keeping the real reason for her shock from her friend, but decided against it. There was no way she could keep something as momentous as her baby's father, prosecuting her brother for murder, from her best friend.

She drew in a deep breath and blurted out the words. "There's something I need to tell you."

———

Colby entered the quiet courtroom, his head reeling. The last person he'd expected to run into was the woman who, for the past fourteen weeks, had haunted his dreams. The knowledge that not only had she materialized in front of him like a beautiful ghost from his past, but she was also the sister of the accused floored him and scattered his carefully prepared opening arguments like dandelion fluff on the wind. He made an involuntary sound of distress in the back of his throat and received a concerned look from his junior counsel.

Collette Croft frowned in his direction. "Are you all right, Colby?"

He glanced at his instructing solicitor. Collette

had assisted him in several other trials and the two of them worked well together. She was young and attractive, smart and ambitious. She was a catch in any man's book. Prior to his week in Fiji, Colby might have been interested, but ever since he'd met his mystery woman, all others paled in significance. And now the sexy Fiji woman wasn't such a mystery woman after all. She was the sister of the accused he was prosecuting, and she was *here*, in Colby's courtroom.

"Colby?" Collette spoke again.

He blinked and forced his thoughts back to the here and now. He hurriedly assured her he was fine and dumped his briefcase on the floor. He turned and helped her unload the files from her trolley onto the bar table. All the time, his mind kept returning to the woman outside.

He'd known she worked in the city. She'd told him she was Jason's PA. He could have picked up the phone any time and contacted her through his brother-in-law and yet, he hadn't. He'd given her his number and unlike her, his hadn't been fake. She could have called him if she'd wanted to. And she hadn't. He could only assume she didn't want to.

In many ways, his decision to enter into a spontaneous holiday fling was completely out of character. He'd never done something like that before. But at the time, he'd fallen so hard and fast for the beautiful stranger, he'd been consumed with the need to spend every available moment with her. He'd quickly established she was single and in his mind, nothing stood between them and a lifetime of love and laughter. How wrong he'd been.

She'd handed him her fake phone number and bid him farewell with a cheery wave as she boarded her plane back to Sydney. He'd wanted to travel home with her, but she'd told him she needed to return earlier than originally planned and insisted he stay and enjoy the rest of his holiday. The tropical island wasn't the same without her and he'd found himself on a plane home the very next day. He'd called her from the airport, hoping to surprise her. That's when he found out her number didn't exist…

She'd lied to him and he didn't know why. He thought they'd both been on the same wavelength, both headed for wedded bliss. At least, that's how he'd felt. It had become immediately clear, standing near the baggage carousel in Mascot Airport, that she didn't feel the same. The knowledge had gutted him.

Even now, the memories of what had happened were enough to fill him with pain. He clenched his jaw against a wave of hurt and determined to force her out of his mind. Whatever he'd felt for the beautiful Monica was over. He could never love a woman with such a deceitful heart.

Once again, resolving to forget her, he focused on the matter before him. He had a murder trial to run and now that he knew his black-hearted ex-lover was intimately connected to the defendant, he was even more determined to see the man convicted of his crime.

The door to the courtroom opened behind him and the defendant and his lawyer strode through. Monica was close behind them. He glared at her, willing her to look his way, to acknowledge the wrong she'd done, but she kept her gaze steadfastly averted.

He tried not to notice how well she looked, almost as if she glowed from the inside out. A faint blush stained her cheeks. He wanted to think it might have been caused by shame, or at least a modicum of embarrassment for the way she'd treated him, but it was impossible to know. She took a seat in the public gallery, behind the defendant.

Colby smiled without humor and anger ignited along his veins. He didn't know if she'd purposefully chosen to sit there in a show of support for her brother, of if she'd merely wanted to sit as far as possible from *him*. Too bad she hadn't shown any such reticence during the hours she'd spent in his arms. Hours when he'd fallen head over heels in love with her, only to have his heart mangled in the most humiliating way.

"Do you have a copy of your opening statement?" Collette murmured, taking a seat.

Colby dragged his gaze away from Monica and pulled out the chair beside his junior counsel.

"Yes. I'm good to go."

"Let's hope the jury selection doesn't take all day. I want to get this show on the road." She grinned as she said it, but Colby's mind stalled. Once again, his head was full of the woman who sat only a handful of seats behind him and to the left. *How the hell was he going to concentrate with her listening to his every word? Breathing the same air?* It was too much to ask of anyone. Unfortunately, no one, including the judge, would care.

CHAPTER 7

Monica sat directly behind her brother in a deliberate show of support. She was still feeling shaky over the discovery that the man who'd unwittingly fathered her unborn child now sat a few yards away and would continue to do so for the foreseeable future as he prosecuted her brother for a murder Tommy didn't commit. She needed to come to terms with that fact and work out a survival plan, but most of all, she needed to remain calm and focused. Colby knew nothing of the baby and that's the way it was going to stay. She just hoped she didn't die from the guilt that even now flooded through her veins.

Which was ridiculous. He'd always known there was a possibility she could get pregnant. He'd been a willing participant that first time when they hadn't used protection. In fact, he'd been the one to suggest it. Though she was relieved he hadn't tried to contact her, it irked her that he hadn't cared enough about the possibility of a pregnancy to even make the most casual of enquires.

Okay, so she'd given him a wrong number and hadn't volunteered the information, but she refused to take all the blame. Besides, she was pleased he hadn't expressed any interest in a possible pregnancy. This baby was hers. She loved the tiny being growing inside her more than she thought possible and nothing and nobody would interfere—and that included her baby's father.

She wasn't quite sure how Colby would react to the news she was pregnant if he ever found out, but in Fiji, he'd expressed a desire to marry and have kids. She didn't want to take the risk that even if he didn't want to spend the rest of his life with *her* (and she most certainly wasn't looking to spend her life with anyone), he might want to spend time with his child. No, it was better for all concerned if the baby remained a secret, just as she'd planned.

Tommy had made mention during one of her visits that Blake anticipated the trial would go no more than a week. She hoped like hell he was right. Another week would see her reach a little over three-and-a-half months and hopefully, she would still be able to conceal her pregnancy from Colby's unknowing gaze.

Pamela dropped into the chair beside her, her eyes still hidden behind her oversized sunglasses. Blake had already taken a seat at the defense end of the bar table, along with his junior counsel. Monica looked up just as Natalie sat down next to her.

"How are you doing?" her friend whispered.

Unwittingly, Monica's gaze glanced off Colby. She quickly looked away. "I'm fine," she reassured her friend. "I guess it was just a bit of a shock seeing him again and especially *here*."

"A shock for both of us," Natalie replied, her tone faintly accusatory.

Monica fought off a stab of guilt. "It wasn't just you I kept it from, Nat. I didn't tell anyone. My baby's father was supposed to remain anonymous forevermore—just like it is when you visit one of those sperm banks. I researched it months ago. The sperm donor can choose to remain completely anonymous."

"Yes, but we're not talking about a sperm donor. We're talking about a flesh-and-blood man who happens to be seated a few yards away," Natalie whispered furiously. "It's not the same at all, Monica."

Once again, Monica stifled a surge of guilt. Okay, so maybe it wasn't fair to keep the news from Colby, but she was now carrying her much-longed-for child. A baby she already loved with all her heart and soul. A baby who would be hers forever. A baby she didn't want to share.

"Please don't say anything to anyone, Nat. I understand you're upset with me and if I didn't want to be a mom so badly, I might even feel the same. It's always possible I could meet the man of my dreams and have a family the normal way, but it's just as likely I won't! I'll be thirty-three before this baby is born. That's way old enough already. I didn't want to wait until I was putting my health and the health of any unborn baby at risk. Do you know the statistics regarding problematic pregnancies, how the risk rises significantly once a woman is over thirty-six. I—"

"Okay, I get it." Natalie cut her off with a shake of her head. "We're going to agree to disagree, but you'll never convince me you've done the right thing. I want you to tell Colby Shearer you're pregnant."

Monica gaped, aghast. "I can't do that!" she whispered crossly. "Haven't you been listening? I don't want a man in my life. I only want—"

"A baby. I get it. But do you know how selfish you sound? What about the father? What about the baby? Don't they deserve to know of each other's existence? To have each other in their lives?"

"I... I don't think that's necessary."

Natalie shot her a look of disbelief. She opened her mouth, as if to continue the argument, but just then there was a loud rap on the door, indicating the arrival of the judge.

As one, the occupants in the room turned toward the bench.

———————

Colby had watched Natalie Johnson enter the courtroom behind Blake Harton and frowned. He seemed to recall something in the gossip pages about Natalie and Blake finding love. The story had used the angle of an unlikely love rising out of the hate and despair of a court case where Nat's ex-husband had been found guilty of murdering their child.

Colby had assisted Greg Villa, a senior crown prosecutor, with the trial. He'd spent a fair number of hours with Natalie, explaining court procedures, going over her testimony, lending her an ear when she needed one. She was a nice person who'd been dealt a tough hand. He was pleased she'd found love with Harton, if indeed the tabloids had printed the truth.

But what the hell was she doing with Monica?

And then he remembered. Natalie worked at Baker & Carr, the same construction company where Colby's new brother-in-law worked. In fact, he was the boss. Monica had told him she was Jason Georgetown's PA. Unless she was lying. She'd already proved she could be deceitful. But, given that Natalie was seated beside her for the first day of the trial, he had to assume she'd told the truth about her occupation, at least.

His gut soured at the reminder of the beautiful blonde's deception. He was even more annoyed at his own gullibility. He should have known their time together on the tropical island paradise was nothing more than a casual fling. It's not like he wasn't aware of that kind of thing happening. Though one-night stands and casual sex had never been his thing, he had plenty of mates who spent more time choosing their business suits than they did their bed partners. Monica was obviously cut from that same cloth.

Cursing irritably under his breath, he turned his

back on her and concentrated on the notes he'd made for his opening statement. With the arrival of Judge Vanessa Sperry, he stood, along with the other occupants of the room. The crowd bowed in the judge's direction in a traditional sign of respect before regaining their seats. The judge made herself comfortable behind the bench and then turned to address Colby.

"Mr Shearer, we're here for the trial of Thomas James Radford on a single charge of murder. Are you ready to proceed?"

Colby pushed away from the bar table and stood. "Yes, Your Honor. The Crown is ready."

Looking over her half-moon glasses, Judge Sperry turned to Blake. "What about you, Mr Harton? Are there any matters we need to deal with before we begin the jury selection?"

It was Blake's turn to stand. "No, Your Honor."

The judge nodded. "Very well." She turned to the bailiff. "Please send in the prospective jurors."

The bailiff acknowledged her request and turned and left through a side door. A short time later, the panel opened and a stream of people filed through. Of all ages, both male and female and representing a mixture of cultural backgrounds, the people whose names had been drawn in the jury ballot quietly came into the courtroom and took their seats. Most looked apprehensive.

Colby had been provided with a list of the prospective jurors ahead of time, including their personal details and background information. It was imperative he do what he could to appoint a jury favorable to his case. In general, men were more sympathetic toward male perpetrators in matters of adultery. As a result, Colby hoped to get as many women as possible on the panel. For a start, they wouldn't look on Thomas Radford with sympathy. Secondly, he had more chance convincing them the adulterous husband could have flown into a rage and murdered his mistress, particularly if he was coming under pressure from his wife to end the affair or if he found out she was pregnant, complicating things.

Colby had no direct evidence that Radford's wife knew about the other woman, but with the affair lasting at least six months, it was likely that Pamela Radford had some knowledge. The police had put together a plausible scenario that was supported by the evidence. It went something like this: Pamela Radford discovered her husband's infidelity. She demanded he end the affair. He, in turn, passed on the disappointing news to his young lover, who hadn't reacted well. They'd gotten into a fight that had turned deadly. Nakamura had come off second best. In fact, from the lack of defense wounds on Thomas Radford's body, his mistress hadn't even landed a blow.

It wouldn't take the jury long to accept Nakamura hadn't stood a chance in a physical fight with her lover. The young girl stood barely five feet tall and weighed next to nothing. Radford was well over six feet, almost as tall as Colby. Throw in the fact the man must weigh more than two hundred pounds and somewhere along the way had produced a knife—well there was simply no contest.

Collette leaned close and lowered her voice to a whisper. "Juror Two and Juror Thirty-seven are both divorced. Juror Nineteen and Juror Twenty-eight are separated. You might want to ask them if they have any personal experience of adultery. We don't want anyone sympathizing with the accused."

Colby nodded, acknowledging her suggestion. He'd already studied the list of prospective jurors and had made notes next to each of them. At least half of them appeared to be ordinary citizens without any bias one way or the other, but he knew from years of experience that no one admitted to all of their prejudices on a jury form—or anywhere else for that matter. It would pay to ask pertinent questions of as many of them as possible and use his peremptory strikes on the ones who seemed particularly sympathetic to the accused.

The defense, of course, would be angling for the opposite. Generally speaking, the kind of juror favored by the prosecution was the same kind of person the defense objected to. It was a game where they lost some and won some and in the end, both sides hoped they'd end up with a fair and unbiased jury they could live with. He prayed this case wouldn't prove to be the exception.

In the end, it took most of the day to choose a jury. He questioned each person at length and so did his counterpart. He and Blake used all three of their peremptory strikes and Colby had challenged more prospective jurors for cause than he cared to remember. It was a sad indictment on society that so many people had personal experience with cheating spouses and had been soured by the experience. Some had even admitted that they wouldn't be able to remain impartial if they discovered the accused had been involved in an affair. Naturally, Blake was quick to eliminate those people from the pool.

Colby leaned back in his chair and swallowed a sigh. It had been a long day and this was only the first day of the trial. Tomorrow, the real work would begin. He snuck a glance across the way and his gaze clashed with Monica's. For an instant, he forgot that she'd given him a fake phone number and remembered only the wonder he'd found in her arms. She was everything he'd been searching for... And then she'd gone and ruined it by making it clear in the most humiliating way that she didn't feel the same way.

It still floored him to think she could be so passionate, so responsive during the hours and days they'd spent together and then give him the flick the moment her holiday came to an end. The thought that she might even have faked her pleasure filled him with irritation and he made a low growl of denial in his throat.

No, he refused to believe she'd been faking it the entire time they'd been together. No one could act that well. She'd felt something for him, even if it was pure lust and he wanted to know what had changed in the time he'd pressed a hundred tender kisses against her skin, drifting off into a sleep filled with sublime contentment, to the moment when she'd bid him a fond farewell with a peck on the cheek and a jaunty wave and smile... And then disappeared from his life.

What had happened during those hours to account for it? For weeks, he'd wracked his brain for an answer and had come up empty. Now she'd stumbled back into his life—well, at the very least, into his courtroom—and if she was going to continue to be present, showing her support for her brother, it would mean he would be sharing the same air for the foreseeable future. The trial was expected to run a week. Plenty of time to get to the bottom of why she'd promised him the sun and the moon in Fiji and had then left without a backward glance, trampling his hopes and his dreams in the process.

———————

Monica felt the weight of Colby's stare and her belly twisted with nerves. It had been bad enough sitting through the hours of legal argument as the barristers selected the jury. From what she could tell, anyone with a past that had been touched by infidelity was excused without cause and that was a good thing. The last thing Tommy needed was a juror who'd been the victim of an unfaithful spouse and was hell-bent on making someone pay. Both Colby and Blake had done a good job of flushing those people out and she was quietly confident they'd managed to get twelve people who would give her brother a fair hearing. It was all she could ask.

Sneaking a peek at Colby from beneath her lashes, she was startled to discover his gaze remained on her. Instinctively, she pressed her clutch purse to her belly and then forced herself to remove it. Her stomach was almost as flat as it always had been. He hadn't seen her since early April. There was no way he'd guess she was pregnant.

Still, it was better not to draw attention to that part of her anatomy. She meant what she said to Natalie. Right or wrong, she was determined to keep the baby a secret from its father and no one was going to change her mind. Now all she had to do was come up with a way of avoiding him for the duration of the trial. Given that he worked for the prosecution and she was barracking for the opposite side, that shouldn't be difficult. Still, she could barely concentrate, knowing he sat such a short distance away.

"I guess that's it then," Pamela murmured beside her.

"Blake did a good job," Monica replied.

Pamela's lips twisted in a grimace, spoiling the perfect shape of her beautiful mouth. "Let's hope it's enough."

Monica nodded. "Will I see you here in the morning?"

Pamela shook her head and Monica's heart sank. It was imperative she and Tommy's wife put up a united front. The jury would notice one of them missing. Tentatively, she sounded Pamela out.

"Pamela, I think it might be best if we both show up every day of the trial. The jury will know who we are. It will help Tommy's case if we're here, supporting him with our presence. Blake was the one to suggest it and I agree. We need to be here for Tommy."

Pamela stared at her. "Tommy was having an affair, Monica. You know it and so do I. He's a total shit who has single handedly destroyed our marriage. Do you really think I want to show up publicly, day after day, and pretend that doesn't matter to me? That I've forgiven him?"

Panic stirred in Monica's belly. She clutched at Pamela's hand. "I understand how upset you are, Pamela, and you're right; my brother's been a total shit. He doesn't deserve you and whether your marriage survives his affair, only time will tell. But we both know he didn't murder this woman. Tommy couldn't hurt a fly. We need to be here and at least offer the appearance of our support until this thing is over. Jurors notice this kind of thing. Blake said so. We owe it to Tommy to let the world know that those closest to him believe in his innocence. How can we expect strangers to acquit him if they think we've already decided he's guilty?"

The last was said on a desperate plea, but it appeared Pamela remained unmoved. She shook her head and terror took hold in Monica's heart.

"You don't understand," Pamela said quietly. "At the moment, I can barely stand the sight of him, but that's not why I'm going to stay away."

Monica frowned in confusion. "What are you talking about?"

Pamela stared at her a moment longer and then sighed. "Blake Harton has asked me to give evidence for the defense." She shrugged. "I guess I'm a character witness. As such, once the trial starts properly, I have to remain outside the courtroom until after I give my testimony."

Relief surged through Monica and she sagged against her sister-in-law. "Oh, thank goodness! I thought for a moment you weren't going to show up because of what he'd done."

"Like I said, at the moment, every time I look at my husband I'm filled with anger and hate. I cry all the time. I question everything. Why did it happen? Why wasn't I enough for him? What am I lacking that he turned to someone else? Then I remember that *he's* the one at fault here. *He's* the bastard who strayed. And then I get angry all over again."

She drew in a shaky breath and eyed Monica solemnly. "But, I'm his wife and he's my husband and I will do what I know is right. Tommy didn't murder anyone and if my presence in this courtroom can help the jury to believe it, then I guess that's a sacrifice I'm willing to make."

"Thank you, Pamela! Thank you!" Monica said, sagging in relief. Unable to help herself, she pulled her sister-in-law close for a spontaneous hug.

"Oh, oh," Pamela replied, slightly taken aback. A faint blush stained the perfect texture of her skin.

Monica understood her reaction. Pamela wasn't exactly known for her touchy feely nature. In fact, it was the first time in all the years she'd been married to Monica's brother that she and

Monica had actually properly hugged. Monica could feel the tension in Pamela's body, but she didn't care. She was going to hug this woman who held the fate of her brother in her hands and that was that.

CHAPTER 8

The sound of water lapping at the shore below Colby's balcony usually soothed him after a long day in court, but tonight, not even the rush of the incoming tide could ease his restlessness and indecision. He stared at his phone and wondered for the umpteenth time if he should call his brother-in-law and ask him for Monica's number. Part of him yearned to speak to her again, to ask her what the hell had happened in Fiji. They'd spent a perfect five days together, most of it spent in bed. And then afterwards... Nothing. She gave him a false number and disappeared without a trace. It was maddening not knowing why.

He wanted to hate her, to despise the way she'd treated him: slept with him, ate with him, led him to believe he was someone special... And then tossed him over in the cruelest of ways and expected him to be fine with it.

With a sound of disgust, he reached for his scotch glass and emptied it in one gulp. The alcohol seared his throat and burned a path down to his belly. He welcomed the feeling and the pleasant numbness he got from his third drink. He wished he could numb his mind to the memory of Monica as easily.

He wondered if she was also a Radford. She hadn't offered him her last name. At the time, it hadn't seemed important. She'd told him she was single, so it was likely she shared the same name as the man he was working hard to send to jail.

The thought sobered him. As if things weren't complicated enough between him and his mystery woman. Now they were on opposite sides of what had all the portents of being a sensational criminal trial. A highly respected university lecturer having an affair with his young foreign student and the story ending with the girl being stabbed to death. To make things worse, the DNA results had come back: The victim had been pregnant with her lover's child.

It read like something out of Hollywood. In fact, Colby could almost hear the phones ringing from LA. The intense media interest would only heighten the tension in what was going to be a sensational trial. And now he had Monica Radford to deal with and all the complications that came with that.

The sound of a car horn was followed by a screech of brakes. Shortly afterwards, angry voices were raised in argument. After a while, they petered out, either moving out of earshot or they sorted it out. The altercation reminded him of the confrontation he had yet to have with Monica. He groaned and then leaned over and poured himself another scotch. He should really take it easy. He had court again in the morning and that's when the real work would start.

Once again, his gaze drifted to his phone where it sat beside him on the couch. *Should he make the call?* Jason would probably ask him questions. Was he ready to provide answers, or should he leave it the hell alone? He'd see her in the courtroom tomorrow. Could he wait until then?

Yes, as much as he wanted to talk to her, he wouldn't involve Jason. He'd speak to her tomorrow and gage her attitude. She seemed hell-bent on avoiding him earlier, but it could have been the shock of seeing him and realizing he was there to prosecute her brother. Murder charges were as serious as they came. She probably had a lot on her mind and dealing with him and their holiday romance was likely the last thing she was prepared to do. He'd give her the benefit of the doubt and try to get her alone at the court house in the morning. Then he'd get the answers he needed. At least, he hoped things would play out that way. Otherwise, he'd be back to square one.

———————

Monica drew aside the curtains that covered her bedroom window and surveyed the new day. The winter sun shone bravely through a smattering of clouds, bouncing off the windscreens of the vehicles parked along her street. Her belly jiggled with nerves at the thought of spending another day in court with Colby.

Smoothing down the fabric of her loosely fitting, white linen pantsuit, she tried not to think about the hours ahead. She'd teamed her outfit with a navy-blue jacket and killer heels. She looked good and she was sure Colby wouldn't have a clue that she harbored a secret that could turn his life upside down.

At the thought of her baby nestled within her belly, she was filled with a rush of love. Tears filled her eyes and she laughed to herself and swiped at them with the back of her hand. Her hormones had been all over the place for weeks. One minute she felt like laughing, the next there were tears streaming down her face. There was nothing she could do about it and like the persistent morning sickness, she just had to ride it out.

She'd already emptied the contents of her stomach into the toilet bowl and was hopeful she'd make it to lunch before the urge to vomit struck her again. Otherwise, she'd just have to excuse herself and leave the courtroom. Thankfully, Colby wouldn't be following her into the restrooms.

The thought of seeing him again sent an undeniable surge of excited anticipation rushing through her. She'd be lying if she didn't admit she found him overwhelmingly attractive. They'd had a physical connection right from the outset and baby or no baby, though they'd only spent a short time together, she genuinely liked him and found him incredibly sexy. If she weren't so determined to remain single and maintain her independence, she might even be tempted to see if they could make a relationship work.

Her parents' marriage had ended in a messy divorce, but that wasn't the main reason she'd taken a stand against commitment and long-term relationships. The truth was, she was happy on her own. She'd had serious boyfriends and one she'd even moved in with—for three whole months. She'd hated every minute of it. Having to compromise on everything from the takeout they ordered to the movies they watched on TV.

Maybe hers had just been a bad experience, but she'd decided long ago sharing her life with a significant other just wasn't for her. The problem was, most guys didn't feel the same way. They dated her for a while and then they wanted to move things to the next level. They wanted to go exclusive, introduce her to their parents, move in together. About then she ended things, letting them down as gently as she could. Never had "it's not you; it's me" rung truer than it did for her at those times.

She'd tried to explain it to Natalie, but her best friend was still hung up on Monica's failure not to tell Colby about the baby. It didn't make things any better that Nat not only knew Colby, but liked and respected him. She'd left Monica outside the courtroom the day before admonishing her to do the right thing and tell him about the pregnancy.

The very thought of coming clean to him sent a wave of nervousness rushing through her. Though he'd been just as aware as she had of the possibility having unprotected sex could result in a pregnancy, she was almost four months gone and hadn't said a word. Each time she remembered Colby telling her how much he looked forward to being married and having kids, her guilt intensified.

Still, this really wasn't the right time. Her brother was facing the toughest fight of his life and even though she remained convinced of his innocence, it was obvious the police and Colby thought they had enough evidence to persuade a jury otherwise. She hadn't been privy to Tommy's meetings with Blake, so she wasn't sure what that evidence was, but the knowledge it must exist made her jittery.

She couldn't wait for the trial to be over. Not only would she be able to put the nightmare involving her brother behind her, she wouldn't have to sit in close proximity to Colby. They'd only managed to get through day one. She didn't know how she was going to endure a week of it.

But endure it, she would, for Tommy's sake. Blake had been adamant she be there, supporting her brother. She would have been, anyway. He was her big brother. He'd always been there for her and now it was time to return the favor. It was as simple as that.

Colby pulled out files from his briefcase and dumped them on the bar table. It was a few minutes before ten. Any minute, Judge Sperry would appear on the bench. The courtroom was slowly filling up with legal personnel and members of the public. The section reserved for reporters was also well occupied. They were there to lap up the juicy details: The teacher involved in an illicit affair with his foreign student. The young girl, barely able to speak English. An honors student. And then there was the beautiful wife who looked like a million dollars.

Colby had yet to speak to Pamela Radford, but he sure as hell had noticed her, as had every other person in the room. He was certain it was part of Blake Harton's trial strategy—and so far, it was working. Colby was sure nobody, not even the jury, was unaware of her identity. The fact that she was in courtroom in an obvious show of support for her husband was gold as far as the defense team were concerned.

The door behind him opened and Natalie Johnson—Harton—walked in. Unwittingly, his gaze moved behind her, automatically seeking out her friend. But the door remained closed and he swallowed his disappointment. Perhaps Monica wouldn't show today? Now that she knew he was the prosecutor, could she have decided to stay away? He wished it didn't matter so much to him that it appeared the answer was yes.

And then an idea occurred to him. He might not be able to question Monica, but perhaps Natalie could help him out? It was obvious the two girls were more than work colleagues. No one would come to support someone through their brother's murder trial unless they were at least good friends. And good friends talked to each other. Especially good female friends. Monica might even have told Natalie about him and the time they'd spent together in Fiji.

Before he could change his mind, he closed the short distance between them and greeted her with a smile. "Hi, Natalie. How are you doing?"

"Hi, Colby. I'm great. It's lovely to see you. You look well."

"Thank you. I was lucky enough to spend a week sunning myself in Fiji a few months ago. It was nice to get away from the hustle and bustle."

She nodded. "Oh, you mean Jason and Katie's wedding? You were there."

"Yes. Katie's my sister."

Her eyes widened in surprise and a smile lit up her face. "Oh, wow! I didn't realize. I knew Jason was getting married, of course, and I've seen Katie come into the office many times, but I didn't realize the two of you were related. Monica told me it was a lovely wedding."

Colby's gut leaped at the mention of Monica's name. "Yes, it was lovely. It didn't hurt that the scenery was spectacular and the weather was beyond sublime. What isn't there to like about celebrating a wedding on a tropical island?"

Natalie laughed. "You're right."

He stared at her and wondered if he was brave enough to take the conversation down a path he so desperately wanted. A second later, he made up his mind and before he lost his courage, dived in.

"Did Monica tell you she and I hooked up at the wedding?"

Almost immediately, a blush stained Natalie's cheeks. She averted her gaze a moment later and found something interesting to stare at on the floor. Finally, she answered.

"Um, yes. I think she mentioned the two of you had spent...some time together after the wedding."

Colby was pleased Monica had spoken about him to her friend. It was a good sign. At least, he hoped it was. Surely better than her not mentioning him at all.

"I'm glad," he said a little hastily and then did his best to slow down. "I thought we had a good time, but she kind of left abruptly and we haven't had a chance to talk about it since."

Natalie squirmed and looked even more uncomfortable. All of a sudden, Colby felt sorry for her. After all, this had nothing to do with her. She wasn't the person he should be grilling about his five days in paradise, followed quickly by three months of hell.

Awkwardly and with heat spreading across his face, Colby nodded farewell to Natalie and turned his back on her. He headed toward the bar table and threw himself down in his chair. If Monica failed to show up in the courtroom, he'd darn well call her boss and force Jason to give him her number so he could get the answers he needed to move past this. After all, the man was now family. It was the least his new brother-in-law could do.

Monica quietly slipped inside the courtroom and took a chair way at the back. The judge was already seated on the bench and Blake Harton was finishing his opening statement. Monica barely paid him any heed. Her attention had snagged on the back of Colby's head. He wore the black gown and ivory wig he'd worn the day before. The fabric of the gown clung to his broad shoulders—shoulders she remembered so well.

At the thought of their magical interlude in Fiji, she sighed and steadfastly forced her thoughts in another direction. Ever since she'd told Natalie about the baby, it seemed she spent far too much time thinking about her decision and the reasons behind it—and second guessing if she'd done the right thing.

Of course she had. Nothing had changed in the time when she'd first realized she was pregnant until now, except for the hormones. This was about her and her baby. It had nothing to do with the child's father. He was never meant to find out about it and that's the way it was going to stay, guilt, be damned.

As if sensing he was the subject of her thoughts, Colby stood and glanced over his shoulder. He spied her at the back of the courtroom and his eyes widened in surprise and then something like cold determination flooded his features. Steel hardened his gaze.

A sliver of apprehension went through her and all of a sudden, she hoped like hell he never found out about the baby. He didn't look like a man who'd blithely abdicate his responsibilities, no matter how much she begged him to. Nor did he look like he was someone who'd find it easy to forgive and forget.

Blake finished speaking and returned to his seat. The judge cleared her throat and looked in Colby's direction.

"Mr Shearer, are you ready to call your first witness?"

With a final narrow-eyed glare in Monica's direction, Colby turned away. Nerves tightened her belly, and this time her apprehension had nothing to do with him and everything to do with the commencement of the trial and the evidence that was about to be presented. The jury would watch and listen and eventually use such evidence to determine her brother's guilt or innocence. The thought terrified her.

Twelve strangers who knew nothing about her brother would decide if he'd murdered his mistress. She straightened in her chair and looked over the heads of the spectators. Tommy sat tall and straight in the dock, focused on the police officer who was climbing into the witness box. Monica's gaze slid further past him and halted on Blake Harton Junior.

He was dressed like Colby, in a black gown and ivory wig. Beside him sat his junior counsel. Monica couldn't remember her name...Teagan? Regan? She caught Monica's eye and gave a reassuring smile. The woman's confidence helped calm Monica's nerves. She drew in a shaky breath and prepared to settle in for another long day and prayed her stomach wouldn't choose this time to betray her.

Colby quickly established the officer's credentials. He was a detective with ten years' experience who spoke with calm authority. His sworn statement was formally entered into evidence and was referenced as he told the court about the emergency call that had been made by one of the victim's neighbors and how he'd attended upon the scene.

"Tell us what you saw, Detective Shepherd," Colby invited.

The officer cleared his throat and looked toward the jury. "It wasn't a pretty sight. I've been present at many crime scenes. This one was particularly violent."

"How so?"

"The victim had been stabbed a total of fourteen times. There was a lot of blood."

"Was there any forced entry to the deceased's premises?"

"No. When we got there, the front door was closed but not locked. There were no signs of forced entry."

"Was a weapon recovered from the scene?"

"A weapon was recovered, but not at the scene. We conducted a thorough search of the area and found a six-inch kitchen knife in a nearby dumpster. It was covered in blood. DNA tests later identified the blood as belonging to the victim."

"Were any fingerprints recovered from the knife?"

"No. It appeared the perpetrator wore gloves."

Colby turned to the lawyer assisting him and she handed him a plastic evidence bag containing a lethal-looking knife. Even from a distance, Monica could see reddish brown stains along the blade.

"Is this the knife recovered from the dumpster?" Colby asked.

The court officer took the bag from Colby and handed it to the witness. The detective glanced at it. "Yes, that's it. It's a Baccarat knife."

"Baccarat being the brand?" Judge Sperry clarified.

"Yes, Your Honor," the detective replied.

"I wish to tender the knife as evidence, Your Honor," Colby said.

With no objection from Blake, the knife was admitted into evidence. As it was passed around the members of the jury, Monica remained tense.

The knife looked deadly. Covered in the victim's blood, it was sure to garner sympathy with the jurors. They couldn't help but think about the poor victim as she was brutally stabbed to death. Still, there was nothing on the knife that linked it to Tommy and she just hoped it stayed that way.

"Was anything else found in or near the dumpster?" Colby asked.

"Yes," the detective replied. "We also found a

single kitchen glove. It was also covered in blood."

Colby turned and picked up a plastic evidence bag from the bar table behind him. "Is this the glove you found, Detective?"

From her place in the public gallery, Monica could see what looked to be an ordinary green-and-yellow rubber glove, the kind that anyone might use while cleaning or doing the washing up at home.

The detective examined the evidence bag and nodded. "Yes. This is the glove."

"And did you have this tested for DNA?"

"Yes, we did. The only DNA we were able to recover was from the blood left on the glove. It turned out to be the blood of the victim, Sara Nakamura."

Colby nodded and then paused a moment. Monica was sure that hesitation was deliberate. It allowed the jury time to think about what had just been said. They were watching him expectantly, their eyes wide with interest. Some of them were frowning in Tommy's direction.

"I seek to tender the bloody glove, Your Honor."

The judge looked at Blake. "Any objection, Mr Harton?"

Monica's hands tightened on her seat. It was irrational to expect Blake to leap up and start arguing about all the reasons why the glove shouldn't be allowed in. The truth was, like the knife, as awful as that was, there was nothing that linked it or the glove to her brother. She just had to keep calm and remember that.

"No, Your Honor," Blake replied.

"All right," the judge replied. "The glove shall be Exhibit C."

Colby nodded and continued. "Were photos taken of the crime scene, Detective Shepherd?"

"Yes."

Colby turned to his junior counsel again. This time, she handed him a bundle of 5 x 8 colored photographs. He handed them in turn to the court officer who gave them to the witness.

"Detective, are these the crime scene photographs?"

The detective took a moment to flip through them. Though Monica sat some distance away, she caught glimpses of red—a lot of red. She could imagine what was in the photos. Fourteen stab wounds were sure to create a mess. She shuddered at the thought of what the poor girl had endured in the moments before her death and couldn't help but wonder how Tommy was feeling. After all, the girl had been his lover. He'd told Monica he'd loved her. And now he had to sit here and listen to the graphic details of her death.

She looked at her brother and saw him slumped in his chair. Tears filled her eyes at the defeat that seemed to radiate from him. She wanted to scream and shout and shake him, tell him to get himself together and show the jury who he was and how he refused to accept the accusations, spoken and otherwise, that were flying around the courtroom. But she couldn't do any of those things and she just hoped his demeanor wouldn't affect the outcome.

Detective Shepherd cleared his throat and

finally answered Colby's question. "Yes, these are the photographs of the crime scene."

Colby nodded. "And when you first entered the bedroom where the victim was found, what were your thoughts?"

"At that stage, I wasn't sure of the number of stab wounds. It was obvious the woman had died a brutal death. The bedclothes were soaked in blood and the headboard and walls nearest to the bed were also liberally stained. It looked like a frenzied attack."

"Tell us, Detective. In your ten years as a homicide detective, what was your gut reaction to the scene?"

"To me, it looked personal. This felt like an attack by someone who knew the victim. Apart from the fact there was no forced entry, crimes of circumstance like from a break-in, don't usually exhibit the same level of savagery. A burglar, for instance, who happens to be disturbed and reacts in a deadly way usually makes the kill quick and clean, as far as possible. He doesn't hang around to inflict fourteen stab wounds on his victim when one or two will do."

Monica watched a couple of the female members of the jury shudder and she knew how they felt. It was a gruesome conversation so early in the morning—or at any time for that matter. She thought of the police officers who encountered such things on a regular basis and was filled with admiration for what they did. Such an occupation certainly wasn't for her. It was hard enough sitting in a courtroom, listening to them talk about it.

The photographs were duly tendered as evidence and were passed around the jury. Monica watched the identical expressions of shock and horror appear on their faces as they went from one to the other. Tension held her nerves taut. She looked at Tommy and saw his head was lowered and tears were sliding down his cheeks. Her heart ached with the need to comfort him. It was obvious he was having difficulty hearing about the brutal death of the woman he said he'd loved.

She tried to remember what Blake had told them—that the prosecution got to present their evidence first. They called their witnesses and everyone on their side testified and for a while, it would feel like the show was one-sided. He urged them to remember that the defense's turn would come and they had to remain strong and positive until that time. Now that the trial had begun, it was easier said than done.

She looked at the back of Colby's head and was filled with a rush of anger. Okay, he was only doing his job, but why did it have to be *her* brother he chose to use his skills against? Especially now that he knew the connection between her and Tommy. Surely he could have excused himself? Explained that he couldn't be involved in this case? Unless of course he had no feelings for her at all, or even worse—wanted an outlet for his hurt and anger.

When she'd given him a false phone number, she'd wanted to believe he didn't care—that their holiday romance had been nothing more to him than it had been to her. At the time, she hadn't known if she were pregnant, but even so, she hadn't wanted to complicate her life with a man and even though Colby had expressed a desire to one day marry and have a family, he hadn't expressed a desire to have that with *her*.

Okay, so maybe he'd shown her in a myriad of ways that he had feelings for her and she refused to acknowledge their existence. That wasn't all her fault. He could have made it clearer that she was more to him than a holiday fling.

She thought of the hope in his eyes as he'd offered her his phone number and was immediately flooded with guilt. The truth was, she *had* known Colby had feelings for her and she'd deliberately blocked that out. Pregnant or not, it didn't suit her to be in a relationship and she'd blithely and selfishly disregarded his feelings on the subject in order to justify her own.

The knowledge filled her with shame, but there was nothing she could do about it right now. They were in the middle of her brother's trial. She wondered if anything she said to Colby about how good and kind and generous Tommy was would make a difference. Would it make him reconsider his prosecution? If only Colby knew there was no way Tommy could have killed his young lover. He wasn't capable of such violence. She knew him better than anyone; she'd known him all her life.

Okay, so she'd been shocked about his affair, but that didn't make him a murderer. No, she'd speak to Colby and make him see the kind of person her brother was and she'd do it soon, before too many other witnesses took the stand and testified against her brother and maybe provided or suggested the crucial link between him and the murder that had so far been missing...

CHAPTER 9

Colby finished with his first witness and returned to his seat. Steadfastly, he refused to look in Monica's direction. He had a job to do and he was determined not to let her presence interfere with it.

Blake Harton stood to begin his cross examination. There wasn't much to ask. The crime scene photos spoke for themselves. If Blake asked too many questions, it would only further reinforce in the jury's mind that there had been a bloody battle between the victim and her attacker and right now, everyone's sympathies lay with the young woman who'd been so brutally murdered. Colby wasn't surprised Blake kept it brief.

"Detective Shepherd, in all your years of investigating homicides, have you ever come across a crime scene as violent and bloody as this one where the perpetrator turned out not to be known to the victim?"

It was a good question. Colby knew the answer

would damage his case. The detective answered honestly.

"Yes, of course. There have been cases where the scene was every bit as violent as this one and it turned out it was a spontaneous attack by a person or persons unknown to the victim, but—"

"Thank you, Detective. Nothing further."

Colby jumped to his feet. "Detective, how common is it that you would come across such a bloody crime scene where the perpetrator was *not* known to the victim?"

"Not at all common. That's why I said before that it was my gut feeling this was done by someone who knew the victim. From my experience, I'd say this was personal."

Colby nodded, satisfied he'd repaired the damage and from the look on Blake's face, he knew it, too.

"Nothing further, Your Honor," he said and returned to his seat.

"Very well, Detective Shepherd, you may step down," the judge said. She shuffled some papers and then looked to Colby. "Mr Shearer, please call your next witness."

Colby stood. "The prosecution calls Detective Joel Craigdon."

The rear door opened and Detective Craigdon made his way into the courtroom. Dressed in full service uniform and standing an impressive six-foot-four, he was a man to be reckoned with. When Colby took him through his evidence, he spoke in a tone that brooked no argument.

"Detective Craigdon, after you became aware

of the relationship between the accused and the deceased, did you conduct a search of his premises?"

"Yes. We carried out a search warrant of both Mr Radford's home and his office at the university."

"What did you find?"

"We found several text messages on his phone that indicated he and the deceased were involved in an intimate relationship. There were also a few pictures in his photo gallery of the two of them naked."

Coby held up an iPhone that was contained in a plastic evidence bag. "Is this the phone you found at the defendant's home, Detective?"

The detective examined the phone and nodded. "Yes."

"I'd like to tender this, Your Honor."

"Any objection, Mr Harton?" the judge asked.

"No, Your Honor."

"All right, the phone will be Exhibit E. Please continue, Mr Shearer."

"During your search of the defendant's home, did you discover anything else?"

"We found an opened packet of kitchen gloves that were identical in brand, size and color to a glove we found in the dumpster, along with what we believed was the murder weapon."

Colby reached behind him and picked up another plastic evidence bag. "Is this the packet of gloves you found in the defendant's house?"

He handed the bag to the court officer who duly gave it to the witness. The detective turned the bag over and then nodded. "Yes, this is it."

"Are you sure?"

"Yes, I'm certain. The evidence bag shows my signature which I applied after I'd sealed the evidence into the bag at the defendant's house."

"Where did you find the gloves, Detective?"

"In a cupboard under the kitchen sink."

To Colby's relief, Blake offered no objection and the gloves were duly admitted as evidence. Colby turned his attention back to the witness.

"Detective Craigdon, was anything else discovered during the search of the defendant's home?"

"Yes. We also found a wooden knife block containing kitchen knives. One of them was missing."

"What brand of knife were they, Detective?" Colby asked.

"Baccarat."

There was an audible murmur through the jury. Colby suppressed a surge of satisfaction, pleased they'd made the connection with the murder weapon. "And what size knife was missing?" he asked.

"From the empty slot in the knife block, I'd guess it was one about the same size as the knife we recovered from the dumpster."

Colby lifted something off the bar table and held it up in front of him. "Is this the block of kitchen knives you found in the defendant's home?"

"Yes."

"And is this the slot that was empty when you found the knife block?"

"Yes."

"I'd like to tender the knife block, Your Honor."

The judge looked toward Blake. "Mr Harton?"

"No objection, Your Honor."

"Very well, that will go in as Exhibit G. Do you have any further questions, Mr Shearer?"

"Yes, Your Honor." He turned to the police officer. "Detective, when you conducted a search of the defendant's office at the university, did you find anything linking him to the deceased?"

"Yes. We found several handwritten notes addressed to the defendant."

"And who had written those notes?"

"They were signed with the name Sara."

"As in Sara Nakamura? The deceased."

"Yes, I believe so."

"What did they contain?"

"They were love letters, the kind lovers write to one another."

Colby turned and picked up several plastic sheets containing paper. Handwriting could be seen on one side.

"Detective Craigdon, can you tell me if these are the letters you found during your search of the defendant's office?"

The letters were handed up to the witness who took a moment to examine them. "Yes, these are the letters. I bagged them myself and after sealing them up, I left my signature. There it is."

He pointed to some writing scrawled across a sticker that had been applied to seal the evidence bag.

"Thank you, Detective." As the letters went into evidence, Colby returned to his seat.

Blake got straight to his feet. "Detective Craigdon, that particular brand of gloves found in the Radford home can be purchased for less than five dollars from any supermarket and corner store, right?"

"That's right."

"In fact, last year there were more than one hundred thousand packets of that very brand of glove sold in this city alone."

The detective shrugged. "If you say so."

"That's a lot of gloves, Detective." Blake paused a moment and then continued. "What size glove was found in the dumpster, Detective?"

"A small size. The same size as the packet of gloves found in the cupboard under the defendant's kitchen sink."

"I see. A small size," Blake repeated and then looked directly behind him at Tommy. Once again, he paused.

"I put it to you, Detective, that the glove you found in the dumpster is too small for it to have possibly been worn by my client."

"I don't believe that's true, sir."

"How many gloves did you find in the packet located during the search of the Radford home?"

"I think there were two."

"Would you like to check?" Blake asked.

The court officer handed the detective the evidence bag that contained the kitchen gloves. He broke the seal and pulled out two identical rubber gloves. "Yes, there are two."

"I see. Not one, not three. *Two.*"

Colby clenched his jaw in frustration. It was a minor point, but one the jury had taken on board if the look of thoughtful comprehension on most of their faces was anything to go by.

"Baccarat knives are very expensive, aren't they, Detective?" Blake continued, taking another tack.

"Yes, I believe they are."

"In fact, a single knife could cost upwards of one hundred dollars, right?"

"Yes."

"Still, plenty of them are sold in Sydney. In fact, when I contacted the Baccarat supplier, they confirmed that several thousand sets of knives were sold in stores in Sydney over the past few months."

"If you say so."

"I put it to you that the knife you found in the dumpster is not the same knife that appeared to be missing from the knife block in my client's kitchen."

"I'm sorry; I disagree."

Blake merely inclined his head. "Detective, you didn't carry out any handwriting analysis on the letters you found in my client's office, did you?"

"No. The letters were addressed to the defendant and signed with the name Sara. Because of the contents of these letters, we accepted them at face value."

"And yet, they could have been written by anyone."

Colby got to his feet. "Objection, Your Honor.

The forensic pathologist will give evidence that the DNA analysis of the semen found at the scene belonged to the defendant. This evidence, coupled with other witness testimony, quite clearly establishes that the defendant had a sexual relationship with the deceased. That isn't an issue."

The judge looked at Blake. "Do you intend to challenge the DNA results of the semen, Mr Harton?"

"No, Your Honor," Blake replied.

"Very well. If you have no further questions, we'll move on. Detective Craigdon, you're excused. Mr Shearer, please call your next witness."

Colby stood. "The prosecution calls Doctor Samantha Wolfe."

From the corner of his eye, Colby saw Blake sit up straighter in his seat. The forensic pathologist's name had been on the witness list Colby provided the defense team some time ago, in accordance with the Supreme Court Rules, but he understood Blake's reaction.

The courtroom door opened and Samantha Wolfe strode in. Her dark hair was pulled back into a bun at the nape of her neck. She wore a charcoal-gray suit comprised of a jacket and skirt that ended at the top of her knees and displayed shapely calves beneath.

Colby had been pleased to discover Samantha had done the autopsy. As the head of the Department of Forensic Medicine in Glebe, she had decades of experience conducting autopsies and determining cause of death. She had an enviable reputation and was considered to be at the top of her field. Blake wouldn't gain any ground by challenging her and both of them knew it. The defense lawyer would have no choice but to accept her evidence for what it was and move on.

The witness was duly sworn in and Colby regained his feet. After establishing her impeccable credentials and the fact that she'd conducted the autopsy on Sara Nakamura, he got into the important stuff.

"Doctor Wolfe, can you tell the court what you found during the course of your examination of the victim?"

Samantha folded her hands in front of her. She looked cool and composed, like she'd done this sort of thing many times before—and she had. When she spoke it was with quiet confidence.

"The victim was identified as Sara Nakamura, a nineteen-year-old Japanese student who attended Sydney University. She'd been in Australia a little over a year. I believe she was studying economics. I examined her body and counted fourteen stab wounds to her stomach and upper chest. She also suffered numerous lacerations to her hands, three of which were considerably deep."

"Can you tell us what caused her death?" Colby asked.

"Several of the stab wounds pierced her chest cavity and entered her heart. It's impossible to say which one provided the deadly blow."

"Have you seen this kind of attack before, Doctor?"

Samantha sighed. "Yes, unfortunately."

"How would you describe it?"

"It was a frenzied attack by someone who was out of control. Like I said, several of the blows were deep enough to have caused death."

"What kind of weapon was used, Doctor?"

"A sharp, long-bladed knife. Not serrated. Some kind of hunting knife, perhaps."

"I'd like to show you a knife that was recovered not far from the crime scene."

The court officer collected the knife from the judge and handed it to the doctor. She examined it briefly.

"Doctor Wolfe, could this knife have caused the wounds you saw on the victim?"

"Yes. Absolutely."

"In fact, the knife was tested and the DNA found in the blood on the knife came back to the victim. Does that surprise you, Doctor?"

"Not at all."

"Doctor, were you able to establish time of death?"

"Yes. In my professional opinion, Sara Nakamura died somewhere between the hours of one and five, the same morning she was found."

"Thank you, Doctor. Was there anything else you found during your examination of the victim?"

"Yes. I discovered the victim was six weeks pregnant."

"And was the DNA of the fetus tested?"

"Yes, it was."

"And who did the DNA come back to?"

Samantha looked over toward the defendant who sat in the dock with his head lowered. She returned her gaze to Colby and then answered. "The DNA proved that Thomas James Radford had a ninety-nine percent chance of being the father."

———

Monica gasped in shock. It was one thing to be told her brother was having an affair. It was quite another to discover his lover was carrying his child, especially after all the heartache both he and his wife had endured during the miscarriage of their baby. It was a cruel blow. Monica wondered if Pamela knew and then immediately accepted that of course she did. This kind of thing wouldn't have been kept from her. If Tommy hadn't come clean about it beforehand, she was sure it would have come out when Blake went through the evidence with them.

Oh, Tommy! What did you do? Poor, poor Pamela... Her heart ached for both of them.

Without conscious thought, her hand went to her belly. *Oh, God, when had life become so complicated?* She was thrilled to be finally pregnant, but guilt over keeping it a secret from the baby's father still weighed her down. And what about Tommy? His girlfriend had been pregnant with his child. A child he hadn't been able to give his wife...

Icy dread crept through her veins and centered in a cold lump in Monica's belly. She knew where the prosecution was going with this. The unplanned pregnancy could have given her brother the incentive to get rid of both woman and child. He was married and as far as Monica knew, he hadn't been about to leave his wife.

She thought back to their very first conversation, when he'd called her from the jail and told her about his marriage difficulties. He'd expressed uncertainty about his ability to make his wife happy, but there had been no talk of leaving. And yet, she was sure Colby was about to bring the jury around to the possibility that her brother had murdered his young lover in order to rid himself of the problem.

The thought sent an agony of shock and protest rushing through her. She knew her brother wasn't capable of murder, but her certainty came from knowing him well his whole life. The members of the jury didn't know him at all... What were *they* thinking?

She forced herself to look across the room and study them. Moving from one face to another, she saw the respect they afforded Colby. They stared at him in concentration, listening as he spoke. A few of the women were nodding.

A wave of urgency went through her. She needed to speak with Colby before any more damage was done. It might not do any good, but she couldn't sit back and stay silent and let him say misleading or untrue things that made twelve strangers believe her brother was a murderer.

Tommy was innocent. She *knew* he was, but right now, she might be the only person in the courtroom who believed it.

To her relief, the judge brought the day to a close. They'd resume again in the morning. As people stood and began to leave their seats, she pushed her way past them and with her handbag placed firmly in front of her stomach, marched up to where Colby stood.

Mindful of his junior counsel who sat nearby, she asked, "Colby, could I have a few minutes?"

He gazed at her in surprise and then his eyes narrowed in suspicion. "Sure."

When he didn't make a move to step away, she motioned with her head. "Do you mind if we speak over there?"

He glanced at the female lawyer beside him and then shrugged before walking a short distance away. Monica held on to her courage and followed him. She kept her voice pitched low.

"You need to bring an end to this."

He blinked in surprise. "Excuse me?"

"You heard what I said. You're making it sound like my brother's a murderer! We both know he didn't do it! My brother's the least violent person I know. Now, you need to put an end to this ridiculousness and you need to do it now!"

He looked at her in amazement. "You're crazy! I mean, I understand that the defendant's your brother, but you're speaking absolute nonsense. *You* might believe in his innocence, but I can tell you, the majority of people in this courtroom don't, including me. And in case you didn't notice, I'm *prosecuting* this case. Now, if you don't mind, I need to get back to doing my job."

A wave of helplessness went through her. He was going to ignore her request! She'd scrounged up her courage to confront him and he'd simply brushed her off. In fact, he looked at her as if she'd escaped from a lunatic asylum. It was too much.

She knew the evidence so far didn't point directly to Tommy's guilt, but Colby was presenting things in a way that implied Tommy had done the deed. And worse, from his reaction just then, she knew Colby likely had something up his sleeve. He must, or he wouldn't be so confident of Tommy's guilt. Suddenly, the awful possibility of her brother spending years of his life in jail for a murder he didn't commit overwhelmed her.

Her chest tightened like a vice had been applied to her ribs. Tears filled her eyes. She tried hard to hold them at bay, but despite her efforts, they slid down her cheeks. She shook her head at Colby.

"He didn't do it! He didn't do it! Can't you see? He's not a killer! He wouldn't hurt a fly. He's innocent! You have to let him go! Please! You have to stop this madness..."

Colby shook his head in disbelief. "Do you have any idea how ridiculous you sound? I'm the Crown prosecutor. It's my job to bring cases like this to trial and if I didn't think I had enough evidence to convict your brother, I would never have taken the matter on. Believe me, today is just the start of it. There is a lot more evidence to come. You'd better do what you need to do to prepare yourself for the fact your brother's likely going to jail and he's going to be in there for a long, long time."

The sobs came harder. Colby looked around, embarrassed. Monica would have felt the same way if she weren't so upset. The hormones going crazy in her body were partly to blame—okay, maybe even mostly to blame—but she knew her brother was innocent and she had to make Colby understand.

Only, she couldn't seem to get her point across.

The thought struck her like a ton of bricks up the side of the head. Colby didn't know Tommy. To Colby, Thomas James Radford was just another defendant he'd agreed to prosecute. Nothing more, nothing less. He'd even said as much. It wasn't personal. It was a case. That was just the way it was...

Her shoulders slumped on a heavy sigh. All of a sudden, she felt exhausted. On top of all that had happened over the past few months, she hadn't been sleeping well. Now, with the stress of the trial and keeping her secret from Colby...she was beyond weary. She wanted to go home and cry herself to sleep. She wanted to close her eyes and forget everything for just a little while. She wanted to go back to a time when her life wasn't so complicated...

Colby cursed softly. "What the hell do you expect me to do, Monica?" he asked.

She sniffed and shrugged. It was all she could manage.

In frustration, he ran a hand down the side of his face. "You heard the witness testimony. She was pregnant with his baby. We've tracked down one of your brother's friends. He's going to tell the jury how scared your brother was of his wife finding out. That's fairly strong motive, if you ask me and I'm sure the jury will agree."

His expression softened and it was all she could do to hold back a fresh wave of sobs before he continued. "Now, if you want my advice, I suggest you either leave now and keep whatever grand notions you have about your brother intact, or brace yourself to hear some rather unpleasant things about the brother you obviously love. That's all I have to say."

He turned away from her and headed toward the exit. Monica stared after him, devastated.

Chapter 10

Colby pushed open the door to the restroom and headed for a stall. While washing his hands, he stared at his reflection in the mirror. He looked like he always did during a trial: somber, focused, tough. He had to be that way to get the job done.

No trial was easy. If the outcome were guaranteed, the matter wouldn't have gone to trial. The prosecution would have offered a plea deal and if the evidence against the accused was strong enough, the accused's lawyer would have persuaded his client to take it. It was only in matters like this one, where the lines weren't quite so clear, that defendants took the risk and went to trial.

He'd told Monica the truth. There was a lot of evidence against her brother, but it was all circumstantial. They had nothing directly linking him to the crime. It was risky taking such a case to the jury, but he'd won other cases with less. He was still confident he had enough to convince the jury of Thomas Radford's guilt.

But now he had the defendant's sister to deal with—a complication he hadn't factored in. Months before, he'd spent a magical week in her arms, hoping it would lead to forever. Then she'd disappeared in a cloud of deception. Now he was in control, and doing his best to convict her brother of murder. Talk about turning things on end.

The devastation on her face as he'd refused to drop her brother's case, sent anguish straight to his heart. He wished things could be different, that their reunion hadn't been like this, on opposite sides of a courtroom... Still, he meant what he'd said. Whether she liked it or not, he was going to do everything he could to secure a guilty verdict. Afterwards, he'd deal with the fallout.

Caught up in a frenzy of panic, Monica pushed through the courtroom doors that led to the exit and made a beeline for Blake. He stood a short distance away in the foyer, surrounded by members of the defense team, including Tommy. Pamela sat off to one side, alone. Monica was glad her sister-in-law hadn't sat through the evidence about Tommy's baby. She knew too well how desperately Pamela wanted a child. Whether Pamela had been told about the pregnancy before the trial, it wasn't the same as listening to it being said by a witness and in front of a roomful of avid listeners.

She glanced at her brother, and not for the first time, was ashamed of what he'd done. He'd cheated on his wife. He was a shit of the first order. But she knew her brother wasn't a murderer.

"How do you think it's going in there?" she asked Blake quietly.

Blake regarded her solemnly. "Do you remember when I told you the prosecution gets to present their evidence first?"

She nodded.

"We'll get our chance, Monica," he replied in a tone so confident he managed to ease some of her fears. "I'm not going to pretend we didn't take some hits in there, but we get a right to reply. There's a lot of evidence against Tommy. There's no denying that's true, but it's all circumstantial. The jury will be made to see that."

She bit her lip against a fresh surge of tears. "It's just so hard to sit in there and listen to them insinuate those things about Tommy. We all know he's innocent!"

"Thanks for the show of support, sis," Tommy murmured.

"You're right," Blake added. "And that's why we need to be patient. There's no point challenging a witness just for the sake of it. I'll only antagonize the jury. Best to leave it for the witnesses I can shake." He paused and eyeballed her. She steadfastly held his gaze. "Do you trust me to be able to do this?"

She nodded again. "Yes, of course. You're the best defense lawyer in town."

"Good. Then let me do my job, okay?"

Monica nodded weakly. She pressed a hand against her stomach. Natalie's gaze followed the motion and a frown appeared between her eyes. Monica ignored her reaction, along with the familiar surge of guilt. This had nothing to do with her baby or the fact its father was the man prosecuting her brother. This was all about Tommy and doing everything she could to help set him free.

Colby exited the bathroom. Steadfastly avoiding a look in Monica's direction, he headed back into the courtroom to pack up his files. He blew out his breath on a sigh.

"Good work today, Colby." Collette smiled at him, a hint of flirtatiousness in her gaze.

He glanced across at her and then returned his gaze to his briefcase. "Thanks. We made some ground."

"Hey, you want to go for a drink?"

"It's a little early to celebrate."

"We don't have to celebrate. Just drink to a good day."

He gazed at her pretty face and tidy figure. She was smart and funny. She had a lot to offer. Monica slid into his mind and he determinably forced her away. A distraction in the form of his attractive junior counsel might be the very thing he needed. He shrugged and gave her a cheeky grin.

"Why not?"

Together, they left the courtroom. Collette pulled the trolley of files behind her. Colby carried his briefcase. From the corner of his eye, he spied Monica huddled together with the defense team. He deliberately averted his gaze, threw his arm across Collette's shoulders and bestowed his junior counsel with a wide smile.

———————

Monica watched Colby leave the courtroom with his arm around the woman who'd sat beside him all day. She had the kind of compact, athletic body that came from hours at the gym. Her dark hair was cut in a pixie style and suited the shape of her face. Monica hated her on sight.

She was immediately annoyed with her reaction to their show of affection. *What did she care if Colby was dating his junior counsel?* It shouldn't irritate her that he'd moved on. She ought to be pleased. She'd purposely given him a fake phone number, for Pete's sake. No matter how much she'd enjoyed his company, she didn't want or need a man in her life. Now, or ever.

She huffed out her breath on an exasperated sigh, still annoyed that her thoughts kept returning to the father of her child. He was meant to remain a nameless, faceless stranger who only provided the necessary genetic material to create a new life. Instead, he was Colby Shearer, a living, breathing man she'd gotten to know far too well and had even felt a reluctance about leaving—

until she'd come to her senses and remembered all the reasons why she wanted to go this alone. Still, it hadn't been as easy in Fiji as she thought to say good-bye to him, knowing it would be for the last time.

And now, he'd reappeared in her life and she was entirely displeased. Well, perhaps not entirely. It was nice to see him again. He looked every bit as sexy in his work clothes as he had in his fancy tux and more casual attire. She wasn't surprised at the eagerness she spied in his junior lawyer's eyes.

"Monica? Are you listening?"

Blake's pointed questions cut through her irritated thoughts. She blinked to clear her head and gave him a suitably somber smile. "I'm sorry, Blake. Do you mind repeating the last part? I didn't quite catch it."

Colby and Collette dropped off their files at the office and Colby divested himself of his gown and wig. "I'll meet you downstairs in five," he said to Collette and she tossed him a cheery wave.

He sat at his desk and logged on to his computer and quickly scanned through his mail. There was the usual assortment of messages from professional bodies, forwarded jokes from office colleagues and a couple of reminders for meetings. Nothing important and nothing that couldn't wait until later that evening, or even tomorrow, for a response.

Pushing away from his desk, he collected his jacket and headed out the door.

———————

The downtown bar was crowded with the usual assortment of suits fresh from the courtrooms and other like-minded professionals. The Supreme Court was situated at the lower end of the central business district, not far from Circular Quay. A winter chill permeated the air, but the ambient temperature in the bar was pleasant. Colby slid onto a stool beside Collette.

"What can I get you?" he asked.

"I'll have a gin and tonic," she replied.

He signaled to the bartender and gave the man their drink order and then turned back to his colleague. She sat with her legs crossed on the stool. Her knee-length skirt had ridden up on her thighs. Her dark hair was short and curled slightly around her ears. Her brown eyes were warm and friendly. Slim and toned, she was very attractive.

They'd worked together on numerous trials and he already knew she was smart. She looked to be a little younger than him—maybe in her late twenties. Old enough to be looking to settle down.

Was that what he still wanted? To settle down? Yes, he *did*. He wanted a wife; he wanted children. He always had. Nothing had changed in that regard. The only thing that had thrown him off course was that he'd met Monica—the woman who'd walked away on a lie. The memory made him frown.

"What's the matter? Are you thinking about the trial?"

Collette's quiet query drew him out of his reverie. He shook his head and offered her a weak smile.

"I'm sorry. No, I was thinking about something else."

"You looked mighty introspective, even a little sad," she replied and shot him a look that invited him to expand on what had captured his thoughts.

He refused to take the bait. "Let's not talk about me, or about work. How about you tell me something about yourself that I don't know?"

Collette grinned and if his head hadn't been so preoccupied by a certain blonde, he might even have responded to it. Oblivious to his thoughts, she replied.

"All right. I come from a family who are all mad about car racing. Me, my dad and my four brothers."

Despite himself, Colby smiled in surprise. "You have four brothers! Wow! Where do you fit in?"

"I'm the baby, of course, so I was mothered and fathered, teased and tormented by every single one of them from the day I arrived home from the hospital. And I can tell you, in the twenty-nine years since, nothing's changed!"

Colby laughed. "I can't imagine what it must be like."

"Do you have any siblings?" Collette asked.

"Yes. I have a younger brother and sister."

"Oh, so you're the oldest. The wise one."

"I'm not so sure about that. In fact, I'm sure my brother would argue that take on things."

"How much younger is he?"

"Three years. We didn't get on so well when we were young."

"And now?"

Colby thought of his brother, Eamon, who'd become a police officer straight out of high school. He'd worked his way up and was now a detective sergeant. Colby couldn't be more proud of him.

"Now? We get on all right."

"Does he live in Sydney?"

"Yes."

"That must be nice. I guess you see each other a fair bit?"

"Yes, although not as often as we'd like. He's a cop. He does shiftwork. We both work long hours. We try to get together at least once every few weeks, but it doesn't always work out like that."

The bartender arrived with their drinks and Colby handed over some bills. He slid Collette's gin and tonic toward her and picked up his beer. She picked up her drink and they clinked glasses.

"Cheers," she said.

"Cheers." He took a sip of his beer and relished the cold, yeasty taste of it on his tongue. He watched Collette suck from her straw. Her lips were full and red and should have stirred his interest, but the spark wasn't there and there was nothing he could do about it.

He swallowed a sigh of regret. She was everything he needed, only... Only she wasn't the one he wanted. Memories of Monica flooded his mind: tall and graceful and naked. Her long slender arms wrapped around him, her lips tasting his skin. Her buttocks clasped in his hands as he thrust himself into her warmth. The way her legs wrapped around his hips, the way she murmured his name...

It had been paradise and then it had been hell. She'd left with promise in her eyes and her smile and then she'd given him a fake number...

He cursed and only realized his companion had heard it when a frown marred the smooth skin of her forehead and her eyes filled with confusion.

"Is everything all right, Colby? Because that's the second time you've drifted off somewhere looking like your best friend just died. You know what? I think I might go. This has been nice, but it's obvious something's on your mind."

Guilt surged through him. He started to protest, but she cut him off.

"Honestly, Colby, it's fine. I understand. You've just started a murder trial. It's always tough going until you know you have the jury on side. Even then, juries can be unpredictable. The pressure's never really off until the guilty verdict comes in. I've worked long enough in the prosecutor's office to know how it is."

He wished he could say something to reassure her that there was nothing wrong, that he was enjoying their time together, but even though that might be true, he was never going to feel for her the things she wanted him to feel. It wasn't fair to pretend otherwise.

She climbed off her bar stool and he stood and bid her farewell.

"Thanks for the drink. I'll see you tomorrow." And with that, she was gone.

CHAPTER 11

Monica patted her mouth dry with a wad of toilet paper and then flushed away the evidence of her morning sickness. Leaving the stall, she rinsed her mouth under the faucet. It was the first time she'd been sick in the past twenty-four hours. Finally, the persistent nausea seemed to be abating. She was grateful for small mercies.

After drying her hands, she checked her appearance in the mirror and patted her hair back into place. It was the third day of her brother's trial and she wanted to look her best. She wanted to believe the hard work she'd put into her appearance—to her carefully chosen pale pink jacket and skirt and matching stilettos to the elegant upswept hairstyle and impeccably applied makeup—had been for the jury's sake. She wanted to look cool, calm and sophisticated. But she was mature enough to admit her efforts had as much to do with the prosecutor as the twelve people who held her brother's fate in their hands.

She left the restroom and entered the courtroom. It was a few minutes before ten. The court was filled with many of the same people who'd been there the day before. Her brother sat in the dock, silent and somber. She'd spoken to him briefly after court the previous day and had expressed her hurt and disappointment that he hadn't confided in her about Sara and Sara's baby. He'd apologized and looked so downhearted and defeated she'd let it go. Besides, she hadn't yet told him about the child she carried. The fact that the baby's father was the Crown prosecutor and Tommy was on trial for murder had a lot to do with keeping it from him, but still…he was her brother. They'd always been close. Under normal circumstances, he would have been one of the first to know. It was frightening how normal seemed so long ago.

Reporters filled the section reserved for the media. Curious strangers took up most of the seats reserved for the public. Blake and his assistant sat on the left-hand side of the bar table. Colby and his girlfriend sat on the right. Okay, she didn't know for sure that the perky little thing was really Colby's girlfriend. But still…

Studiously ignoring them, she took a seat not far from Tommy and settled in. If yesterday was any indication, it was going to be a long and difficult day. A loud knock on the door announced the arrival of the judge. The crowd stood on request and bowed toward the bench.

"Good-morning, Mr Shearer, Mr Harton. I trust you're ready to continue?"

"Yes, Your Honor," both men murmured simultaneously.

"Good. Well, let's get on with it. Sheriff, please send the jury in."

In short order, the twelve men and women who held Tommy's fate in their hands filed in through a side door and took their seats. Monica stared at each of them, trying to determine what they were thinking. Some of them glanced in Tommy's direction, but most of them kept their gazes lowered. Monica tried not to read anything into that. They'd only heard evidence from a handful of witnesses and all of those had been called by the prosecutor. It was far too early to determine what they'd feel about her brother's guilt or innocence at the end of all this.

"Mr Shearer, please call your next witness," the judge requested.

Colby got to his feet. He looked strong and capable and oh-so-sexy in his wig and black gown. "The prosecution calls Akari Higashi."

The door behind Monica opened and a young Japanese girl walked through and took her place on the witness stand. She was petite with long black hair. Her bright red turtleneck contrasted starkly with her pale skin.

The court officer swore her in and the girl took a seat. Colby glanced over his notes and Monica's hands tightened into fists. She wasn't sure what the girl was about to say, but the fact she was Japanese made it likely she'd known the deceased.

Colby led the witness through the formalities, including having her confirm her full name, age and occupation and just as Monica had guessed, Akari Higashi stated she was a student at Sydney University and Sara Nakamura's best friend.

"Miss Higashi, were you aware that Sara was having an affair with her teacher?" Colby asked.

"Yes. Sara and I were very close. She told me everything. For months she kept trying to get Mr Radford's attention. She'd leave him notes and little gifts—pieces of candy, chocolate bars and the like. She thought he was hot."

"Did you ever have any conversations with her about it?"

"Yes. I thought she was being silly. He was a teacher, after all. It wasn't right."

"Did you tell her that?"

"Yes."

"And what did she say?"

"She laughed. She said *I* was the one being silly. She told me we were in Australia now—and that Mr Radford liked her and she could prove it."

Colby paused and Monica knew it was a tactic used to get the jury's attention. It worked. All twelve of them regarded the witness with interest, waiting to hear what she'd say.

"Did you ask her how she was going to prove it?"

"Yes. She showed me her term paper. It had been graded by Mr Radford. He'd given her an A and there was a handwritten note next to the mark."

"Did you read it?"

"Yes. It asked her to meet him the next day after class to discuss her results."

"Had Mr Radford ever asked you to meet him after class?"

"No."

"To the best of your knowledge, had he ever asked *anyone* else to meet him after class?"

"No. Not until he asked Sara. He was usually the first to leave after the lecture ended. He wasn't a teacher to hang around after the bell."

"Then what happened?"

"Sara met with Mr Radford. Things kind of went from there. She told me she'd kissed him in his staffroom when no one else was around. It didn't seem long after that she told me she was sleeping with him."

"Did she tell you anything else about the affair?"

"Just that he was good in bed. Later, she told me she'd asked him to leave his wife, but he refused."

"Did she know before the affair started that he was married?"

The girl nodded. "Yes. I remember she asked him in class one day, long before they got together. He told her yes."

Colby nodded, as if satisfied with her answers. "Thank you, Miss Higashi. No further questions."

Blake got to his feet. "Miss Higashi, you were close friends with Sara Nakamura, weren't you?"

"Yes, she was my best friend."

"In fact, you said she told you everything."

"Yes. We didn't keep secrets from each other."

"And yet, you didn't know she was pregnant, did you?"

The girl's eyes widened in surprise. "No, I didn't."

"So, she *didn't* tell you everything, did she?"

"Well… I thought she did. She was my best friend."

"And in fact, sometimes, she didn't tell you the truth."

The girl's eyes flashed in anger. "Sara would never lie to me!"

"I put it to you, Miss Higashi that Sara *did* lie to you. In fact, she lied when she told you Mr Radford wasn't going to leave his wife."

"I… I don't believe that. She told me he'd refused. She was so upset…"

"In fact, Miss Higashi, Thomas Radford had a conversation with Sara only hours before her death. He told her of his intention to leave his wife."

"I'm not sure what happened that night. I hadn't seen Sara for a couple of days. We were busy studying for mid-term exams. We hadn't talked much during that time and certainly not about Mr Radford."

"So you accept that my client could have told Sara the night of her death that he was going to leave his wife?"

The young girl shrugged. "I… I guess so."

"Thank you, Miss Higashi. I have no further questions."

After asking Colby if he wished to reexamine the witness and Colby answering in the negative, the judge excused the young woman and she stumbled from the witness box and headed toward the exit. Monica sighed. She wasn't sure if the young woman had done Tommy's case harm or good. She'd certainly reinforced in the jury's mind that Monica's brother was a sleaze of the highest order—not only cheating on his wife, but with a student, a girl nearly half his age. To make matters worse, he'd gotten her pregnant and might or might not have agreed to leave his wife. Some of the jurors were gazing at him with looks of disdain and Monica understood their reactions.

She recalled her conversation with Tommy the day he was arrested, how he told her he and Pamela had been having problems and he wasn't sure he loved her enough to try for the baby Pamela longed for. And all the time he was having an affair with his student—an affair he'd given no indication of during that conversation. In fact, the way he'd told it, the deceased student was no more than that—one of his students. And all along, he'd known the girl was pregnant with his child... She couldn't help but wonder what else he'd lied about—or at least, had actively concealed.

She still didn't believe he was capable of murder, but it troubled her that the jury might also be wondering about Tommy's moral compass and his willingness, or otherwise, to tell the truth.

The judge cleared her throat. "I note the clock, gentlemen and I think this might be an appropriate time to take a break. We'll reconvene again at two."

The jury departed through the side door from which they'd entered and a moment later, the judge rose and also disappeared. Monica eased her breath out on a quiet sigh and absently rubbed her belly. The stress of the trial was already taking its toll. They were only part way through the third day and already she was feeling fatigued. She wanted to be there to support Tommy and to listen to the evidence that was put forward against him, to reassure herself that the prosecutor had nothing that would cause a jury to convict him, but even at this early stage, she was fearful the jurors might not read things the way she did.

Seated beside her, Natalie reached over and squeezed her hand. "How are you doing?"

"I'm okay," Monica murmured.

"You look a little pale."

Monica gave her a weak smile. "It's tough sitting here and listening to what's being said."

"Yes. I can't imagine how it must feel."

"I never thought Tommy was a saint, but having an affair with his student..." Monica shook her head.

"I wish you didn't have to hear this stuff," Natalie said quietly.

"Me too, but I have to be here. I have to show the jury that I believe my brother's innocent. He might have made some immoral decisions in his personal life, but he's not a murderer."

"Stay strong, Mon. Blake's very good at his job. I'm sure he'll make them see the truth of it."

Monica blinked back a sudden surge of tears. It was too easy to cry with her hormones all over the place. She bit her lip to still its trembling and nodded. "I hope so."

Natalie leaned over and gave her a hug.

Monica appreciated the show of support. "Are you going somewhere for lunch? Do you want some company?" Natalie asked.

"Yes, I'd kill for a coffee and my stomach might even tolerate a sandwich. I think the morning sickness is finally easing."

Natalie smiled. "That's great. I might just have a quick word with my husband first. I'll meet you outside." Natalie moved past Monica and headed in Blake's direction. Monica made her way to the exit.

She leaned her shoulder against the wooden panel and pushed. At the same time, someone on the opposite side pulled the door open. Monica stumbled in her high heels. She swayed forward, grappling for balance. Before she realized what was happening, she felt herself toppling forward.

"Oh! Oh, no!" she yelped.

The carpet came up to meet her. At the last minute, she had the presence of thought to twist her body sideways and so she took the brunt of the fall on her shoulder. Pain, hot and immediate, radiated down her arm. She heard the distinct sound of a bone breaking and cried out again.

"Monica! Oh, my God! Are you all right?"

She blinked into Colby's face. He leaned over her, his expression filled with concern. She tried to sit up, to reassure him she was fine and another shaft of pain raced down her arm.

"Ouch!" she cried and grabbed her injured arm.

"Take it easy," Colby urged. He put his hand under her head, pillowing her.

A rush of warmth flooded through her. She tried not to think about how good it felt to have him so close that his cologne tickled her nose and she could count the freckles on his face.

"Where does it hurt?" he asked gently.

"My arm."

"You fell pretty hard. Is it only your arm you hurt?"

She nodded and then became aware of a warm wetness between her thighs. Realization of what could be happening filled her with horror. "Oh, my God! Please, no! Please!"

Colby's expression became more concerned. "What is it, Monica? Please, tell me what's going on?"

"My baby!" she cried. "I think I'm losing my baby!"

CHAPTER 12

Colby stared down at Monica in shock. He hadn't even realized she was pregnant. She didn't look pregnant.

"How far along are you?" he whispered, his voice hoarse.

She stared at him. "Fourteen weeks."

It took him a millisecond to count back the weeks since Fiji. He shook his head in disbelief. "Are you saying it's *mine*?"

She nodded. Fear and uncertainty warred on her face. "I'm sorry. I... I didn't mean for it to happen."

"When were you going to tell me?" he asked, still raw with shock and disbelief.

She shrugged helplessly and the movement caused her to cry out in pain. "Ouch! It hurts, Colby. It hurts so badly!"

Knowing this wasn't the time or the place to have this out with her, he sat back on his haunches and looked around. Pockets of people were gathered outside the courtroom, but no one appeared to be paying them much heed.

"We need an ambulance. Will somebody call an ambulance?" he shouted. "This lady's been hurt."

Almost immediately, he and Monica were surrounded and several people pulled out their phones. He kept his hand under her head and urged her to remain calm.

"The ambulance is on its way, Monica. Just hang in there, honey. You're going to be fine, don't worry."

The mindless words spilled out of his mouth. He was hardly aware of what he was saying. All he knew was that he cared for this woman and his baby that she carried. His mind spun with the knowledge he was going to be a father and then he remembered her concern that she was miscarrying and silently urged himself to be cautious. There was no sense getting his hopes up until they knew exactly what was going on. Besides, he had a million questions…

"Oh, my God, Monica! Are you all right?"

Colby looked up and spied Natalie Johnson. She ran over to where Monica lay and kneeled down beside her.

Monica gave her a weak smile of reassurance. "I think so. I fell and hurt my arm and…"

"The ambulance is on its way," Colby added.

Natalie nodded and then looked at Colby. "You're needed inside. The judge has returned to the bench."

"But—"

"It's fine," Natalie interrupted. "I'll stay with her."

He looked down at the woman on the floor

and struggled with indecision. He wanted to go with her, to talk about the baby, to ask her why she hadn't told him, to find out so many things... But he was in the middle of a trial. He could hardly go and plead for an adjournment because the sister of the accused required medical treatment.

He nodded grimly. Natalie was right. He was needed inside. Monica would be fine. She had Natalie and the paramedics were on their way.

"I'll speak with you later," he said to Monica.

She looked at him, residual fear still obvious in her eyes, though she whispered, "Okay."

Slowly, he removed his hand from beneath her head and rose to his feet. With a last look in her direction, he resolutely turned away. Fielding a curious glance from Collette, he took his place at the bar table.

"Nice of you to join us, Mr Shearer," the judge said, an edge of sarcasm in her tone.

Colby fought off a blush. "I apologize, Your Honor. There was a slight incident outside."

"Is everything all right?" the judge asked.

"Yes, paramedics are on the way. I'm sure everything will be fine."

"Are you ready to continue with this trial?"

"Yes, Your Honor. The prosecution calls Alexandra Mison."

The rear door opened and a young woman with blond hair and eyes too large for her small face took the stand. Colby quickly established the preliminaries, including the fact the woman was thirty-one years old and was a close friend of Pamela Radford's.

"How long have you known the defendant's wife?" Colby asked.

"Most of my life. We met in high school."

"You socialized together as adults?"

"Yes, we regularly meet for coffee. Once a week, we play tennis."

"Were you aware Pamela and her husband were having marriage difficulties?"

The woman grimaced. "Yes. Pammie wanted a baby so badly. She lost one and it really tore her up. She was having a hard time convincing Tom to give it another go."

"Did she tell you her husband was having an affair?"

The witness glared at the defendant who sat in the dock with his gaze lowered to the floor. "Yes. She told me. She was devastated."

"Did she raise the possibility of divorce?"

"No, in fact, just the opposite."

"What do you mean?"

"She didn't want him to leave their marriage. He'd messed up, but she loved him."

"Did you find that strange?"

The woman shrugged. "It wasn't up to me to judge."

"What else did she tell you?"

"She told me Tom had promised to end the affair and to work harder on their marriage. She was hopeful he might even be willing to try for another baby."

"Are you sure of that?"

"Of course I'm sure! That's what Pammie told me and she's never lied to me before."

Colby paused. "What would you say if I told you someone else was just as certain the defendant was going to leave his wife?"

The woman sat up straighter in her seat and turned to face the jury. "I'd say they were mistaken."

Colby nodded, satisfied with the response. "No further questions, Your Honor."

Blake jumped to his feet. "Ms Mison, Pamela Radford never told you her husband was going to end the affair, did she?"

"Of course she did! I remember the conversation well. I expected her to tell me she'd tossed him out on his ear. That's what I would have done! Instead, she told me they were trying to work things out and that she was giving him another chance."

"I put it to you, Ms Mison, that my client had no intention of ending his affair or working on his marriage. He was in love with Sara Nakamura and he wanted to be with her. Permanently."

"That's not what Pammie said. She was convinced they could make things work."

"Thank you, Ms Mison. I have no further questions."

Colby got to his feet. "Ms Mison, would you consider Pamela Radford to be an honest person?"

The witness nodded. "I've known Pammie a long time. I've never known her to lie."

"Thank you, Ms Mison. Nothing further."

Colby returned to his seat. The woman climbed down from the witness box and sat in the public gallery. He wondered fleetingly about Monica and hoped she was all right. He looked at the clock and then checked with Collette to ensure their next witness was ready to go. She answered in the affirmative. He got back on his feet.

"The prosecution calls Salim Haddad."

The back door to the courtroom opened and a young man with a neatly trimmed black beard and thick black eyebrows walked toward the witness box. Colby took him through the preliminaries and established that Salim Haddad was a twenty-one-year-old college student who lived in the apartment across the hall from Sara Nakamura.

"Mr Haddad, I want to take you back to the night of April tenth. Were you home that night?"

"Yes. I was studying for my mid-term exams."

"Did you see anyone in the neighborhood or in your building that night?"

"Yes. I was studying at my desk. It looks out on the street. I saw a man come into the building. A short time later, I heard someone outside Sara's door."

"Do you see the man in the courtroom today?"

"Yes. He's sitting over there."

Colby looked up at the judge. "May the record reflect that the witness has pointed to the accused, Thomas Radford, as the man he saw enter the deceased's building."

"So noted," the judge replied. "Please continue, Mr Shearer."

"Was that the first time you'd seen the accused, Mr Haddad?"

The man shook his head. "No. I'd seen him plenty of times before. Someone told me he was Sara's boyfriend. I didn't know if that were true, because he was so much older than her, but that's what I understood."

"Did you see anyone else enter the building that night?"

"No. I got up briefly for a bathroom break, but otherwise, I was there most of the night."

"Did you hear anything unusual?"

"Not at first. I heard Sara's door open and close and then nothing for quite a while. Then I heard arguing and finally, the screams." The man shuddered, as if recalling the moment when Sara had been brutally attacked.

"Could you tell what was being said during the argument?"

"No, I only heard voices."

"Could you tell if the voices were male or female?"

"I definitely heard the sound of Sara screaming. Before that, I'm not sure. I think I heard male and female voices. After all, I knew Sara's boyfriend was in her apartment."

"Did you do anything?"

"Yes. I was scared. It sounded like Sara was in trouble. I called the police."

"Did you see the accused, Thomas Radford, leave Sara's building?"

"No. As soon as I called the police, I went into my bedroom and hid."

"Did the police interview you about this?"

"Yes. They knocked on my door about an hour

after I called them. I spoke to a couple detectives."

"Mr Haddad, did you make a formal statement?"

"Yes, I did."

Colby turned back to the bar table and picked up some papers. He handed them to the court officer who handed them to the witness.

"Is that the statement you gave to the police?"

The witness took a moment to look it over and then nodded. "Yes, this is it."

"Your Honor, I'd like to tender Mr Haddad's statement."

The judge looked over to Blake. "Any objection, Mr Harton?"

"No, Your Honor."

She nodded. "Very well, the statement is tendered as evidence and will be marked Exhibit I. Do you have any further questions, Mr Shearer?"

"No, Your Honor."

"Mr Harton, are you ready to cross examine the witness?"

"Yes, Your Honor."

Blake came to his feet. "Mr Haddad, you said you were at your desk studying when you heard the argument coming from across the hall, is that right?"

"Yes."

"It was in the middle of the night. Do you usually study in the middle of the night?"

The witness stared at Blake defiantly. "Yes. I often work shifts around my classes during the day. Sometimes, the only time I have to study is through the night. I had exams coming up. I was hitting the books pretty hard."

"So you were up in the middle of the night. You must have been tired."

"Yes, I was tired. It had been a long day."

"I put it to you that when you heard the sound of people arguing, that you didn't hear my client."

"I'm pretty sure I heard a man's voice."

"Yes, but it wasn't the voice of Thomas Radford."

"Maybe. I guess I couldn't say for sure."

"You've never spoken to my client, have you?"

"No."

"So you wouldn't know what his voice sounded like, would you?"

"No."

"In fact, it could have been anyone, couldn't it?"

"Yes, I guess so."

"And you told us at some stage that night you went to the bathroom, correct?"

"Yes."

"So it's possible my client left the building while you were otherwise occupied, correct?"

"Yes, I guess so."

"In fact, it's also possible that someone else might have come into the building while you were in the bathroom."

"Yes, I guess so," the man conceded.

"By the time you heard the screams, you'd already been to the bathroom and returned, right?"

The man scrunched his brow in thought. "Yes, I think so."

Blake paused and eyeballed the witness. "Thank you, Mr Haddad. I have no further questions."

The judge looked at Colby. "Any re-examination, Mr Shearer?"

Colby shook his head. As much as he didn't want to end the testimony with the jury wondering who exactly Salim Haddad had seen and heard, there was nothing more to say.

"No, Your Honor."

The judge nodded in acknowledgement and cleared her throat. "Do you have any other witnesses, Mr Shearer?"

"No, Your Honor. The prosecution rests."

"Very well. I note the time. We have less than an hour to go before the day is over." She looked at Blake. "Mr Harton, please have your first witness ready to go in the morning. We'll adjourn until ten o'clock. Bail to continue."

With that, her gavel came down. The jurors filed out silently and a moment later the judge disappeared back into her chambers. Colby sighed and stretched his arms over his head.

"You did well today," Collette said, offering him a smile.

He smiled back at her, glad there was no uncomfortableness between them. She must have worked out that they were only ever going to be work colleagues—and she seemed fine with that.

"Thanks. I think we made an impact on the jury, but it's going to come down to which story they believe. The one thing we have on our side is that the defense haven't offered an alternate killer. They say Thomas Radford didn't do it, but they don't have anyone else. That's got to help us."

"Yes."

Collette began to pack up the files. Colby shoved his papers in his briefcase. "Listen, do you mind taking all this back to the office? There's something I need to do downtown."

Collette looked a little surprised, but nodded. "Of course."

"Great. I'll see you in the morning."

Hurrying from the courtroom, he tugged out his phone and scrolled through his contacts until he found Natalie Johnson's number. She answered after the third ring.

"Natalie, it's Colby Shearer. I was just wondering how Monica was doing?"

"She's fine, apart from a broken arm. We're at the emergency department of Sydney Harbour Hospital. She's been seen by the doctor. We're just waiting for someone to come and put a plaster cast on."

He paused and then asked, "What about the baby?"

Natalie sounded surprised. "Oh, you know about that, do you?"

"Yes. Monica told me. She was worried she might be having a miscarriage."

"It was just a scare. A small amount of bleeding, but they've done a scan and everything's fine."

Relief surged through Colby. He drew in a deep breath and blew it out. "That's great news. Listen, court has finished up for the day. I'd like to come and see her. Do you think that would be all right?"

"I'll ask her."

There was silence on the other end of the phone for so long, Colby nearly died from waiting.

At last, Natalie came back.

"She said that would be okay."

Once again, relief flooded through Colby's veins. He grinned into the phone. "Great. I'll be there soon." Without giving Natalie time to reply, he ended the call.

―――――――――

Monica stared at Natalie as her friend tossed her phone back into her handbag. She couldn't believe she'd just agreed to let Colby come and visit her in the hospital. He knew about the baby. He'd have a million questions.

What was she going to tell him?

There was no way a man like Colby Shearer would make such a discovery and then forget about it. He'd want to know why she'd given him a fake phone number and most of all, he'd want to know why she kept the news of the baby from him.

Another wave of anxiety went through her as she remembered the way she'd lied to him about her lack of condoms. It had only happened the once, but as it turned out, once had been enough.

Natalie saw her concern and spoke. "What are you going to tell him?"

"I don't know."

"Well, you'd better think of something. He's on his way over."

Panic surged through her and she suddenly

wished she hadn't agreed to let him come. Perhaps Colby might accept her need to do this on her own. *Yeah, right.* She'd known right from the moment she started talking to him at the wedding that this guy was a stayer—someone who would stick around through thick and thin. Oh, hell.

"Would it be so bad if you told him the truth—about everything?" Natalie murmured.

"You mean about how I lied to him about not having any condoms?"

"Yes, and the fact you want to raise this child on your own."

"What if he doesn't accept that? He's the father, after all. He has rights. This is why I didn't want to tell him in the first place."

"Well, now he knows and you're going to have to deal with that. Honey, Colby's a great guy. You'd be hard pressed to find anyone better."

Monica's face heated with embarrassment. "But I don't want to be in a relationship, no matter how eligible the man might be," she protested. "And it's not my intention to trap anyone either."

"I don't know what you want me to say, Mon. He's the father of your baby. He's a part of your life now, whether you like it or not. I know Colby Shearer. He's a good and decent man. There's no way he's going to turn his back on his responsibilities."

Monica brought her good hand up to her face and groaned. "Oh, my goodness! What have I done? How did this get so complicated? I should have simply gone to a sperm bank like I originally planned and fallen pregnant with a random donor, someone I never had to meet. I always meant to raise this baby on my own, providing for its every need, loving it as much as two parents ever could. Now everything's such a mess. What am I going to do?"

Natalie's expression gentled. "Would it be so terrible to let Colby into your life? Not necessarily as a life partner, but couldn't you learn to let him be the father of your baby, help you out where he can? What's so wrong with that, Mon?"

Once again, Monica let out a groan of despair. "I don't *want* a man in my life, Nat! I don't want someone telling me what to do! I like my life just as it is."

"Honey, do you have any idea how selfish that sounds?" Natalie asked quietly. "You're going to have a baby. Another person with wants and needs even more important than yours. Have you thought about that? Have you thought about what you're going to tell your son or daughter when he or she asks about their dad?"

"Oh, Nat! I don't know what to do!" She shrugged helplessly and then yelped as she remembered her injured arm. She'd gotten herself into a terrible mess and she didn't know how to get out of it. And all this while her dear, but foolish, brother was fighting to clear his name… It was too much.

Tears of helplessness and frustration burned behind her eyes. She blinked hard, but they filled her eyes and ran down her cheeks. Natalie leaned over and gave her an awkward hug.

"Oh, honey, don't cry. We'll work something out. I always say, when in doubt, stick with the truth. You can't go wrong with that."

"But what if he hates me?" she wailed.

"He might be upset at first. Hell, if you hadn't lied about not having a condom there wouldn't even be a baby. But I'm sure he won't hate you. Like I said, he's a good and decent guy." She shot Monica a sly look. "And sinfully good-looking. Hard to beat that, you know."

Monica rolled her eyes. If she could have thrown something at her friend, she would have.

Natalie merely chuckled. "I wonder how long the doctor is going to be."

"I don't know, but I wish they'd hurry. The painkillers are starting to wear off."

"It's too bad they can't give you anything stronger than paracetamol. How about I go and see what's keeping them?"

"Would you?"

"Yes, of course. Hold tight."

Natalie pulled open the curtain that surrounded Monica's bed. She had a brief glimpse of the patient across the room before Nat closed the curtain again. Monica leaned back against the pillows with a sigh. Not only did she now have to contend with Colby and his knowledge she was pregnant with his baby, she also had to deal with a broken arm. How would she cope?

The radiologist had informed her the break had occurred halfway up her left humerus. Being left-handed, she wasn't sure how she was going to manage. She lived alone in a three-story walk-up.

She barely knew her neighbors by name. Carrying groceries or anything else from the car would also be tough.

And then there were the more basic things like dressing and undressing, showering, opening cans and jars, sweeping the floor, using the dustpan... Driving would also be difficult. She'd have to leave at least half an hour earlier if she were going to catch the train and she hated getting out of bed. It was just another thing she'd have to deal with.

"*Uggh!*" She groaned aloud and squeezed her eyes shut. *When had life gotten so darn difficult?*

Chapter 13

The sound of the curtains being opened snagged her attention. Monica's eyelids snapped open. Colby stood at the foot of her bed, the curtain behind him gaping.

"I take it things aren't going so well?" he murmured.

"W-what are you doing here?" she stammered and ignored the heat that crept across her cheeks.

"I spoke to Natalie. She told me you were okay if I dropped in for a visit." He gaze turned serious. "It is okay, isn't it?"

Monica sighed and waved him closer. "Yes. Of course it is. Thank you for coming. You didn't have to."

"I know. I wanted to. How are you feeling?"

"Sore," she admitted. "I'm waiting for someone to come and set my arm in plaster. The doctor said it will be five or six weeks before I can use it."

Colby winced. "Ouch. It sounds like a bad break."

"Yes. I snapped the humerus clean through. One good thing though, it isn't displaced. No need for surgery."

"That's good."

An awkward silence fell between them. Monica frantically tried to think of something to say.

"I'm sorry about—"

"Why don't you tell me about—?"

They spoke simultaneously. Monica offered him a wry smile. Colby chuckled. "I'm sorry," he said. "Ladies first."

Monica drew in a breath and gathered her courage. The moment she'd dreaded was upon her. She looked up at him and for a time, got lost in his chocolate eyes.

"You were saying?" he encouraged.

She nodded. "I just wanted to say how sorry I am for blurting out the news of the baby like that. It must have come as a shock."

He blew his breath out on a quiet sigh and moved further into the space occupied by her bed.

"Do you mind closing the curtains?" she asked.

Colby turned and pulled them shut. He took the seat recently vacated by Natalie. "Talk to me, Monica."

She shot him a helpless look. "I don't know what to say."

"How about you start at the beginning? I thought we had something going, a real connection and then you gave me that fake number. Now I find out you're pregnant with my baby... I'm confused."

There was a roughness to his tone. She realized he'd been hurt by her decision not to give her real phone number. "I panicked," she said and was relieved that in this at least, she was telling the truth.

He frowned. "I don't get it. Why would you panic? I thought we were getting along well."

"We were. We did. We had a wonderful time together, but... We were on holidays on a tropical island. It wasn't real life. I got to thinking about who we really were and what life in the real world was like and...I panicked."

"So you decided I was good enough for a holiday romance, a fantasy fling, but after it was over, you didn't want to see me again." Once again, she detected the hurt in his voice.

"It wasn't like that, Colby!" she protested. She stared at the sheet. Guilt ate into her heart.

"How was it then, Monica? Because from where I stand, that's exactly what it looks like."

She shrugged in an effort to buy time. "I don't know. Those five days were overwhelming. We dived in head first and barely came up for air. I hardly knew anything about you and you knew just as little about me. We weren't our real selves there. I got scared that if you discovered the real Monica Radford, you wouldn't want me."

The lies rolled off her tongue like she'd practiced them forever. Guilt flooded through her, prickling the pores of her skin, but she paid it no heed. She couldn't tell him that all along, she'd hoped to get pregnant with his baby and that she'd lied when she'd told him she didn't have any condoms.

"Wouldn't *want* you?" Colby cried, his eyes wide with disbelief. "Why wouldn't I want you in the real world? I couldn't *wait* to get to know you better! I left the island early and I called you from the airport the moment I cleared customs. That's when I discovered you'd given me a false number."

His voice hitched with emotion on the last few words. Once again, she was filled with guilt.

She shook her head. "I'm sorry. I can't explain it."

He reached over and took her hand in his. Her heart skipped a beat. The feel of his warm skin against hers sent an avalanche of memories rushing through her head.

"Would you tell me about the baby?"

She tensed. Keeping her gaze averted, she nodded. "What would you like to know?"

"We used condoms except that first night. I take it that's when it happened?"

"It must have been."

"Wow. What are the odds?"

"Who knows?" she murmured and then cleared her throat. "Listen, Colby, I'm sorry you found out the way you did, but it doesn't change anything. I'm having this baby and I'm quite willing to raise it on my own. I don't expect anything from you, emotionally, physically or even financially. I have my own place in Parramatta. I can—"

"Of course you won't be raising this child on your own," he interrupted. "Okay, so I didn't plan on starting a family this way, but I'm not unhappy about it. I've always wanted to get married, have kids. There's no way I'm going to step aside and let all of this fall on you."

Real panic rushed through her. She pulled her hand out of his and tried to sit up. "Ouch!" The pain in her shoulder intensified. She bit back tears.

Colby was there in an instant. "Hey, take it easy. Let me help you." Gently, he drew her forward and stacked more pillows behind her back. "How's that?"

"Better, thanks." She drew in a couple of deep breaths. Calmness and control were key. She needed to convince Colby that she could do this; that she could be a single mom, but first of all, she needed to get her damn arm set so she could go home.

"I appreciate your offer, Colby, but I've got this. When I found out I was pregnant, I knew keeping the baby would mean raising it on my own. I'm good with that. In fact, I welcome it. I didn't want you to feel responsible. I didn't want the baby to be the reason we were together."

She eyed him steadily and continued. "My parents divorced when I was three. I grew up without a dad. I adjusted. It was fine. A lot of my friends grew up in single-parent homes. In fact, I seem to recall you did, too."

"Yes, but—"

"The odds are against us, Colby. Marriages just don't last anymore. In Australia, one in three come to a sorry end. I don't want to be another statistic. Our child won't suffer for not having both parents in his life. That I can guarantee. I've thought about this long and hard." She stared at him, trying to make him understand.

His expression grew increasingly bewildered.

Toward the end of her monologue, anger glinted in the dark depths of his eyes.

"You talk as if I have no say in this, Monica. I'm the father! I *want* to be part of my child's life! Okay, so we didn't plan to become parents, but now that we are, I'm going to do everything I can to be the best dad I can be, including taking care of you."

Monica shook her head. "Colby, you're talking nonsense. I'm thirty-two years old. I'm pregnant. I'm not disabled. I can take care of myself and my baby."

"Except now you have a broken arm and if my memory serves me right, you're left handed. Right?"

She compressed her lips and reluctantly offered him a nod.

"That's your dominant arm. Do you live alone?"

"Yes."

"How do you think you're going to cope with only one hand? Who's going to look after you?"

"I already told you, I don't need looking after," she cried.

He ignored her outburst. "How far away do you live from the nearest public transport?"

"Two blocks to the bus stop. A little further to the train."

"And you think you're going to be able to carry groceries home that far?"

She stared at him defiantly. "I'll take a cab."

"For six weeks?"

"If I have to."

Colby blew his breath out in an obvious sign of

frustration. "This is madness, Monica. Let me take care of you! I *want* to take care of you! I have a two-bedroom place in the city. You could easily walk to work—and the court house. I'm not suggesting anything permanent, but you're in a fix. I'd like to help you out."

Monica regarded him—full of indecision. This was everything she'd hoped to avoid. Her plan to find an anonymous baby daddy and disappear when the deed had been accomplished had seemed so straightforward, easy even. Now she was faced with the problem of having the baby's father in her life—and involved in the life of her unborn child.

How did she get herself into such a fix? It was never meant to be this way. And yet, here he was, her knight in shining armor, wanting to take care of her, to look out for her, to help her... And because of her arm, there was no doubt she needed help. Many everyday chores would be impossible to accomplish with her injury—juggling shopping bags one-handed while struggling onto a bus held absolutely no appeal.

Perhaps she could take Colby up on his offer, just until after her arm had healed? She'd keep him at a distance, treat him no more than she would a friend. She'd make it clear so he knew that. Then, when the plaster was removed, she'd thank him for his kindness and resume her present life.

She might be forced to let him have more to do with their child than she initially bargained, but whether she accepted his help or not, she could tell he wasn't the kind of guy to walk away from his responsibilities. It was clear he wasn't like her father. He'd never walk away from his child. She was stuck with Colby Shearer in her life in some shape or form and she'd better get used to it. She sighed heavily.

He frowned. "Would it really be so awful for you to live with me for a while?"

"No, I guess not, but let's get something straight. First of all, we're not going to be living together. I'm merely taking you up on your offer to make use of your spare room while I'm...indisposed. Secondly, we will *not* be taking up where we left off in Fiji. That was then; this is now. Thirdly, the fact that I'm pregnant changes nothing. I have a life and so do you. We'll remain independent of each other, as best we can. You go about your business and I'll go about mine. We need not check in with each other or otherwise rearrange our schedules to suit each other. We'll be roommates, nothing more."

"Except I'm prosecuting your brother for murder and I've noticed you in court on all three days. I'm assuming you intend to be present in the court for the duration of the trial?"

She nodded reluctantly. "Yes, I *know* he's innocent. I need to be there to support him."

"So for the short term at least, we'll both be heading to the same destination."

"You said the court was within walking distance of your place. I can make my own way there."

"Fair enough. So does this mean you're taking me up on my offer?"

Despite her earlier thoughts, she was filled with a flood of misgivings. Moving in with Colby was the last thing she wanted to do, not the least because he was prosecuting her brother for murder. But he was right. She was going to struggle with her dominant arm in plaster. She wasn't too proud or too stupid to accept help. She couldn't move in with Tommy and Pamela. They had enough going on and she didn't want to add to their burden by asking them to assist. Her mother hadn't been well for some time and simply didn't have the room. Besides, she was too far away.

She could probably ask Natalie. She had a spare room and Monica would love to spend some time with Nat's boys. They'd stayed with her during their father's trial and Monica had grown close to them. She liked to think Bailey and Darby felt the same about her.

Yes, staying with the Harton family was a much wiser choice. Besides, it was only for six weeks. She looked up at him, at the expectant look on his face, and gave him her answer.

"Um, actually, I think it would be better if I stayed with Nat."

———

Colby was unable to hide his disappointment. He'd been stunned to discover Monica was pregnant with his baby, but now that the shock had worn off and he'd kind of gotten used to the idea, he was beyond excited. *He was going to be a father!* It was finally going to happen! And as much as Monica now pretended they had nothing special together, he knew differently and he was determined to prove it to her. Getting her under his roof was the first step in his plan. Except, she'd just turned down his offer.

The curtain behind him slid open. Natalie appeared in the gap. She looked startled at the sight of him. "Colby! You're here."

"Yes. I told you I was on my way over."

Natalie shot a glance in Monica's direction, as if checking to see if she were okay. "Yes, of course. I... I just didn't expect to see you so soon."

He shrugged.

"Colby offered to let me stay with him until the plaster comes off," Monica stated in a casual tone.

Natalie's eyebrows rose in surprise. She looked from Monica to Colby. "Wow, um... That's very kind of you, Colby. I would have offered already, but the boys are home sick with the chickenpox."

"Oh," Monica replied, her tone laced with disappointment. "That's too bad. I was going to add that I declined Colby's offer. I thought I could stay with you?"

"I'm sorry, Mon. I wish you could. With a sitter there night and day we're tight as canned sardines. And have you had the chicken pox before?"

"Yes, but I guess being pregnant, I probably shouldn't take the risk."

"You're right," Natalie agreed. "You don't want to expose the baby unnecessarily."

Colby cleared his throat and was quick to side with her. "I agree, Monica. You need to think about the baby. My offer still stands." He turned to Natalie. "I'm sorry to hear your kids are unwell, but I hope they're doing okay."

She nodded. "They're fine. Blake and I both had it when we were kids, so we're already immune. I hired a nanny-nurse to look after them so I could be with Monica in court."

Monica smiled softly and her eyes filled with tears. "Oh, Nat! You should have told me! I had no idea!"

Natalie brushed away her concern. "It's fine. You had much more important things on your mind."

Colby cleared his throat. "Well, that's settled. Monica can move in with me. I have plenty of room and I *don't* have chicken pox."

He said it lightly, but Monica shot him a narrow-eyed look. "I'm not *moving* in. I'll just be residing in your spare room until my arm heals."

Colby shrugged as if her take on things was of no consequence. "Whatever."

She could keep her distance and do what she had to do to make herself feel better about the situation, but he'd chip away at her defenses until she'd be forced to admit they were good together and that the best thing they could offer their baby would be two parents who were committed to and maybe even loved each other.

Love? Could he love Monica? Of course he could! He was already halfway there. All he needed to do was convince her she felt the same way. He was confident if he was given a fair opportunity, he could make it happen.

Natalie continued to stare down at her friend, her brow creasing in concern. "Mon? Are you *sure?*"

Monica smiled back at her, but Colby noticed it didn't reach her eyes. *He had some work to do.*

"Of course, Nat. It's a sensible solution. Colby has room and he lives in the city. I can walk to the court house and to work. It sounds...perfect."

"In fact, as soon as you finish here, I'll take you back to my place and get you settled," Colby added.

Monica frowned. "I need to go home and get a few things. Some clothes and other stuff."

"I can do that for you," Natalie offered.

"It's fine, Natalie. I don't mind swinging by Monica's on the way home." He turned back to Monica. "Or, you can give me a list and I'll pick things up for you."

A blush crept up Monica's neck. She averted her gaze. He couldn't believe she was embarrassed at the thought of him packing her a suitcase. He'd seen her naked, for Pete's sake.

"It's okay," she murmured. "If you can drive me home and get the suitcase from out of the top of the cupboard, I'll be able to take it from there."

He shrugged. It didn't matter to him how she accomplished it. All that mattered was getting her ensconced in his home. Hopefully for a hell of a lot longer than six weeks.

CHAPTER 14

After what seemed like an eon, the doctor eventually arrived and plastered her arm from shoulder to wrist and then stabilized it in a sling. Colby collected her handbag and together they left the emergency department, headed for her home.

She gave him the key and he opened her front door. She was relieved to discover she'd folded last week's laundry and put it away and that there were no dirty dishes in the sink. She wasn't exactly untidy, but she wasn't as fastidious about housekeeping as some people were. Still, she didn't want him to think she was a slob.

He commented on the stylish furniture and the pretty rug on the living room floor. He also recognized the Ken Done print she had on the dining room wall. Her job at Baker & Carr Construction didn't earn her a hefty pay packet, but she was a thrifty shopper and often found bargains in second-hand stores. She also had a natural flair for decorating and could tell what might go with what. The result was a stylish and comfortable apartment, a place she was proud to call home.

"This is very nice," Colby commented, looking around.

"Thank you. It's home."

He nodded. "Where do you keep your suitcases?"

"In the cupboard down the hall."

He headed in that direction and a short time later, reappeared with a suitcase in hand. "Where do you want to start?"

"Put it on the bed in the spare room. I have my things stored in the closet there. The room's second on the right."

He disappeared again and she took the opportunity to check her answering machine for messages. There were none. It wasn't surprising. Most people called her cell phone. Knowing she didn't want to leave Colby alone in her bedroom too long, she hurried down the hall. He met her at the door on his way out.

"I opened it for you and left it on the bed, like you asked."

She murmured her thanks and tried not to remember the last time they were together in the vicinity of a bed. From the way he quickly averted his gaze, he was remembering, too. She was filled with a sudden surge of longing to feel him hard and urgent against her once again but quickly suppressed the urge. They were friends, nothing more. *Had she made the right decision when she agreed to move in with him?* It wasn't too late to change her mind. She was sure she could find somewhere else to stay...with a little creative thinking.

As quickly as she could, she packed her things. Within moments they were on their way to his place. He insisted on carrying her luggage and placing it in the trunk of the car and for all her reluctance to accept his invitation, she was grateful for his assistance.

He lived in one of the modern steel-and-glass structures that had begun to pop up around the city. The building was a stone's throw from the courts and within easy access of her workplace. She followed him to the entrance and into the lobby where they were greeted by a concierge and waved to the elevator. A collection of specialty shops comprising a dry cleaner, a pizza place, a café and a hairdresser were situated on the ground floor. The two- and three-bedroom condos were built above them. She leaned against the shiny wall's surface of the elevator and tried to take it all in.

"Are you all right?" Colby's gentle query brought her back to the present. She straightened and moved away from the wall of the elevator and gave him a semblance of a smile.

"Just tired, I guess. It's been a long day."

He nodded. "You can say that again."

"What did I miss at the trial?" she asked, suddenly wanting to know.

"I called two more witnesses. The first one was a woman by the name of Alexandra Mison. Do you know her?"

"I'm not sure. The name sounds familiar."

"She's a close friend of Pamela Radford. The two of them have known each other since high school."

"Oh, yes, I remember her. I met her a couple of times at social functions held at Tommy's home."

"Yes, well she gave evidence to the effect that your brother promised to end the affair with his student and work harder on his marriage. The defense tried to get her to admit she was mistaken, that your brother was intent on leaving his wife, but she remained firm."

Monica frowned. She recalled the conversation she'd had with her brother the day he was arrested; how he hadn't been convinced he loved his wife enough to try for another baby. And this was before Monica had a clue about the affair and everything else that had been going on.

"I also called a witness who lives across the hall from Sara Nakamura's apartment. He was the one who called the police the night of the murder."

Her mind was still stuck on his earlier statement. "What makes you so sure Tommy intended to honor his marriage vows?" she asked.

"Because if he were going to leave his wife for his mistress, he and his lover would hardly end up in a fight that resulted in murder. I've never had a mistress, but if I did and I told her I was choosing her over my marriage, I would think that would be cause for celebration, not for a fight—and certainly not a fight that ended in one of us dying in a pool of blood."

She glared at him. "Okay, I agree with the logic. But the other explanation is that someone else did it. Tommy didn't kill that girl."

"So you keep saying and I understand why you feel that way. He's your brother. It's your job to defend him. I applaud your loyalty. I hope my siblings would be there to defend me, too, if I were ever to find myself in need of it. Unfortunately, the evidence dictates otherwise."

Anger flared inside her. "Tommy's *innocent*. Your evidence is only circumstantial. I'm sorry you don't agree with me and I guess it's your job to see him put away, but just so you know, you're *wrong* and I don't give a damn what the evidence shows."

Her breath came fast. Her chest felt tight. Mindful of her baby, she brought her uninjured hand up and pressed it against her heart in an effort to slow its pace. Colby's expression immediately changed to one of concern.

"Monica, are you all right? You look flushed."

"I'm fine," she managed.

Colby blew his breath out on a sigh. "I'm sorry. I shouldn't have said anything."

Monica breathed in deeply and eased the air out. When she felt more in control, she spoke again. "I'm sorry, too. You're just doing your job. But you don't know him like I do."

"I think it might be best if we refrain from speaking about this case again, outside the courthouse. I understand that you're not on the witness list, but still... We're on opposing sides. At least where this is concerned. Once the trial's over, we can put it behind us and concentrate on what's really important." He pointed to her belly. "This little guy."

A frisson of alarm went through Monica, but she forced herself to smile. There would be time enough later to establish the ground rules of how this shared parenting thing was going to work. Right now, though it was difficult for her to admit, she needed Colby's help.

The elevator door slid open and they stepped out into a carpeted corridor. Colby led the way. Three doors down, he came to a halt and set her luggage down to fish in his jacket pocket for a key. He inserted it into the lock and turned the door handle. Picking up her suitcase and bag, he indicated for her to enter ahead of him and then closed the door behind them.

Monica walked down a short hallway and came into an open concept kitchen and living room that stole her breath. Marble tiles buffed to a high gloss covered the floors. Plate glass windows made up one entire wall. The view of Sydney Harbour was spectacular. She could see a balcony off another exit near the kitchen and couldn't wait to step outside.

"You have a nice place," she murmured, mimicking what he'd said to her an hour earlier.

He smiled and gave a modest shrug. "It's home."

She turned toward the window. "Your view is spectacular. It must be hard to leave here every morning."

"Yes, it is pretty good, isn't it? I like to sit out on the balcony and take in the night."

"I love my place in Parramatta, but it would be nice to be closer to the harbor. I've always loved the water. I'm a Cancerian. It's in our blood."

"I'm a Pieces. I love the water, too."

They shared a smile that was only broken when Colby looked away and cleared his throat. "I'll put your things in the spare room. It's right down the hall."

He disappeared down the corridor. She followed slowly behind him. The rest of the apartment was equally luxurious. She'd kicked off her shoes in the living room. Her feet sunk into thick pale-gray carpet. Expensive artwork lined the walls. A family portrait took pride of place halfway down the corridor. Monica recognized Colby and his brother and sister from the wedding. Jason was also there, as well as a smartly-dressed older woman who looked enough like Colby, even with her graying hair, that Monica guessed she was his mother.

"That's a nice picture," she murmured.

He came back to stand beside her and looked at the photo. "Yes. It was taken right before we left for Fiji."

His gaze snagged hers and as much as she wanted to, she couldn't look away. Her heart thumped. Adrenaline surged through her veins. He was so close, if she swayed forward just the tiniest bit, she might even be able to kiss him.

His dark eyes flashed with desire. His mouth parted. She heard his indrawn breath. He lowered his head toward hers, his lips just inches away.

She stepped back just in time.

"I-I'm sorry," she stammered. "I..." Her cheeks

burned. She stared at something behind him and wished the floor would open up.

He recovered more quickly than she did. In fact, his voice was remarkably steady when he spoke. "No, Monica, *I'm* sorry. You've already made it clear that whatever went on between us before is over. You're my roommate. I respect that. It's just that, for a moment, all I could remember was how you tasted, how it felt to have you in my arms. I guess I got caught up in the memory. I promise you, it won't happen again."

He stepped away and continued down the hall. She at once felt bereft of his company. She was annoyed by her reaction and was left to wonder—not for the first time—if she'd made the right decision to keep him at a distance and out of her life. But this time, her thoughts had nothing to do with the reasons why she should stay away and everything to do with what it might be like to throw her arms around him and pick up where they'd left off.

———————

Tommy Radford stared across the table at his lawyer and tried to contain his nerves. It was the fourth morning of his trial. The prosecution had finished with their witnesses. It was now the defense's turn. Today, he would take the stand.

"You don't have to do this, Tom," Blake said. "I've explained this to you before. You're entitled to a presumption of innocence. It's up to the prosecution to prove you committed this crime. You can choose to remain silent. The judge is under an obligation to instruct the jury not to read anything into the fact you haven't given evidence. They can't hold that against you."

Tommy nodded impatiently. "I understand that, Blake, and I appreciate your position, but I need to tell my story. I've listened to everyone else. The police believe I did it. The prosecutor believes I did it. Hell, I think even my wife has doubts about my innocence. But the truth is, I *didn't* do it. I don't know how the hell Sara died, but it wasn't at my hands. I loved her."

His voice hitched and he paused and dragged in a breath in an effort to get a hold of himself. He still mourned the loss of his Sara. He'd loved her so much! They'd only known each other six months, but somehow they'd clicked and every minute he'd spent with her had lightened his life.

His only regret, other than the death of his lover, was that he'd hurt Pamela. He'd thought he was in love with her once, but then she'd suffered the miscarriage and he'd realized the baby was the main reason they'd gotten married. He'd tried hard to make their marriage work, but the stresses of life had intervened and then he'd met Sara... Only then had he realized what it truly felt like to be in love; to think about that person every single minute of every single day; to want to be with them and even when he was, for it not to be enough.

"Tom, you need to understand that if you give evidence, you won't just be telling your story. The prosecution will be entitled to cross-examine you. They can ask you nearly anything they darn well feel like. They'll accuse you of lying to Sara. They'll argue that you had no intention of leaving your wife. They'll say that you argued with Sara about that fact, that she didn't take it well, that you fought and you pulled a knife..."

Blake gave him a hard look. "It's their *job* to pin this on you, Tom. That's what we're doing here. Colby Shearer's a clever prosecutor. He plays to win. Lucky for you, so do I, but I only take calculated risks. You, getting up there and giving evidence is risky. It would be easier for me if you kept your mouth shut."

Tommy regarded his lawyer steadily. "I have to do it."

Blake stared back at him. "I understand your need to have your say, to clear your name as best you can. I'd want to do that, too, but I have to look at this from a professional point of view. And as your lawyer, I would be remiss if I didn't tell you you're opening yourself up to a lot of risk. I can help deflect the questions as often as I can, but the judge might overrule me and you'll be forced to answer. I want you to be clear about what could happen. You might come off the stand worse than before you dared to speak."

Tommy regarded his lawyer solemnly and carefully considered what he'd said. Blake was an excellent barrister and Tommy was grateful to have him on his side. He took his advice seriously, but at the end of the day, it was Tommy's reputation and freedom on the line. He'd heard enough from the prosecution and couldn't sit by and let Colby Shearer build an even stronger case against him without speaking out.

"I appreciate your words of wisdom, Blake, and I'm sorry if I'm going to make your job more difficult, but like I said, I *need* to do this."

Something in his earnest tone or perhaps the desperation on his face appeared to resonate with Blake. The lawyer stared at him a moment and then, with his expression filling with resignation, he sighed on a heavy release of breath. "All right, we'll do it. I'm not happy about it, but I understand."

He glanced at his watch. "We have less than twenty minutes before we're due in court. We need to go over a few things and prepare ourselves for the kind of questions you might get from the prosecution." He paused and shot Tommy a solemn look. "Are you sure you're ready for this?"

Tommy filled his lungs with air and slowly eased it out. He stared Blake in the eye and nodded.

"Bring it on."

Monica hurried to keep up with Colby's long stride. She understood his need for haste. He was due in court and they had mere minutes to spare. She'd spent a restless night in an unfamiliar bed, vacillating between dreams of lying naked in Colby's arms on the sun-whitened beaches of Fiji to having him stand over her, angry and demanding, staking a claim on her child. She'd tossed and turned until the early hours and then had overslept, despite her alarm. She'd only woken when Colby had knocked on her door, telling her it was eight o'clock and asking if she was all right.

She'd flown out of bed and had dashed to the shower. There, she'd come up short. She needed someone to wrap her plaster in plastic to keep it from getting wet. With a sigh, she found Colby in the kitchen and explained her predicament. With cool efficiency, he wrapped her arm in a plastic bag and sealed it with masking tape.

Then came the really embarrassing moment after her shower, when she'd had to ask him for help with her bra. Once again, she'd found him in the kitchen and once again, he'd quietly and efficiently applied himself to the task. Her face had burned with embarrassment, but he didn't seem to notice. It was ridiculous to react so violently to a man who'd seen her naked plenty of times, but it was just the way it was. She hurried out of there as soon as she could.

It was only when she pulled a skirt and blouse from out of the closet that she realized she hadn't had her usual moment bending over the toilet. *Had the morning sickness finally passed?* She could only hope.

Awkwardly, she'd managed to pull on her clothes one-handedly, but like the hooks on her bra, there was no way she could deal with the buttons. The blouse had a whole row of them running from top to bottom. Her skirt had a zipper, as well as a button. Besides, her arm was already aching from the activity. Once again, she was forced to seek Colby's assistance and this time, she was a little peeved when he completed the task with clinical efficiency, touching her only when necessary. She was grateful, even if she wouldn't have minded if his fingers had slipped a little...

Thoughts like that were just plain stupid. She didn't want him in her life. She didn't want *any* man. It was just the way it was. *Wasn't it?* Right at that moment, she could hardly remember her reasons for wanting to strike out on her own and that realization annoyed the hell out of her.

"Watch your step," Colby murmured, interrupting her thoughts. He reached out to take her right elbow and helped her up the stairs that led to the front of the Supreme Court.

His fingers were warm—their warmth leaked through the thin fabric of her jacket. She relished the feel of him and the spicy scent of his cologne as it wafted toward her on the light breeze. The air smelled of salt from nearby Circular Quay. The morning sun warmed her face. If she wasn't about to take a seat in a courtroom and sit through the fourth day of her brother's murder trial, she might even feel happy.

From a distance, she caught sight of a crowd of reporters and accompanying cameramen. Her belly clutched with nerves as the reality of the situation came back to her in a rush. Instinctively, she moved closer to Colby. He bent his head and spoke close to her ear.

"It might be best if you go in ahead of me."

She looked at him and nodded, understanding what he meant. They were on opposite sides of a serious legal battle. If the press saw them entering the building together, who knew what they might suggest? Both she and Colby might seek opposing outcomes, but neither of them wanted to jeopardize the trial.

She pushed her way through the crowd of onlookers and ignored the questions tossed at her from members of the press. With her head down, she went through the glass doors that opened onto the Supreme Court foyer and made her way directly to the elevators. As she stepped inside the first one to arrive, she sent a silent prayer heavenwards that things would go Tommy's way. Nothing on earth would convince her he'd committed murder. She just hoped Blake could make the jury feel the same way.

CHAPTER 15

Tommy watched the jurors file in. Some of them glanced in his direction. Most of them didn't. Blake had explained it was always a good sign if the jury maintained eye contact with the defense. Tommy didn't know what to make of the fact the majority averted their gaze, but he refused to dwell on it. If anything, it made him even more determined to tell his side of events.

The judge dealt with some preliminary matters and then told Blake to call his first witness. Blake got to his feet.

"The defense calls Thomas Radford."

There was a stir of interest in the courtroom. It wasn't often that a defendant in a criminal trial took the stand. But Tommy wasn't the everyday criminal. He was innocent of the crime and he was determined to convince the jury to set him free.

He took a seat in the witness box and was duly sworn in. Blake shuffled through his notes. Tommy took the time to survey the occupants of the courtroom. His sister was in her usual seat behind the dock. She was dressed stylishly, but there were dark circles beneath her eyes and her arm was casted and in a sling from the fall she'd taken the day before. He felt a stab of guilt at the knowledge that he was the reason she was losing sleep.

His gaze moved further back and he noted the members of the press. The judge had banned filming in the courtroom, but an artist had been brought in to create pictures of the proceedings that could be used on the six o'clock news and they were already sketching Tommy's features.

Of course, Pamela wasn't there. Blake had explained prior to the trial commencing that as a defense witness, Pamela wasn't allowed to listen to anyone else's evidence until such time as she'd testified. Tommy understood the rules, but he wasn't sure she'd be there anyway. They'd barely spoken since he'd confirmed Sara's baby news.

Idly, he wondered what Pamela would say when it came time for her to give evidence. *Would she tell the truth, like he would?* He hoped so.

Blake cleared his throat, signaling he was ready to begin. Tommy curtailed his restless thoughts and focused on his lawyer.

"Mr Radford, can you state your full name and date of birth?"

Tommy provided the information. Blake asked another handful of mundane questions, establishing the fact that Tommy was married to Pamela, was an economics lecturer employed at Sydney University and had known a woman by the name of Sara Nakamura.

"How did you and Sara meet?" Blake asked.

"She was one of my students."

He and Blake had talked about Tommy owning up to the affair. While it was immoral and unsavory, it wasn't illegal and after Tommy's semen had been found at the scene, claiming anything other than that he was involved in an illicit affair would be suicide.

"Did you have an affair with Sara Nakamura?"

Tommy stared straight ahead toward his lawyer. "Yes."

"How long did it go on?"

"Six months. We were still involved when she died."

"Did your wife know about the affair?"

"Not initially, but she eventually found out."

"How?"

"I told her."

"How did she react?"

"She was upset and angry. She was shocked and hurt. She was lots of things and I completely understood her reaction."

"Did you offer to move out?"

"Yes, I did."

"What did Pamela say?"

"She told me she didn't want me to leave. She still loved me and believed in our marriage. She was sure we could work through this, go to therapy, do whatever needed to be done."

"How did you feel?"

"I wanted to please her. I felt incredibly guilty about what I'd done. I was willing to agree to anything."

"Did you believe your marriage could survive this?"

"I wasn't sure. I believed Pamela wanted to do everything she could to make things work."

"What did you tell Sara?"

"I met with Sara the next day after class. I told her about Pamela, how she'd found out. I told her Pamela had asked me to end the affair and I'd given her my word that I would. I told Sara it was over."

"How did she react?"

"We were still in the classroom. There were a couple of people about. She was upset, but she didn't shout or scream or do anything like that."

"So, in your mind, the affair was over?"

"Yes, though I wasn't happy about it. I was completely torn. I didn't want to destroy my marriage and bring further hurt and pain to my wife, but I'd fallen in love with Sara. She was everything to me."

"What happened next?"

Tommy sighed and ran a hand tiredly through his hair. His sister wasn't the only one having trouble sleeping.

"I agreed to see a therapist who specialized in couples. Pamela and I went two or three times. She made the appointments, I showed up, but I really didn't want to be there. All I could think of was Sara and how I'd broken her heart. Sara continued to send me letters, texts, pictures, begging me to take her back. She'd turn up to my classes and wait until the end. She'd blow me kisses, leave me gifts. She told me she loved me...

I felt the same way about her."

"Did you resume your affair?"

"Yes. I tried hard to stay away, but I couldn't. Pamela and I were barely speaking to each other and I knew that was all my fault, but I couldn't help resenting her and the restrictions she'd placed on my life. I had to check in with her three times a day. If I didn't pick up when she called, I'd be grilled for hours on end. I understood her trust in me had been destroyed and it would take a long time to build it back—*if* I ever got it back—but it was difficult to put up with her insecurities, just the same. In the end, I couldn't take it. I went back to Sara."

"What happened the night Sara was murdered?"

"Pamela and I had gotten into another argument. By that time, Sara had told me she was pregnant. I was shocked, but overjoyed. I was more certain than ever that I couldn't continue with the farce that was my marriage. The night Sara was murdered, I told Pamela about the baby."

"How did she react?"

Tommy grimaced at the memory. He could almost hear the screaming and the sound of breaking glass. "She already knew about it. She told me she'd found one of Sara's letters in my office at work."

Did you argue?"

"Yes. It was awful. There was a lot of shouting, a lot of crying. Eventually, I left. It was late, but all I could think of was being with Sara. I wanted to tell her I was leaving Pamela. I was through with our marriage."

"Did you go to Sara's place?"

"Yes, I did. She was asleep, but I managed to wake her and she let me in. I told her what had happened. We celebrated by making love."

"What did Sara say about your plans?"

"She was excited, of course. All she wanted was for us to be together."

"Did you argue with Sara that night?"

Tommy shook his head in disbelief. "Of *course* we didn't argue. Sara was beyond herself with joy. She cried tears of happiness when I told her Pamela and I were through. Straight away, she began making plans for the two of us to find a place together."

"What time did you leave Sara's place?"

"About two in the morning. I'd left Pamela in an awful state and I didn't want to stay out all night. I'd already decided to end my marriage, but I didn't want to throw it all in Pamela's face."

"So, you went home?"

"Yes."

"Did you say good night to Sara?"

"Yes, of course. I left her dozing in her bed."

"So she was alive when you left her?"

"Very much so." His voice hitched.

"What time was it when you got home?"

"About three."

"Did you see Pamela?"

"No. The house was dark and quiet. It was late. Pamela was in bed upstairs. I cleaned up the broken glass she'd thrown at me earlier and fell asleep on the couch in the den. That's where I was when the police came calling a few hours later."

Blake turned away for a moment and picked up a plastic evidence bag that lay on the bar table. He gave the bag to the court officer.

"Mr Radford, would you mind looking at this?"

Tommy took the bag and turned it over.

"Can you tell us what it is?" Blake asked.

"It's a rubber glove."

"Indeed, it is. It's the glove found by Detective Craigdon in the dumpster not far from Sara's home."

"What's your point, Mr Harton?" the judge grumbled.

"Judge, if I might request a favor from the court. I'd like Mr Radford to try on the glove."

Colby shot to his feet. "Objection, Your Honor. Mr Harton is asking permission to tamper with evidence."

"No, Your Honor," Blake responded. "I merely want to demonstrate for the jury whether my client's hand fits into that glove. The prosecution has presented evidence implying that Mr Radford wore this glove when he murdered the victim. I want to see for myself whether or not the glove fits and I'm sure the jury does, too."

The judge nodded uncertainly. "Very well, Mr Harton. I'll allow it."

"Thank you, Your Honor," Blake replied and turned back to his client. "Mr Radford, are you right or left handed?"

"I'm right handed."

"Will you put that glove on your right hand?"

The courtroom was deadly silent while Tommy opened the evidence bag and pulled out the glove. He tried for several minutes to fit it over his hand. The glove wouldn't go on.

"Is there a problem, Mr Radford?" Blake asked.

"Yes. The glove's too tight. It won't go on."

"You mean to say, the glove doesn't fit. Is that right, Mr Radford?" Blake asked.

"Yes. It doesn't fit."

Blake paused and eyeballed the jury and then spoke slowly, enunciating each and every word. "The glove doesn't fit. The glove doesn't fit." He paused a moment and then turned to stare hard at Tommy. "Thomas Radford, did you kill Sara Nakamura?"

Tommy held his gaze without flinching. When he answered, his voice was strong and clear. "No, I did not. I loved her."

Blake nodded. "Thank you. I have no further questions."

———————

Monica eased out a breath she hadn't realized she'd been holding, and sunk back in her seat. Relief flooded through her. Tommy was still the good and decent man she knew and loved. She'd been on tenterhooks listening to his testimony, wondering if he'd say something that would go against him. Instead, he'd come off sounding honest and straightforward, if a little lacking in morals. Still, immorality wasn't a crime and she hoped the jury would recognize that.

She saw the judge nod toward Colby and he

slowly got to his feet, his black gown fluttering around him. Once again, Monica held her breath.

"Mr Radford, you consider yourself an honest man, don't you?" Colby asked.

Tommy nodded cautiously. "Yes."

"It isn't honest to deceive your wife, is it?"

"No, it isn't."

"And yet, that's exactly what you did. You lied and cheated on her—all for your own personal gratification—and even after giving her your *word* that you'd bring the affair to an end, you didn't, did you?"

"I tried. I tried to stay away."

"But you didn't. You continued the affair and all the while, your wife thought you were working as hard as she was to save your marriage."

Tommy hung his head in shame. Monica's hands clenched into fists. She felt his pain. It hadn't been his fault he'd fallen in love with his young lover. She was sure he hadn't set out for things to end that way.

"How old are you, Mr Radford?"

"I'm thirty-seven."

"And how old was Sara Nakamura?"

Tommy paused. "She was nineteen."

"Nineteen. A young girl. You were almost twenty years older than her!"

Blake got to his feet. "Objection, Your Honor. What is the relevance of this? Miss Nakamura was a consenting adult. There's no basis for such a question."

The judge nodded. "I agree, Mr Harton." She turned to address Colby. "Mr Shearer, ask another question. I'm not going to direct the witness to answer anything more along those lines."

Colby nodded, but didn't appear deterred. "Mr Radford, I put it to you that you were lying when you said you told Sara Nakamura you were leaving your wife."

"No, that's not true. Of course I told her. She was so happy. We were going to be a real family."

Colby continued on as if Tommy hadn't spoken. "In fact, not only didn't you tell her you were leaving your wife. You went over there and told her it was over between the two of you."

"Yes. No."

"Which one is it, Mr Radford?"

"Yes, I told Sara we were over, but that was before, when I thought Pamela and I could work things out. But after, when I started seeing her again, no, I didn't tell her it was over between us. In fact, I told her the opposite. I told her I was leaving my wife."

Once again, Colby ignored him. "You see, Sara's neighbor heard the fighting. And then he heard the screams. He called the police. By the time they arrived, you'd left. You returned home, showered and cleaned yourself up. Somehow, you disposed of your bloody clothes. When the police arrived the next morning, you pretended you'd just woken up."

Tommy was shaking his head more vehemently and his cheeks were now flushed an angry red. Monica sat tensely, praying he wouldn't explode. The last thing the jury needed to see was her brother's temper. She knew from experience that it was formidable.

"No! You're making this up! That's not what happened!" Tommy shouted.

Blake jumped to his feet. "Your Honor! The prosecutor is badgering the witness! These questions have been asked and answered."

"That's true, Mr Shearer. Move on," the judge replied.

Colby stared implacably at Tommy. A moment later, he said. "Nothing further, Your Honor."

"Any re-examination, Mr Harton?" the judge asked.

Blake was back on his feet. "Yes, Your Honor." He turned to Tommy. "Mr Radford, did you kill Sara Nakamura?"

Monica gripped the seat. Tears formed in Tommy's eyes. He slowly shook his head. He stared at her for a long moment as if willing her to understand. When he spoke, his voice was heavy with pain and grief.

"No, I didn't kill Sara Nakamura. I *loved* her. We were going to have a baby! We were going to build a life together. I loved her and now she's *dead!*"

Burying his face in his hands, he sobbed loudly in the stillness of the courtroom. Monica's heart went out to him. She wished she could go to him and offer him comfort. A moment later, the judge intervened.

"Thank you, Mr Radford, you may return to your seat. Your testimony is over. The judge looked toward the bar table. "We'll take the lunch break." With a bang of her gavel, she stood and departed.

Chapter 16

Colby had a quick word with Collette and then headed toward the exit. Monica had already left. He wondered how she felt after listening to her brother's testimony. It couldn't have been easy. He hoped she understood his cross examination had to go that way.

It was unfortunate fate had seen fit to throw them together on opposite sides of a murder trial, but that's the way it was. It didn't change the way he felt about her or his unborn child. The trial was an unnecessary complication, and one he could have done without, but he was determined to keep his personal and professional lives separate. He just hoped Monica was prepared to do the same.

He spied her on the opposite side of the room, standing in the same small group of people she'd been with all week. As if sensing his attention, Monica lifted her head and looked at him. Colby's heart skipped a beat. She looked so beautiful in her simple pale-gray suit—a suit he'd helped her into.

He'd done his best to keep his touch impersonal, but it had been hell to touch her like that while trying his best not to notice how good she smelled, how soft the silk of her blouse, like the silky softness of her skin. He'd noticed the pulse that fluttered in her neck and had been pleased she hadn't remained unaffected. He was still determined to prove to her that they had something special and wasn't prepared to give up until she accepted that.

The look she gave him now was cool, but he couldn't detect any anger in her gaze and that had to be a good thing. His cross examination of her brother had gone well. He could have done without the glove demonstration or the teary entreaty at the end, but that's the way things went. He hoped the jury would focus on the fact the man was a lying, cheating adulterer who'd lost his head in an argument with his mistress and had stabbed the poor girl to death. There were certainly a number of jurors at the end of the defendant's testimony who looked at him openly with disgust. That was a good sign, but only time would tell.

Colby pulled out his phone and checked his messages and returned a couple of calls. He should really go and get some lunch, but he didn't feel like eating. He'd rather concentrate on dinner and what the evening might bring with Monica.

He glanced at her again. She was still surrounded by members of the defense team. Hell, she was part of the defense team. He could hardly stride over there and ask her what she wanted for dinner in front of them all. Still, he wanted her to know he was thinking about her. With that thought in mind, he sent her a text.

Sorry about earlier with ur brother. Hope ur ok. What would u like 4 dinner?

She'd given him her real cell phone number the night before. He was pleased she trusted him enough to provide it. The expectation of professional distance seemed odd given that she was carrying his child, but still, they were making progress. He couldn't complain.

From across the room, he saw her pull out her phone and look down at the screen. A few minutes later, his beeped to indicate a new text.

My tummy's feeling more settled this morning. Might even keep something down. I love fettucine carbonara.

He smiled down at the message. She made no reference to her brother. He hoped that meant she understood. And she loved Italian food. His mother would be thrilled. It was a good thing she'd taught him how to cook. He started mentally composing a shopping list. There was a well-stocked deli not far from where he lived. He could stop by on his way home. He looked up and once again caught her eye. With his heart feeling lighter than it had for a long time, he smiled.

Monica surreptitiously kept an eye on Colby from across the room. Blake was going over their game plan, including calling their next witness. Darren Stevenson was a good friend of Tommy's and it was hoped he'd be able to make the jury see that Tommy wasn't a bad man. To the contrary, he was a good man who'd had an affair and it had caused the breakdown of his marriage. A marriage that hadn't been working, even before all this began.

She thought about Colby's text offering to cook dinner and couldn't help but smile. He was another good man who was trying to do a difficult job. She understood that. She wished it wasn't the father of her unborn baby who was trying to put her brother away, but neither of them had been given that choice. It didn't make him a monster or someone to be despised. She was mature enough to see it from both sides. Besides, he didn't know Tommy like she did. He didn't know Tommy at all. If he did, he'd know just as surely as she knew that her brother wasn't guilty of this crime.

She looked across at him and saw he'd been joined by the same young woman who'd been assisting him throughout the trial. Colby bent his head and said something to her and they both laughed. The woman reached out and touched his shoulder in a familiar way. Jealousy, hot and instant, poured furiously through Monica's veins.

She immediately turned away and hoped no one had noticed. She tried to get her heart rate back under control. Heat crept up her neck and spread across her cheeks and she frowned with annoyance. She had no claim on Colby and no right to feel jealous. She'd told him they were nothing more than friends and she'd meant it. She didn't want a man in her life, even one as smart and sexy and kind as Colby. As far as she was concerned, he was free to see whoever he wanted.

Another peal of female laughter coming from Colby's direction set her teeth on edge. *What was it that the woman found so funny?* They were in the middle of a murder trial, for Pete's sake! Didn't she have any decency? The defendant's family stood less than ten yards away. *Did the stupid woman think they couldn't hear the sounds of her mirth?*

Embarrassed and ashamed by her ungracious thoughts, Monica forced Colby and his assistant from her mind. What did she care who he spent his time with? So what if she was still attracted to him? It was only natural for her to have feelings for him, especially after the five exquisite days they'd spent together in Fiji. And he was the father of her child.

They'd barely come up for air during that magical time at the wedding. They'd made love in every conceivable position and most locations around their rooms. The shower, the balcony, the bed. He'd even taken her up against the wall of the compact living room. The memory of their sizzling encounters heated her flesh and left her tingling, needing, longing for more. She stifled a moan.

Would it be so bad to have him in her life? To take up where they left off? Was she crazy for even thinking about it? She didn't know, but all of a sudden she was more than keen to find out. Dinner that evening seemed like the perfect opportunity.

In no time at all the court officer came out to tell them the judge was ready to continue. Monica returned to her usual spot behind Tommy. Natalie sat beside her.

"How are you holding up?" she asked.

Monica sighed softly. "I'm okay. I'll be glad when it's all over."

Natalie nodded. "I know how you feel. It seems like just yesterday that I was here for Ian's case." She shuddered. "That was a nightmare I'd much rather not repeat."

Monica regarded her friend with compassion and understanding and reached out and squeezed her hand. Natalie's ex-husband had murdered their young daughter. He'd been convicted and sent to jail and everyone was glad. Monica could only hope the same thing didn't happen to her brother because, unlike Natalie's ex-husband, Tommy wasn't guilty.

The judge entered the courtroom and asked for the jury to be summoned. They filed in silently and took their places. Blake called his next witness.

Darren Stevenson was in his mid-thirties, but a paunch and balding head made him look at least a decade older. The man lumbered into the courtroom and climbed into the witness stand. Blake took him through the preliminaries and established that the man was a thirty-four-year-old accountant who'd been friends with Thomas Radford for nearly ten years. Monica knew him well.

"Are you and Mr Radford close?" Blake asked.

The man shrugged. "I guess so. He's my mate. We do stuff together. Hang out on weekends, go to football games. The kind of thing mates do."

Blake nodded. "Do you share confidences?"

"If you mean, do we tell each other stuff, yeah, we do. I told him when Lucy, my seven-year-old had to have braces. Do you know how much those things cost? And insurance barely makes a dent."

"Thank you, Mr Stevenson," Blake replied. "Did Mr Radford share anything personal with you?"

"Yes, sometimes. He told me he was having a few problems at home."

"Did he elaborate?"

"He said he and Pamela were arguing a lot."

"Do you know what they were arguing about?"

The man looked uncomfortable, but answered the question. "I think it had something to do with the fact Pamela wanted a baby. Tom wasn't so keen."

"Did my client tell you he was having an affair?"

Once again, the witness squirmed in his seat. "Yes."

"What did he tell you?"

"He told me he'd fallen in love with one of his students and that he was sleeping with her."

"How did you react?"

"I was shocked, of course. Tom's a decent bloke. I didn't expect that of him. Still, I didn't judge him. He's had it tough at home."

"Because he told you that, right?" Blake said.

"Yes, he told me, but I witnessed their arguments for myself. You couldn't be around the two of them for long without one of them picking a fight."

"Did Pamela know about the affair?"

Colby got to his feet. "Objection, Your Honor. Hearsay."

"Your Honor," Blake protested. "Pamela Radford is expected to give evidence. There should be adequate opportunity for Mr Shearer to put these questions directly to her if he requires firsthand clarification."

The judge nodded. "I agree, Mr Harton. I'll allow the question."

Blake cleared his throat and asked the witness again if Pamela Radford was aware her husband was having an affair.

"I believe she was. Tom certainly told me he'd confessed to his wife."

"When did this happen?"

"Must be three or four months ago, at least."

"How did Pamela react?"

"Like you'd expect. She wasn't happy."

"Did she ask Mr Radford for a divorce?"

"No. I think she wanted him to stay."

"How did Mr Radford feel about that?"

Stevenson shrugged. "I'm not sure. He was torn. He was really into Sara, but he didn't want to bust up his marriage. It was tricky."

"Did he talk to you about it?"

"Yes. That's how I know he was torn."

"Did he tell you whether he'd discussed the issue with the deceased?"

"Yes. He said he'd told her they couldn't be together anymore. That his wife knew about them and it had to stop. Later, when he was telling me what he'd said, he was already second-guessing his decision. He was in love with Sara. He wanted to be with her, but he didn't want to hurt his wife."

"What about later? Did Tom talk with you about his situation again?"

"Yes. A couple of months ago, he told me he'd had it with Pamela. He'd tried to make things work, but they were arguing worse than ever. He was in love with Sara. He wanted to be with her. He told me he was going to tell Pamela it was over."

"What did you think he meant by that, Mr Stevenson?"

"I think he was going to leave Pamela for Sara."

"Thank you, Mr Stevenson. I have no further questions." Blake sat down and Colby got to his feet.

"Mr Stevenson, I put it to you that at no time did the defendant tell you he was in love with Sara Nakamura."

The witness frowned in confusion. "Well, I'm not sure if he actually said the words, but I could tell he'd fallen hard. He'd talk about her all the time and he'd get this smile on his face..."

Colby shook his head. "See, Mr Stevenson, that's where you're wrong. The defendant had no intention of leaving his wife. He'd told her he was ending the affair with his student and he meant it. He went over to the deceased's place the night she died. They had sex and then he told her it was over. They got into a fight and he killed her. That's what happened, isn't it?"

"No, I don't think so. Tom could never do something like that. He just co—."

"Thank you, Mr Stevenson. I have no further questions."

The judge looked at Blake. "Any re-examination, Mr Harton?"

Blake compressed his lips. "No, Your Honor."

Judge Sperry addressed the witness. "Very well, Mr Stevenson, you're excused." She glanced at the clock on the courtroom wall. "I note the time. Let's call it a day and reconvene at ten on Monday. Have a good weekend."

After continuing Tommy's bail, the judge brought the gavel down. The jury departed, along with the judge. Monica sighed quietly in relief.

It was the weekend. They had two days of reprieve. Two whole days where she didn't have to sit and listen to court testimony and wonder if these were the last days her brother would be free. Two whole days where she'd do her best not to think about the evidence that had been presented and the evidence that was yet to come. Two whole days where she was determined not to contemplate the twelve jurors and what they thought about Tommy and the decision they'd been charged to make. Two whole days where she could spend time thinking about Colby and whether she wanted him in her future and what that would mean.

The courtroom had quickly emptied. Apart from the clerk and the stenographer who was quietly packing up recording equipment, she and Natalie were the only other people who remained.

"How's it going over at Colby's house?" Natalie's softly spoken question interrupted Monica's thoughts. She looked across at her friend.

"It's fine. He's perfectly hospitable and offers help when I need it without leaving me feeling suffocated. It's working out better than I expected."

"I guess that's a good thing."

"Yeah, I guess so, but it hasn't made things any easier."

"How so?" Natalie asked quietly.

Monica sighed. "I told him we were roommates, nothing more. He's been keeping his distance. Except when he has to help me with my bra or do up the buttons on my blouse. He's very cool and calm and professional and of course and that's what I wanted—at least, I thought it was. But the feel of his hands... All I can think of is Fiji. Now I'm getting jealous of any woman who comes within a mile of him and I'm more confused than ever!"

Natalie's eyes widened in surprise, followed quickly by a calculating gleam. "You're jealous of the women Colby keeps company with?"

"Yes!" Monica cried. "And it's driving me *insane!* I never wanted to be part of a couple. I never felt the need for a man in my life. I was quite happy with who I was and where I was going. I knew what I wanted to achieve out of life and I was more than happy to get there on my own. Now I don't know what I want and its turning me upside down."

"Hey, calm down, Mon. It isn't as bad as that, I'm sure. And anyway, there's nothing wrong with plans changing. That's part of life. Would it be so awful to let Colby in? To see if you could share a life? Who knows? You might not even like each other that much. Just because you had a rollicking time on holiday, doesn't mean you have what it takes to go the distance. Most of life is the monotonous drudgery of the everyday. We're not on holiday all our lives. You need to work out if you can stand each other through the day-to-day stuff. That's if you want to try and work things out with him at all."

Monica sighed heavily. She rested her hand on her belly, curving her fingers over the slight rounding that signified where her baby lay. *Would it be so awful to have Colby in her life?* And what about him? How did *he* feel? Would he be willing to take things to another level? To see if they had what it took to make things work?

She sighed softly. Colby had left ahead of her. She understood the need for them to keep their distance in public, especially outside the courtroom. She'd make her way back to his place and see how the night developed. She was filled with a surge of hope that Colby would be as keen as she suddenly was to see if what they'd found in Fiji was deep enough to last the distance.

CHAPTER 17

The smell of frying bacon should have turned Monica's stomach, but instead, she inhaled its greasy smell and smiled. Colby was busy at the stove, a striped apron tied around his waist. His jacket and tie had been discarded and he'd rolled up his sleeves. He looked so sexy with his hair ruffled and a five o'clock shadow darkening his cheeks. It was Friday night and she was in the mood to forget about her stressful week.

"Hi," she said, suddenly unaccountably shy.

He turned and spied her in the doorway. He smiled a slow and sexy smile that curled her toes and sent heat rushing to her core. It had been too long since she'd been with a man, been with Colby. Her chest tightened on a surge of need.

"Hi, yourself. You made it home all right."

"Of course," she replied, setting her handbag on the table and moving closer to the stove. "That smells wonderful."

"You said you like carbonara."

"Yes. And you can't have carbonara without bacon."

His gaze swept over her, lingering on her belly. "How are you feeling?" he asked, his voice husky with concern.

She thought of everything that had gone on in recent times and most especially her fears for Tommy, but there was no point in raising them now. He was the prosecutor and they'd agreed not to speak about the trial. She gave him a one-shouldered shrug. "I'm fine."

"Are you sure? It's been a rough week. First the trial and then breaking your arm; putting up with me." He shot her a teasing smile, but she could tell he sought reassurance. She was happy to give it to him.

"You've been the best part of the week. I'm not sure how I would have managed having to get by on my own. For a start, the commute from the city would have killed me. You're so lucky to live close to your work."

"Yes, it comes in handy. I never complain when the alarm goes off. It's set for exactly eighteen minutes before I'm due at the office."

He chuckled and she laughed along with him. It felt good to share normal conversation. Just the two of them, going over their week while dinner cooked on the stove.

"Do you like to cook?" she asked. There was so much she didn't know about him.

"Yes. My mom's a great cook. Her parents were both born in Italy. They passed on their culinary secrets along with their dark hair. Mom still makes her own chorizo. She hangs it in the garage to dry."

Monica laughed again. "Really? That's fantastic! I bet it tastes better than anything you can buy in the shops."

"Oh, yes," Colby agreed. "You won't taste any better than the sausage my mom makes."

She sidled closer. He had a pile of fresh dough rolled into a ball on the counter. She smiled in surprise. "You make your own pasta?"

He looked affronted. "Of course! What self-respecting Italian buys their pasta off the shelf?"

She giggled and it felt so good. With all the strain of her brother's trial weighing on her mind, she couldn't remember the last time she'd felt so happy, so carefree.

Yes, she could... Back in Fiji. Her smile faded. Colby noticed.

He frowned. "What's the matter? Did I say something wrong?"

"No, no, it's nothing like that. I... I was just thinking about something else."

"Do you want to share?"

She thought about his offer. She could hardly talk about Fiji without talking about the baby and if she talked about the baby, she'd remember how she'd deceived him and that would ruin her night. No, better not to say anything and just enjoy this time with him while she could. She forced a smile and waved away his concern.

"It's nothing," she said. "Please, tell me more about your family."

"Well, they were all there at the wedding," he replied. "Mom and Dad sat at different tables, but they're still civil toward one another. My brother, Eamon, made a fool of himself in the speeches by blubbering all over the place—he's way too in touch with his feminine side." Colby rolled his eyes and Monica giggled. "You wouldn't think he was a hard-nosed detective, would you?" he added.

She shook her head in disbelief. "Really?"

"Yes, really. He works in the city. But he's a softie at heart."

"I think you told me he wasn't married, right?"

"Yes, he's still single."

"How old were you when your parents divorced?"

"Eight. Eamon was five. Katie was just a year old."

"Did you live with your mom or your dad?"

"Mom got custody. We visited Dad every other weekend."

"Did you miss having him around?" She posed the question casually, but tension held her in its grip as she waited for his answer.

"Yeah, of course. For all his failings as a husband, he was a great father. My parents sheltered us from many of the arguments. Sure, we could often feel the tension and it wasn't hard to work out something was wrong when you got up in the morning and your parents couldn't look each other in the eye, but we weren't subject to much of the awfulness kids are forced to witness when marriages go awry."

"You were lucky," she said softly.

"Yes, we were."

"I guess I could say I was lucky, too," she added quietly. "I don't remember my father at all. I suppose Tommy would have different recollections. He's five years older than me."

"Have you ever talked to him about it?"

"No. It wasn't something that interested me. Mom kept a few of my father's pictures—for us kids, I guess—but my father was nothing to me."

"Do you have a relationship with him now?"

"No. He died when I was thirteen."

"I guess you can't miss what you never knew," Colby mused.

"Right."

The expression in his eyes intensified. Her belly jumped with nerves.

"I don't want that to happen to our baby, Monica."

Her belly tightened with nerves. She wasn't sure if she was ready to have this conversation with him. "Colby, I—"

He held up his hand as if to stop her. "I know we've talked about this, but we need to talk about it some more. Though my father didn't live under the same roof for most of my childhood, he was still an important part of my life. Whatever happens between us, I want my child to know who I am, to have a relationship with me. Is that so hard to understand?"

The intensity in his eyes filled her with guilt. *How had she ever supposed she could get a man to father her child and then walk out of her life? She hadn't counted on that man being Colby Shearer. And now she was stuck with him. It was funny how* that realization didn't send her into the same kind of panic it would have a week ago.

"No, Colby, it's not so hard to understand," she said quietly. "In fact, I think it's admirable that you want to be part of this child's life. You hardly know me."

He nodded. "True, but I know everything that's important. I know you're good and kind and honest. I know you have a good job and good friends. You love your family and you know what it's like to be loyal. They're all very admirable qualities and I look forward to discovering more. Besides, it wasn't like this baby was planned. Somehow it happened and now we're going to be parents. I'd like to think we're mature enough to want to do the best we can by our child. If that means co-parenting and sharing all the responsibilities, then that's fine with me. I'd like it even better if you'd move in with me permanently."

He held her gaze. Her heart skipped a beat at the hope that filled his eyes. She tried to ignore the rush of guilt his words instilled in her. What would he think if he knew the truth…?

"W-what are you saying?" she stammered.

He set the spoon in his hands down on the counter and drew closer. "I think you know what I'm saying."

He closed the distance between them until there was nothing left but a whisker of air. His shirt brushed her jacket. She drew in a sharp breath. His gaze remained locked on hers as he reached out and tilted her face upwards. At the same time, his head came down.

His lips grazed hers, softer than a whisper. He tasted of bacon. Unable to help herself, she opened her mouth and deepened the kiss. His touch remained light on the back of her head. At any moment, she was free to pull away. Only, honestly, she didn't want to.

Her good arm crept around his neck and she drew him slowly toward her. She couldn't get as close as she wanted because of her broken arm in the sling, but the kiss continued. Sweeter and hotter than it had ever been, she couldn't get enough. And then it was over.

Colby set her gently aside, his breath coming fast. "I'm sorry, Monica. I didn't mean to do that. I know you said we were nothing more than roommates, but I... I couldn't help myself."

She sucked in some air in an effort to catch her breath. "It's okay, Colby. You don't need to apologize. I didn't exactly fight you off."

His expression filled with relief. "Are you sure you're okay with it? I thought I might have blown it."

"Of course I'm okay with it. In fact, I...enjoyed it. I haven't kissed anyone since Fiji."

Her admission slowly sank in and his eyes flared with emotion. His voice turned husky. "You don't know how good that makes me feel."

She shrugged. "It's true."

"I'd really like to kiss you again," he said.

"I'd like to kiss you again, too."

They stared at each other for a long moment. Colby was the first to look away. "I'd better finish dinner. I promised you fettucine carbonara and that's what you're going to get."

Monica frowned in confusion. How could he think about dinner when she was dying to throw herself in his arms and kiss him senseless and beg him to take her to bed? Did he not find her attractive? Her body had changed, it was true, but she was barely showing. Did it really matter to him that much? Oh, God! What if it did? She made a small noise of distress.

Colby glanced at her and his face was filled with remorse. "Monica, I'm sorry. I know what you're thinking and believe me, there's nothing more I'd rather do than make love to you all night long, but... I want to take things slowly this time round. I feel like we've been given a second chance and I want to do things right, the way they should have been. Fiji was amazing, but it wasn't real. You told me you were scared that real life wouldn't measure up. Well, this is real. Let's see if it can."

She stared at him and slowly shook her head. Tears pricked her eyes. She blamed the hormones, but the truth was, she was overwhelmed with feelings of worthlessness. She didn't deserve this special man and yet, she was fast getting to the point where there was no way she could give him up. Silently, she vowed to be the best person she could, to live up to his expectations, to be the woman he thought she was, the woman he deserved—and maintaining the illusion that she was a good person. She could never ever tell him the truth about that first night they'd spent together, how she'd been so desperate for a baby, she'd lied about the condom.

At the sight of her tears, he frowned. "What's the matter? What did I say?"

"N-nothing!" she stammered and cried even harder.

He stepped forward and mindful of her injury, gently folded her in his arms. She rested her head against his broad chest and took solace in the fact that he cared. He cared about her and he cared about their baby. It was a nice feeling.

Gradually, her tears subsided. She pulled away from him and offered him a shaky smile. "I'm sorry for blubbering all over you like that. I don't know what came over me. It must be the hormones."

"Hey, there's no need to apologize. I've never been around a pregnant woman before, but I know enough to know it can be a bit of a rollercoaster ride. If you feel like crying, cry away. It won't worry me."

She reached awkwardly into her pocket and retrieved a tissue. She wiped her eyes and blew her nose.

"Better?"

She nodded. "Better."

He winked at her. "Are you still up for some of the best fettucine carbonara you've ever tasted?"

Her smile widened. "You bet."

Colby returned to the stove and tended to the carbonara. She watched with interest while he rolled out the pasta dough and ran it through a machine that turned it into strips. He boiled water, poured cream, added herbs and spices. Last of all, he dropped the freshly cut fettucine into the pot of boiling water... Within minutes, he announced it was done.

"Dinner is ready." He bowed toward her with a flourish.

She sniffed the air. "It smells divine."

"And it will taste even better."

She raised a single eyebrow. "You're pretty confident."

He smiled. "With reason. Just you wait."

And with that he took two large bowls from the cupboard and filled them to the brim. He carried them over to the small dining table where two place settings were already laid and after setting the bowls on the table, he pulled out her chair.

She took the proffered seat, murmuring her thanks.

"Would you like some parmesan?" he asked.

"Does anyone eat pasta without it?"

He grinned and headed back to the kitchen. He returned a moment later with a small grater and a chunk of freshly cut, aged parmesan cheese. With impressive efficiency, he grated a generous amount of cheese over her carbonara and repeated the action over his own. Dropping the cheese and the grater on the counter, he finally took his seat.

"Let's eat!"

She picked up her fork and twirled a small amount of pasta around the tines. Bending low, she brought the fork up to her mouth and took a bite.

"*Mm*, you were right! This is delicious!"

He grinned. "Did you doubt my expertise?"

"Never!"

They ate in companionable silence. She was relieved to discover that her nausea had stayed away. In fact, she'd gone a whole day without vomiting. *Perhaps she was done with that.* She could only hope.

Colby reached for the pepper the same time she reached for the salt. Their fingers touched and a shiver of awareness ran tingling up her arm. Night had fallen around them and the plate glass window framed a perfect sight. A full, round moon, glowing golden, rose slowly in the sky. It glinted off the water and ran in silver trails to the shore. It reflected the soft and gentle mood that had fallen between them. Monica hardly dared to breathe lest she disturb it.

"What would you like to do tomorrow?" he asked, breaking the comfortable silence.

"I'm not sure. I usually spend Saturdays doing laundry and catching up on housework. Occasionally I run to the shops and stock up for the following week."

"My, what an exciting life you lead, Miss Radford."

She poked her tongue out at him. He burst into laughter. The sound of it warmed her through and sent heat straight to other, needier parts of her anatomy.

"Okay, Mr Smarty Pants. What do *you* do on a weekend?"

"If it's a nice day, I might head to The Rocks markets. I usually find something worth bringing home. I might also go for a stroll along the waterfront, enjoy coffee on the pier. At other times, if I'm busy with a case, I head off to work. On those occasions, I barely even notice what kind of day it is, let alone that it's a weekend."

"Ah, that's real life again, raising its ugly head," she murmured, smiling.

"You said it, but we don't have to worry about that now. I'm all sorted as far as the trial goes. We can spend the day however you like."

She frowned slightly at the reminder that he was working hard to send her brother to jail and then pushed the thought aside. He was what he was. She just had to believe in the legal system and hope that justice would prevail. Blake was confident they were doing well. She hoped his confidence wasn't misplaced.

"The markets sound like fun," she ventured.

"You're right. They are fun. All right, that's decided. Weather permitting, we'll visit the markets and see what treasures we can find."

Chapter 18

The day dawned bright and sunny. Monica rolled over and squinted at the light that shone through the window. She'd been so preoccupied with the fact Colby had merely pecked her on the cheek by way of a good-night kiss, that she'd forgotten to draw the curtains. She had to give herself a stern talking to; that was merely his way of taking things slow and had nothing to do with her desirability. Still, it had taken some convincing and she'd lain awake for hours after he'd left her at her door.

The fact that he'd helped her undress and then assisted while she put on her pajamas and all the while remained calmly aloof didn't help matters. She wanted to feel his hands on her in passion, like she had during their time in Fiji that now felt like so long ago. She wanted...

She groaned in frustration. She didn't know what she wanted. She thought she wanted to go it alone, to maintain her independent life. Now, after only two nights sharing Colby's place, she remembered how nice it had been to share dinner and talk and wondered if she could get used to such an arrangement.

The sound of the TV tuned to a morning breakfast show slowly infiltrated her thoughts. And then she heard whistling. It was Colby. He was whistling. *How cute.* Throwing off the covers, she padded down the hallway, following the smell of coffee.

"Please tell me you have some of that left," she said and pointed to the pot.

"Of course. It's freshly brewed." He poured her a cup and added cream and sugar. She'd only been there a couple of nights and he already knew how she took her coffee. It was just another example of his thoughtfulness.

He handed her the cup and she gratefully took a sip. "Ah, that's heaven."

He smiled. "How did you sleep?"

"Great," she lied. "And you?"

"Like a baby."

"It must have been that pasta. You were right; it was beyond divine."

"The best you've ever tasted?"

"Yes, the best I've ever had."

They laughed together and then returned to their coffee. A moment later, Colby spoke again.

"What would you like for breakfast?"

"I'm not usually much of a breakfast person," she admitted.

His eyes widened in mock horror. "Not a breakfast person? How will this ever work? I eat cereal and toast and two poached eggs every morning. Breakfast is—"

"The most important meal of the day," she interrupted, rolling her eyes. "Yeah, I've heard it all before."

"And yet, you blindly ignore it!" he continued, amusement glinting in his eyes. "What about our baby? Shouldn't you think of him?"

She frowned in disquiet. "Please don't think you have the right to tell me what to eat just because I'm carrying your child."

He quickly realized she was serious. He hastened to reassure her. "Of course not. I was joking. I'm sure you know better than I do what's best for you and our baby."

The tension eased out of her and she took another sip of coffee. It was good and hot and strong and was just what she needed after her restless night.

"Are you still keen to go to the markets?"

"Absolutely. It looks like a beautiful day." She turned as she spoke and took in the perfect blue of the harbor dotted with white sailboats outside the window. This time, it was the golden rays of the sun that sparkled off the water, sending shards of diamonds into the sky.

"Great. We'll go straight after breakfast. That is, after I've finished my eggs. Are you sure I can't get you something?"

"No, thanks. I'm fine."

"Okay, then. Feel free to use the shower first. Do you need a hand with your cast again, or getting dressed?"

He spoke the words so casually, but heat rushed through her veins. The thought of him touching her filled her with desire. A shiver of need puckered her nipples and sent tingles down to her core. She *wanted* to be touched by him, caressed, kissed, tasted. She wanted him to make love to her like he had in Fiji, like he'd simply die if he didn't have her. She'd felt the same way.

He continued to regard her with a bland expression and she realized his thoughts were a long way from hers. She wasn't sure if she could stand another impersonal encounter, but the fact was, she needed his help.

"Um, yes, thanks. That would be great. It's my bra that poses the greatest challenge. All those hooks." Heat crept across her cheeks "And the buttons, of course," she quickly added, refusing to look at him.

He nodded and taped the plastic over her cast. "No problem. Let me know when you're ready."

She set her coffee cup down on the counter and escaped his casual regard. It was obvious he was oblivious to her torment and that was fine. He wanted to take things slowly. Fine. She could do slowly. She *would* do slowly. Even if it killed her.

Colby watched Monica depart and slowly eased out his breath. He'd been fighting the urge to take her in his arms and kiss her senseless from the moment he set her away from him the previous night. He didn't know how he'd managed to serve up dinner, converse and even eat. His gut had been in a turmoil of nerves and need.

He'd told her he wanted to take things slowly and that was mostly true. He did think they'd rushed headlong into a passionate holiday fling in Fiji. But this was real life and he wanted it to last a hell of a lot longer than five days. With that being the case, it was important for them to slow things down and get to know each other before they ravaged each other again.

Still, it was testing every ounce of his self-control not to sweep her into his arms and take her to the nearest bed. His or hers. He wasn't fussy, as long as he could love her again. She looked so beautiful in her pale pink shorty pajamas—pajamas he'd helped pull on—and the faint blush that colored her cheeks. He'd had to stay behind the counter so she couldn't see the evidence of just how much he wanted her.

And now he had to remain unmoved while he undressed and dressed her all over again. How was he going to manage it? And then there was the day to come. They were about to spend a full ten or twelve hours, maybe more, together. How was he going to keep his hands off her?

The sound of the shower running filled his mind with even more erotic memories. They'd made love in the shower in Fiji at least twice. He'd run the soap all over her body and massaged it into her skin. Her generous breasts, glossy with water and bubbles, had filled his hands to overflowing. He'd caressed every inch of her silky skin and her hands had been busy, too. Finally, he'd taken her up against the shower wall with her legs wrapped around his hips.

Their lovemaking had been fast and furious. They'd climaxed together among a torrent of shouts and relief. Afterwards, he'd dried her off with a towel and wrapped her up in a sheet. He'd carried her to bed and had held her close all night. He'd already been half in love with her then and that night he'd dreamed of forever.

Okay, so things hadn't quite gone to plan and he didn't get his fairytale ending, but that was then and this was now. She was here with him and seemed to be enjoying his company. He thought of the day ahead of them and was filled with a sudden surge of anticipation. He'd do all he could to make it a day to remember. He'd force her to think about how good it could be between them—how good it *had* been. She'd told him she was scared the magic of Fiji couldn't be replicated in everyday life. He was determined to show her it could be.

———

Monica tilted her face up toward the sun and breathed in the scent of sea and salt. The Rocks Markets were an open-air market nestled between the picture-perfect harbor and the Sydney Harbour Bridge. The historic cobblestone laneways and ancient buildings added to the air of old-world charm and a slower pace of life. People wandered in a casual and relaxed manner, as if they had all day to discover something special in one of the many stalls showcasing things such as handcrafted jewellery, textiles, housewares, original art works, beauty products, fashion, photography and more. And of course, there were the food stalls.

The smell of barbeque made Monica's mouth water. She'd turned down Colby's offer of breakfast and now she was starving. Everywhere she looked, there were food vendors offering exotic samples to eat. From homemade preserves, seasoned cured meats, mouth-watering burgers and traditional gozleme, there was something to tempt everyone's tastebuds. She turned to Colby and smiled.

"Everything smells so wonderful. I think, during the months of almost constant morning sickness, I forgot how good food could be."

He smiled back at her. "I'm sorry to hear you had it so bad, but I'm glad the worst appears to be over. You haven't been sick this morning, have you?"

"No. In fact, this is the second day I've woken and been able to think about food, and even consider eating it."

He looked around at the collection of food stalls. "Friday is the best day to come down here to eat. In fact, the locals call it "Foodie Friday." There are even more things on offer than today. Still, I'm sure we'll be able to find something to satisfy your hunger. Do you like Indian food? There's a great curry place over there."

She grinned. "I *love* Indian food. The spicier, the better!"

He laughed and shook his head. "Between my Italian heritage and your penchant for curry, this kid's going to have one hell of a sophisticated palate."

Monica smiled and instinctively curved her good hand over her belly. In a few weeks, she'd have her scan. She hadn't decided whether to ask them to disclose the sex. She wondered what Colby thought.

The very fact she was even giving consideration to his opinion was a miracle in itself. She'd been so determined that the father of her baby would have no involvement in its life and now she was contemplating inviting him to her scan—and the possibility didn't send her into a panic.

Was she coming to accept that having Colby a part of her baby's life wouldn't cause the world to stop spinning? That she might even enjoy sharing the parenting responsibilities, joys and fears with him? It was a sobering thought and one that definitely required more serious contemplation.

When she'd set out on her baby plan, she never dreamed she'd want the baby's father in her life and yet, the more she thought about it, the more she wanted Colby to be there—not only for her baby, but for *her*. The realization was illuminating and a little disconcerting. After all, she'd laid the ground rules, made it clear they were roommates. Well, perhaps that idea had been diluted a little after she'd returned his kiss...

She stole a look in his direction. He'd been so kind, inviting her to stay with him, cooking her dinners, seeing to her every need. They'd spent last evening in comfortable companionship, and apart from the fact she was burning to kiss him again, the time they'd spent together had been surprisingly nice. Everyday life with Colby was so much better than she'd expected and it made her wonder what she'd been so afraid of in the first place.

He hadn't tried to take over her life, or tell her what to do—other than at breakfast and he'd quickly backed down over that. He'd been interested in her job at Baker & Carr and had shared a few stories about her boss. They'd steered clear of any discussion of the trial, but even that had become less of a bone of contention between them. She put her faith in the justice system that the truth would win out and her brother would be set free. Either way, it no longer had any bearing on how she felt about the man who stood so close that if she reached out, she could touch him.

A cool breeze blowing in from the ocean ruffled her hair and sent gooseflesh across her skin. Colby noticed instantly and asked if she wanted to pull on a jacket. He'd packed one of his, just in case and she was grateful for this thoughtfulness when he explained that hers likely wouldn't fit over the cast.

Gently removing her sling, he worked the jacket over her shoulder. She tried to ignore his nearness, but it was impossible. His fingers were warm on her skin, his scent filled her nostrils. He was so close she could count the few freckles on his nose. He replaced the sling with casual efficiency and when he was finished, he stepped back and turned away. She swallowed a soft sigh of disappointment.

"Hey, look over there!" he cried. "They have a stall of handmade baby clothes. Do you want to check it out?"

He looked at her with shyness and uncertainty, but she saw the hope that filled his eyes. *He wanted to go and look at baby clothes.* It didn't get any cuter than that. Her heart melted on a smile.

"Sure. In fact, I don't have anything for the baby, yet. I guess it's still so far off, and I've had other things on my mind."

Colby nodded in silent understanding. Taking her hand, he pulled her toward the stall, his enthusiasm, infectious.

"Oh, look at this!" he exclaimed and held up a tiny sailor suit, complete with sailor hat.

She laughed and joined in the fun. Her eye was caught by a playsuit made from white linen and emblazoned with red and pink hibiscus flowers. It also had a matching hat. She picked it up and turned to Colby.

"Oh, Colby! How cute is this? It's so bright and beautiful. I can just imagine our baby wearing this."

"I'm assuming you think you're having a girl?" he said, laughter glinting in his eyes.

"Of course. Would you mind if it was a girl?"

"Not at all. Boy or girl, it doesn't matter to me. As long as it's healthy."

She rolled her eyes and smiled. "That's such a cliché."

He chuckled. "You're right and I used to hear people say that and think the same thing. But, now that I'm in that position, with a baby on the way, I realize how true it is. Who cares about the sex? A healthy baby is all that matters. Don't you think?"

Monica's expression grew solemn. "Yes, it *is* all that matters," she admitted softly.

Unbidden, she moved her arm and cradled her bump with her good hand. She blinked back a rush of tears. She looked back at Colby. He was staring at her belly, his dark eyes glittering with emotion. He stepped closer and put his hand over hers. On sudden impulse, she moved it until it rested inside her jacket, with only her T-shirt separating his hand from her skin.

The warmth from his hand seeped into her and set off a burning rush of need. It had been so long since they'd touched each other intimately, pressed together, skin to skin. His hand moved slightly and her lips parted on a sudden intake of breath. She wanted to lean into him, to hold him, kiss him, love him. Fire rushed through her veins to her center. She blushed from the heat of it.

They were in the middle of the markets, a public area filled with people and all she could think of was pulling him close, tearing off his clothes and having her way with him. She blamed it on the hormones. She'd read in one of the pregnancy books she'd downloaded that a woman's sex drive often went into overdrive during pregnancy, especially during the first three months. Well, she was now fifteen weeks and hadn't had sex since Fiji. It wasn't any wonder she was desperate for a man's touch.

No, that wasn't fair. It wasn't just a man's touch she yearned for. She wanted Colby. She wanted to run her hands through his thick dark hair, press kisses against his full lips. She wanted to trace the clearly defined muscles in his chest and caress the flat smoothness of his belly. She wanted to encircle his erection with her hand and take him in her mouth. She wanted to give him pleasure and be pleasured by him in return. She wanted him hot and hard and ready. She wanted to feel him pounding away inside her while she clung to his shoulders and hips. She wanted the indescribable feeling of reaching the pinnacle and crashing over the other side. She wanted him shouting out his relief. She wanted...

With a sound of impatience, she stepped back and forced the images away. This was madness! They were surrounded by people. She couldn't do any of those things. Besides, she'd told Colby they were over, that they were roommates, nothing more. *What would he say if she suggested they go back to his place and spend the rest of the day in bed?* Her blush deepened.

"Monica? Are you all right?"

Colby's brow was creased in concern. She forced a smile. "Yes, of course." She gestured toward the baby clothes. "Have you found something you like?"

He grinned. "As a matter of fact, I have. What do you think of this?"

He held up a tiny white onesie. The words "My mommy and daddy are the best!" was printed on the front in blue. She smiled and lifted an eyebrow. "Blue?"

He shrugged. "Hey, it comes in pink and orange and yellow, if you want something else. Besides, girls can wear blue, can't they?"

"Of course." She sent him a cheeky grin. "Girls can wear anything they darn well want!"

He laughed and put his arm around her shoulders and drew her close. Handing over some bills, he paid for the onesie and tucked it into the back pocket of his jeans. It felt so good to be with him like this, like they truly were a couple.

"When are you due?" the man behind the stall asked.

Monica smiled proudly and touched her belly. "November twenty-first."

"Ah, a little way to go yet," the man replied.

Colby chuckled. "Just as well. We have a lot to do to get ready before then."

"Well, he's going to be a handsome little fellow, that's for sure," the vendor said.

Colby's smile broadened. "Or a beautiful little girl, just like her momma."

He looked down at Monica with an expression so full of tenderness. Her heart filled with warmth and once again, tears threatened. She couldn't believe she'd ever wanted to keep him out of her life. Then she thought of the way she'd deceived him and was filled with shame. If she could only turn back time... Still, there was nothing she could do about that now. All she could do was be the best person she could be and pray that Colby never found out the truth.

CHAPTER 19

Colby poured himself a scotch from the well-stocked bar he kept in his living room and picked up Monica's cup of tea. He headed outside to the balcony that wrapped around his condo. The day had drawn to a close and night was settling in. Stars poked through the darkness, way up in the sky. A light breeze drifted in across the harbor and he was glad Monica had kept his jacket on. He didn't want her to get a chill. She looked up as he set the cup of tea on the low table beside her.

"Thank you," she murmured and favored him with a smile.

He took the seat beside her and sipped from his drink. The scotch burned a familiar, fiery path down his throat. After the markets, they'd walked along the promenade, all the way around to the Opera House and back. They'd shared pleasant conversation, beef vindaloo and butter chicken and lots of laughter. It had been a wonderful day. Just remembering it, he sighed in contentment.

Monica turned to face him. "It's been such a lovely day, Colby. Thank you for taking me out."

"It was my pleasure. I enjoyed it as much as you."

She nodded and sipped at her tea. He turned to stare out across the water, struggling with the need to tell her how he really felt. Today, they'd felt like a couple, like two people enjoying each other's company and looking forward to the birth of their child. He liked the way he felt when he was around her and he was already in love with the baby she carried.

It amazed him how quickly he'd taken to the idea of fatherhood. He'd always wanted a family and at thirty-three, he'd been increasingly impatient to have one, but he never knew just how much the reality of it would mean to him—and he had Monica to thank for it.

But it wasn't just about the baby. He'd fallen for Monica, too. Even back in Fiji, he'd known she was special, that she was more to him than a holiday fling. If she hadn't given him a fake phone number, they might already be together.

She'd explained that she'd panicked about real life not measuring up, but he was confident he'd shown her today just how good real life could be. She certainly seemed to enjoy the day in his company. The way she'd smiled and laughed and took his hand. The signs were positive that she might be coming around to the idea of them as a couple. He could only hope it was true. He needed to find out for sure.

Before his courage could fail him, he set his drink down beside him and then turned to face her. Taking the tea cup out of her hand, he put it on the table. She started in surprise.

"Colby?"

He leaned closer and put a finger to her lips. "*Shh.*"

Her eyes widened, but he saw only anticipation and excitement in her gaze. And then her eyes lowered to his mouth. She paused there before moving lower, skimming across his chest and lower still. His body tensed. Fire coursed through his veins. Blood pounded in his ears and exploded in his groin. His cock hardened almost painfully and all he could think about was how desperately he needed to touch her. The words he'd intended to say completely escaped him.

As if oblivious to the torrent of need coursing inside him, her gaze slowly came back to his.

"Kiss me, Colby."

The whispered words ignited his desire like nothing else could. Hope that she felt the same way flooded through him. Mindful of her injured arm, he stood and drew her slowly up beside him. He cupped her ass and pressed her against his erection. At the same time, he lowered his head and kissed her.

It was meant to be a kiss of awakening, of rediscovery, but it quickly turned into so much more. She opened her mouth and their tongues tangled. She returned his kiss with equal passion. She brought her good hand up and buried her fingers in his hair. He splayed a hand across her back. Except for the arm in a sling in front of her, they were as close as they could get.

His heart was thumping, but he couldn't drag himself away. She felt so good in his arms. So *right*. It was just like the days they'd spent together in Fiji. She was perfect. This was meant to be. Finally, he set her gently away. He was pleased so to see she was breathing just as heavily as he.

"I want to make love to you, Monica." His voice was husky with emotion, but it was important to him that there be no mistake about what was going to happen. He wanted her to be fully on board with any decision. It took everything he had, to stand there calmly and await her answer. It seemed a long time coming.

"I want to make love to you, too, Colby."

Her words filled him with elation. He almost *whooped* for joy. And then he remembered the baby. His excitement dimmed.

"What about the baby? Is it okay to...you know...?" He flushed with embarrassment.

She merely smiled. "Of course. You can't hurt the baby, I promise."

This time, he did let out a cheer. Picking her up in his arms, he carried her to his room. He lay her gently on the bed and then stepped back and removed his shirt. His boots came next, followed by socks and jeans. When he came back to her, he was clad only in his underwear. He sat on his haunches beside her.

She immediately reached up and scraped her nails across his chest satisfied when his nipples puckered from the contact and he sucked in his breath.

"You're so beautiful," she murmured.

He gave her a lop-sided smile and shook his head. "Men aren't beautiful."

"You are."

She said it with such certainty, he believed her. The knowledge that she found him so desirable filled him with satisfaction. He'd never given much thought to his looks before, but he was glad she found them pleasing.

Her hand moved lower, her fingers splaying across his abdomen before following the trail of dark hair that disappeared beneath the waistband of his boxers. She slid her hand beneath the elastic and caressed his cock.

He sucked in a breath and his heart skipped a beat. Blood pounded in his ears. Her fingers tightened around him and then released in a rhythm that drove him wild. He was so hard, he thought he might explode. He hadn't been with a woman since Monica and her actions were seriously testing his self-control. When she released her hold on him, he almost cried out in relief.

Gently, he took her hand and brought it up over her head. He held it in place and then bent over her and kissed her on the lips. Slow and tender, he relearned the shape and texture of her mouth. Soft and full, her lips parted under his. She kissed him back just as slowly. It killed him to hold back.

But she was injured and he wanted to take things slow. If he were lucky, they'd have a lifetime of loving each other. The night was young. There was no rush. He wanted to cherish every moment, to bask in the feel of her in his arms. Knowing she wanted this, wanted him as much as he wanted her, filled him with wonder.

Pulling back, his hands went to the sling. He undid the clasp and eased her arm out. Next came the jacket. Carefully, he worked her good arm out of it and then eased it off the broken one. He tugged at the bottom of her T-shirt. The soft cotton fabric molded to her breasts and he took a moment to admire the view. His hands reached out and cupped their fullness. The pads of his thumbs scraped across her nipples.

The large nubs immediately pebbled and Monica emitted a gasp. He remembered from their first time together how sensitive they were. Once again, he gently lifted the T-shirt over her head and tossed it to the floor. Underneath, she wore the same lacy white bra he'd secured earlier that day. He'd never been more pleased to remove it.

Sliding his hands along her ribcage, he released the hooks on her bra one by one and tugged it off her arms. Her breasts bounced with the movement, large and unfettered. The dusky pale pink of her nipples had darkened to a chocolate brown. His gaze drifted lower, to her belly. It was softly rounded. He marveled silently at the changes in her body.

His gaze came back to hers and he caught a flash of uncertainty in her eyes. "What is it, sweetheart?" he asked.

"You haven't seen me like this before... pregnant. Do I still look all right?"

He shook his head, amazed she could even ask

the question. Instinctively, knowing his actions would speak louder than words, he bent his head and kissed his way across her chest until he reached her belly. His hands cupped the rounded bump that was their baby and he was filled with awe at the sheer wonder of it.

She was carrying his baby! He was going to be a daddy!

Flooded with feelings of awe and wonder, tears burned behind his eyes. He pressed his lips against the silky softness of her belly and thought of the child who lay within. A surge of protectiveness flooded through him. He vowed silently to keep both mother and baby safe and loved and cherished for as long as he lived.

She stirred restlessly beneath him and he knew how she felt. His cock still pulsed with need. Desire filled his veins. But there were still clothes to deal with.

She'd kicked her shoes off not long after they arrived home. He made short work of her jeans and panties and they went the way of the rest of their clothing. Shucking off his boxers, he came back to her and drew her in his arms. They both sighed with contentment as they came together, skin to skin.

"You feel so good," she whispered.

He pressed a kiss against her hair. "I've missed you."

And just like that, the passion between them reignited and once again his lips found hers. They kissed like ravenous teenagers, his fingers buried in her hair. And then she pulled away from him and perched herself above him, straddling his thighs.

He thought about protection and then remembered she'd told him she was clean. He'd given her the same assurance he was disease free and they hadn't been with other partners. A moment later, she lowered herself on his cock and all thoughts but the feel of her warm, wet heat surrounding him, disappeared.

She moved up and down on his length and he reveled in the feel of her above him. She set the pace, slow and steady and he gritted his teeth. It had been so long since they'd been together, all he wanted to do was drive himself into her and lose himself in her heat, but it wasn't all about him and she needed to do this her way. Besides, she was injured. He could hardly push her up against the wall and have his way with her, no matter how much his body demanded he do just that.

Her breasts bounced up and down above him. He reached up and squeezed them, rubbing her nipples in the way she liked. She let out a little moan and moved faster. It was excruciating, waiting for her to come. He was in heaven; he was in hell. He was lost. She was the only one who could save him.

"Come for me, babe," he murmured, his voice low and husky with need.

She opened her eyes and stared down at him. Her hips moved up and down faster and faster until she cried out her release. The whole time, she looked at him and that hot gaze was one of the most erotic things he'd ever experienced. Her face tightened and then relaxed as the tension inside her found an escape.

Slowly, her breathing returned to normal. She looked down at the place where they were still joined and offered him an uncertain smile.

"I guess it's your turn, now."

He needed no further encouragement. With his cock rock hard to bursting, he took hold of her hips and thrust up hard inside her. She rocked against him, urging him on. It didn't take long.

He surged frantically upward once, twice, three times and then cried out as he climaxed and filled her with his seed. Carefully, and still joined, he rolled them over and pulled her in against his side. He'd never felt so replete.

Nuzzling her neck, he fell asleep.

Monica woke to the unaccustomed sensation of having someone else beside her in the bed. The last time that had happened, she'd been with Colby in Fiji.

Colby.

Memories of their night of lovemaking came rushing to the fore. She blushed as she recalled her wantonness and then pushed her embarrassment aside. She and Colby had always been passionate when they came together. It was one of the things she loved about him.

Love? Was she in love with Colby Shearer? After all the plans she'd made, her determination to keep him at a distance and out of her life? *How had this happened?* She had no idea, but somehow, he'd crept into her heart and captured her soul and now she couldn't imagine having him anywhere else but by her side. And when her brother's trial was finally over, and Tommy was free, she hoped they could shout out their feelings to the rooftops.

"Hey, there sleepyhead."

She turned at the sound of his voice. He smiled at her and reached out to gently move a strand of hair out of her eyes. The tenderness in his expression stole her breath.

"Good morning, to you, too," she replied.

"It *is* a good morning, isn't it?"

His hand slid lower and his thumb ran across her swollen-from-being-kissed lips. Almost immediately, her body responded to his touch. Desire ignited inside her and she reached out for his cock. It was already hard and ready. Another wave of desire rushed through her. She wished her broken arm didn't restrict her so. She wanted Colby to take her hard and fast and leave both of them gasping.

As if reading her mind, he rolled her onto her uninjured side so that she was facing away from him. His hand slid down her back, across her buttocks and then moved lower until his fingers parted her cheeks. He stroked his way down until he found the warmth between her legs.

Opening them wider to allow him access, she gasped when his fingers slid inside her.

"*Mm*, it feels like you were dreaming of me," he murmured and stroked her slick flesh.

She smiled, feeling naughty. "Maybe I was."

His cock pressed against her buttocks, hard and hot and urgent. She pressed back against him and was rewarded with a low growl. And then he moved until it was the tip of his cock probing her entrance.

He held her hips still. A moment later, he thrust inside her, stretching her wide. She gasped.

"Oh! That feels so good."

"*Mm*. I can't think of a better way to start the day."

He moved inside her, stroking in and out. The pressure built inside her. His hand came around to cup her breast and his fingers tweaked at her nipple. The rhythmic movement of his hips, coupled with the magic in his fingers sent her toppling over the edge. She cried out and climaxed, her inner muscles tightening around his cock.

Thrusting harder and faster, Colby picked up the pace. Moments later, he gave a shout of relief and collapsed against her, replete. She wasn't sure how long they lay there, but the sun seemed higher in the sky when they woke again. She removed the arm he'd flung around her and made a move to get up.

"Are you hungry?" he murmured.

"Yes. And I have to go to the bathroom."

She returned a short time later. Colby was sitting up with his back against the headboard. He beckoned her over and she climbed back into bed, sighing in contentment when he drew her into his arms.

He pressed a kiss against her hair. "What would you like to do today?"

"Whatever you like. I'm easy. I'm just as happy to spend the day like this."

He chuckled and tightened his arms about her. "A woman after my own heart."

"Actually, there's one thing I need to do," she said.

"What is it?"

"I forgot to pack my vitamins. I'm taking a few extra ones that are supposed to be good for pregnant women. I left them behind."

"No problem. I'll go over to your place and get them for you, if you like."

She smiled up at him. "I can come with you."

"There's no need. Go back to sleep. We had a late night and I promise you, it's going to be another late one tonight."

With that, he gave her a cheeky grin and releasing her, climbed out of bed. The thought of spending another hour or two in bed was immensely appealing.

"Are you sure you don't mind?" she asked.

"Of course not. Give me your house keys. I'll be back before you know it. Is that all you need?"

"Yes, I think so."

"I'll leave straight after I take a shower."

He headed toward the bathroom. Monica sighed in contentment and closed her eyes.

CHAPTER 20

olby hummed along with the morning radio and tried to keep the smile off his face. He couldn't believe how well things had turned out. Not only was he with the woman he loved, it seemed like she felt the same way. He couldn't believe how far they'd come since yesterday. Of course, she hadn't actually said the words, but he hadn't either. It didn't mean they didn't feel that way about each other. He couldn't be happier.

He flipped on his indicator and turned into Monica's street. Taking the stairs two at a time to her apartment, he let himself inside. The place looked just as they'd left it a few days earlier. Had it only been a few days? It felt like a lifetime had passed.

She'd told him the vitamins were in the top drawer of her nightstand. He walked into her bedroom and was immediately assailed by the smell of her perfume. Sweet and exotic, it reminded him of the soft spot between her neck and shoulder which he'd kissed repeatedly the night before. His body hardened at the memory and all of a sudden, he was eager to get home again.

Making a beeline for the nightstand, he pulled open the drawer. Rummaging through notepaper, pens, packets of gum and a couple of letters, he finally found the vitamins. Pulling them out, he sat them on the bed and then spied a diary that lay open there. The pen was still in the middle of the book, like she'd been disturbed while writing an entry.

He paused. Curiosity burned through him. He wondered what she'd written about their time in Fiji. For him, it had been the most amazing five days of his life. For her, doubts had crept in. His gaze returned once again to the open pages. It was her diary, her private thoughts. Reading them without her permission was wrong on so many levels.

He pushed away from the bed and stood, the vitamins in his hand. He was two steps across the room before he remembered he hadn't returned the things to her nightstand. The notepaper, pens, gum and letters still lay in a pile on the bed, right next to the diary.

Once again, curiosity warred with the need to do the right thing. *Leave it there, Shearer. Put her things back where you found them and get the hell out of there before you do something stupid. It's her diary, for Pete's sake.*

Her diary.

The sound of the phone ringing in the next room startled him. He jumped like he'd been scalded. Guilt rushed through his veins, setting them on fire.

He hastily returned her things to the nightstand drawer. The diary still lay on the bed. He stared at it, unable to believe he'd even contemplated reading it. No, he'd take it with him and ask her to share her thoughts with him. That was the right thing to do.

With the diary and vitamins in his hand, he made his way back down the hall and into the kitchen. The answering machine had kicked in and he paused as Natalie Johnson's voice came on the line.

"Hi, Mon. Listen, I've been thinking about this thing with you and Colby. I think this could be the real deal. You'd make the perfect couple. But you need to tell him the truth about what happened in Fiji. A relationship shouldn't start out on a lie. Trust him and trust me when I say he'll forgive you. Don't forget he was a willing participant in the unprotected sex. Stop beating yourself up about lying to him and come clean. You'll be glad you did.

"Oh, I just remembered you're staying at Colby's. You probably aren't going home much to check your messages. Listen, I'll call your cell again. Perhaps you'll pick up this time. Okay, I'll talk to you soon. Bye."

The phone call ended. Colby stared at the machine in shock. The diary burned in his hand. *What the hell was Natalie talking about? What had Monica done that he might or might not forgive?* All of a sudden, he was filled with cold foreboding. Something was off and it could be huge. *Did he even want to know?* It might mean the end for him and Monica. Did he want to take that risk and find out, or was it best to leave the past in the past? Still, like Natalie had said, relationships shouldn't start out on a lie. If he had any self-respect, he'd demand to know the truth.

With that thought filling his mind to the exclusion of all others, he hunted around for Monica's house keys and found them on the counter where he'd left them. Near the phone sat a pile of brochures. Something about the front cover of the one on top caught his eye.

With dread coursing through him, he picked it up. It took a moment for the words to sink in. They were brochures from a sperm donor bank, a private clinic that could see to a woman's every need—a woman who wanted a baby but didn't want the hindrance of a man.

His gut churned with nausea. *She'd been canvasing baby options.* He could only assume she'd collected the brochures before her trip to Fiji. After all, she'd returned pregnant with his baby. No more need to visit a sperm bank. She'd gotten what she wanted: a gullible man to father her child. A man too blinded by her beauty to smell a rat. And he'd been the lucky guy.

Too bad she hadn't found some anonymous donor to do the trick. Then he wouldn't be feeling like he'd been betrayed in the worst possible way by a woman he'd fallen in love with; wouldn't feel like his heart had been ripped out of his chest; wouldn't feel like screaming in agony at the injustice of it. He, a lawyer, who held justice in the highest of esteem.

She couldn't have treated him worse...

With a muffled howl of agony and anger, he picked up the brochures and along with the diary and vitamins, strode out the door determined to get answers and this time, the truth.

Monica heard Colby's front door open and smiled in anticipation. She couldn't wait to see the look on his face when he realized she'd made him breakfast: cereal and toast and two poached eggs, just like he'd told her he had every morning. He rounded the corner into the kitchen. The look on his face gave her pause.

"Colby, what's the matter? What happened?"

"I'll tell you what happened."

He shoved something toward her. His face was dark with anger and pain. She looked down and saw what he held in his hands and her stomach somersaulted with fear.

Her diary and the brochures.

She gasped in horror and icy fingers of fear clutched at her heart. Stumbling backwards in shock, she came up hard against the counter. She thought of all the things she'd written in the pages of the leather bound volume and dread nearly overwhelmed her. She saw the fury in his eyes and froze. Panic ratcheted the speed of the blood flowing through her veins.

"Colby, please. Let me explain."

"In case you think I stooped low enough to

read your diary, I'm telling you right now, I didn't. At least one of us knows what it is to be honorable. Now, are you going to tell me what the hell is going on? Before you try and deny it, let me tell you this. Natalie called your apartment while I was there. She left a message on your machine. She told you to come clean about what you hadn't told me. She said that no relationship should start out on a lie." His eyes burned into hers, the fury in them almost palpable. "So don't try telling me there's nothing to talk about because I know darn well you lied about something. Maybe I'm not the father. Is that it?"

Monica's world tilted on its axis. A buzzing noise sounded in her ears. It was as though she was hearing Colby through a thick fog, where everything echoed. She clung to the counter behind her and tried to maintain her balance. All the while, she frantically tried to think of something to say.

"No, Colby! God, no! Of course you're the father! It's not that... I'm sorry. I should have told you from the start."

His glare didn't waver. His voice was cold as ice. "Then speak now and by God, you'd better tell the truth."

Distress surged inside her. Tears burned behind her eyes. Her chest felt so tight she could barely breathe, but she knew she had to come clean and she hoped he'd forgive her when she told him the truth.

"For a long time now, I've been thinking about having a baby. I'm not getting any younger and there is only a small window of opportunity for this to happen, if you know what I mean. I wanted a baby, but I didn't want the complication of a relationship. I started canvassing my options. One of those was to visit a sperm bank."

"Well, you obviously dropped by long enough to collect some brochures. What happened? Did none of the donors catch your eye? Not good looking enough? Too short? Too tall? What is it, Ms Radford that changed your mind and set you on your journey to find a real-life sperm donor?"

The sarcasm in his voice tore strips off her heart, but she bravely withstood the pain. He had a right to be angry and he didn't know the half of it, yet.

"A sperm clinic was one option I looked into, yes. Then I attended the wedding and met you."

She saw him tense and watched the wave of pain wash over his face. She hurriedly continued. "Please believe me when I tell you I didn't set out that night to find someone to father my child. The night I met you was amazing. We danced and drank and shared stories. It was only a short time, but we seemed to click. When things progressed to your room, I was just as eager as you were to make love. Then you asked me about a condom."

His eyes narrowed on her face. "You told me you didn't have any."

Guilt surged upwards and sent heat rushing across her face. "Yes."

His eyes widened in sudden comprehension. "You *did* have a condom, didn't you? You lied about it because you *wanted* to have unprotected sex with me. Maybe with whoever you ended up with that night...?"

Her face burned hotter. She wanted to look away, but his furious gaze pinned her in place. "Yes, I lied about the condom and yes, I wanted to have unprotected sex, but only with you." She shook her head and tears crowded her eyes. She was frantic to make him see.

"I was desperate to have a baby! So desperate, I'd even sabotaged my condoms by pricking holes in them with a pin. Yes, they were in my purse, waiting to be used. But when you asked me about them, I had an attack of conscience. It wasn't fair to deceive you like that. So, I pretended I didn't have any and *you* suggested we do without."

The more she thought about it, the more she was certain she wasn't the only one responsible for the unplanned baby. She glared at him as her arguments picked up steam. "You were prepared to take the risk as much as I was, Colby. You knew there was a chance a pregnancy would result. Yes, I was desperately hoping that might happen, probably as much as you thought it wouldn't. The odds were definitely against it, but it happened just the same. I'll accept the blame for the fact we didn't use a condom, but no one forced you to have sex without using protection." Her voice lowered to a whisper. "And now, we're having a baby."

At the thought of the miracle growing inside her, she smiled a sad smile and laid a protective hand on her belly. With or without Colby's support, she was going to be a mother. The knowledge filled her with quiet joy.

Anger and pain continued to war on Colby's face. With clenched fists, she waited for him to respond. His next words would make or break them. *Had Natalie been right? Would he find it in his heart to forgive her?*

"You should have told me. You should have told me right from the outset that you weren't interested in a relationship and that you wanted a baby. All along, I was a holiday fling, with the slim chance of a pregnancy thrown in for good measure. There had been no mad panic at the end. You deliberately gave me a fake phone number. You had no intention of continuing things after we returned home, regardless of whether or not you were pregnant."

His voice was so cold, she wanted to protest. "Colby, I—"

"Why did you bother to pretend you were so into me?" he interrupted, his voice harsh. "Why didn't you tell me the truth? I would have been disappointed, but I'm a big boy. I could have handled it. Instead, you led me to believe we might have a future and you gave me a fake phone number. Do you have any idea how much that hurt? We were two consenting adults enjoying a holiday romance. It wasn't like you'd promised me forever while you'd lain replete in my arms. I made the mistake thinking the two of us were on the same page. It was my bad, but then when we ran into each other again, you *still* didn't tell me the truth. You gave me some weak explanation that you'd panicked at the thought of me not liking the real you. It was bullshit from start to finish, wasn't it?"

"No, Colby! It wasn't like that!" she cried, swiping at the tears on her face. "I really, *really* liked you. I had a wonderful time, but... Sharing my life with a man at that time just wasn't something I wanted to do. Now..." Her voice drifted off. She shrugged with her good shoulder. "Now, I wonder whether it would be so bad if we made things work together."

His eyes widened in disbelief. He shook his head back and forth. "Are you crazy? How could I ever trust you again? You lied to me! All along, you were seeking a baby daddy. Whether it was me or some anonymous donor, you had it all planned out. I came along at a convenient moment and even though I agreed to have unprotected sex, I had no idea you were desperately trying to get pregnant."

"Would it have made any difference?" she cried.

"Who knows? But that wasn't your call to make. You decided all on your own that I'd make the perfect candidate to father your child. And stupid me, I fell for it. I was flattered by your attention, by your willingness to throw caution to the wind and engage in a passionate affair with a stranger. And all along, you'd been scheming behind my back, using me, deceiving me..."

"No, Colby! Please, it wasn't like that!"

"Did you care for me at all?" he shouted, his voice ragged with pain.

"Of course I did!" she protested, but he wasn't listening.

The look he threw at her was so cold and distant, her chest tightened on a sob.

"There's nothing you could say to me to make this better, Monica. I'm going out. When I get back, I want you gone. Understand?" With that, he turned on his heel and stormed from the room.

The sound of the front door slamming made her jump. The tears came faster. She stumbled into the living room and sank down on the couch. With her head in her hands, she cried like her heart had broken. She cried for Colby and for the pain that she'd caused. She cried for their baby who might never know his dad. And most of all, she cried for herself and for the foolish choices she'd made. Natalie had warned her things wouldn't end well if Colby discovered the truth on his own, and she was right. Monica hadn't counted on it hurting so much.

When had she fallen in love with him? She'd been bound and determined to keep him out of her life. Now she'd ruined everything and the knowledge devastated her. She couldn't imagine ever feeling happy again.

Still, she refused to go down without a fight. Colby wanted her to slink away like a criminal, disappearing into the night, but she wasn't of a mind to do that. She loved him and she knew he loved her. And if it wasn't love he felt, he definitely cared for her a great deal and he cared for their unborn child.

There was no way he'd manufactured those feelings or the tenderness in his eyes. No, she'd stand her ground and have her say and beg him to understand. And then she'd plead with him to forgive her. If that failed, she didn't know what she'd do.

To Colby's relief, Monday finally dawned. He left his condo early, before the feeble winter sun had even peeked above the horizon. He'd spent the remainder of Sunday working in his office. He'd needed somewhere to go to escape Monica and the awful realization that everything between them had been a lie. He'd pounded the streets for a while, but eventually sought refuge in his job. The trial of Thomas Radford was drawing to a conclusion. He used the time to work on his closing arguments.

Even so, his mind kept returning to their argument. He still couldn't believe she'd systematically set out to find someone to father her a child. Lucky him, the suitable sucker who just happened to stumble into her path. And she'd had the nerve to tell him the pregnancy had been unplanned; that it had been his decision as much as hers to have sex without the use of protection. What a joke! There probably wouldn't even be a baby to consider if she hadn't lied about her lack of condoms.

A fresh wave of anger rolled over him and he felt justified all over again for shutting her out. He'd been beyond irritated to find her still in his home when he finally returned early Sunday evening. He hadn't even looked in her direction when he headed straight to his room.

Now in a few hours, he was due to see her again—in the courtroom. It was the fifth day of her brother's trial. No doubt she'd be there to support him, like she had on all the days before. So be it. He was there to do a job and by God, he'd do it and all the while he'd continue to ignore her until she got the message that he never wanted to speak to her again.

He thought of his baby and was filled with sadness. He never imagined having a baby with a woman he wasn't sharing a life with and the knowledge that his son or daughter would grow up living between two homes flooded him with heartache. It should never have happened this way. It wasn't fair to him and it sure as hell wasn't fair to their child.

How could she have been so selfish? To think of nothing and no one but herself? It blew him away that she could be so self-centered; that she could so blithely deceive him and sleep with him as if even that weren't a lie. Okay, he conceded his part in the debacle. She hadn't forced him to have sex without a condom, but it had been a heat of the moment thing. He'd wanted her badly and she'd told him she didn't have anything they could use. She'd deliberately deceived him in the hope that she might fall pregnant. Had she *ever* planned to tell him the truth? He'd never know.

———————————

Monica struggled to pull a dress over her head and cursed softly under her breath. Without Colby around to attend to the buttons, she'd been forced to choose something she could put on without assistance, including swapping her usual bra for a crop top. Still, it wasn't easy and she breathed a sigh of relief when she'd managed it. Smoothing out the pale blue linen fabric over her hips, she surveyed herself in the bathroom mirror.

Her baby bump had become more noticeable. She should tell Tommy. He'd be upset if he realized she'd deliberately kept it from him. She hoped the end of the trial would clear his name and restore his liberty and that sometime in the near future, she could share her news with him.

Inevitably, at the thought of her baby, her thoughts turned to Colby. He'd come in last night and had stalked past her without speaking. This morning, she hadn't heard him leave. It was obvious he was still furious with her and she understood his anger. She just hoped he'd give her a chance to explain, although she didn't have a clue what she'd say—to him or to Tommy. What would she tell her brother when he asked about the baby's father? She sighed. She'd deal with that problem when the time came. For now, she needed to get to court.

Walking the short distance from Colby's condo, she arrived in time to pass through security and take a seat in her usual place in the courtroom just before Colby strode through the door. He was followed by his assistant. Monica stared at him, trying to catch his eye, but he didn't once look in her direction. She swallowed her disappointment.

Blake and Natalie arrived shortly thereafter, followed by Tommy. Monica greeted her brother with a hug and a kiss and assured him she was fine and she was looking forward to all of this being over. He agreed.

"Where's Pamela?" she asked.

"She's still waiting outside. Blake's calling her next to give evidence. She's my alibi witness."

Monica started in surprise. She'd never thought to ask her brother where he'd been during the hours the forensic pathologist believed his mistress had died. She knew her brother was innocent. It hadn't occurred to her to ask him if he had an alibi. She'd assumed that since Tommy hadn't seen his wife upon his return home that fateful night, that the same was the case for his wife. She was relieved to discover that wasn't the truth.

"That's great," she replied. "How's she holding up?"

Tommy shrugged and avoided her gaze. "I'm not sure. We're not exactly talking."

"Oh, Tommy! I'm so sorry! This has been such an awful time for you, and not just because of the charges against you. If I'm to believe you and Darren Stevenson, you were in love with this poor girl and to discover she's been brutally murdered... You must be devastated. On top of that, your marriage is over and you've been subject to this trial... It's so awful for you. How are *you* doing?"

He offered her a strained smile and sighed quietly. "Yeah, I've had better weeks, that's for sure. Pamela and I were already on shaky ground and this trial—well, I have to put my trust in Blake and my faith in the legal system that justice will prevail. But the thought of what happened to Sara..." He shook his head sadly. "No one should die like that."

"No." Tears burned behind Monica's eyes. She hadn't even known the girl, but she'd heard enough to know that Tommy was right. No one should have been made to suffer that way.

The sharp rap on the wooden panel behind the bench indicated the arrival of the judge and after another quick hug, Monica left her brother and took a seat beside Natalie. She barely had time to murmur hello when the judge walked into the courtroom.

"All rise."

After a few preliminary matters had been dealt with, the judge instructed that the jury be sent in. The fifth day of Tommy's trial was about to begin. Monica snuck a look toward Colby, but he had his head down, intent on the notes spread before him on the bar table.

Blake got to his feet and cleared his throat. "The defense calls Pamela Radford."

CHAPTER 21

Natalie reached across and squeezed Monica's hand. Monica appreciated the silent show of support, just as she was grateful Natalie had hired a nurse to take care of her sick sons and had taken a week of her vacation time to sit with Monica in court.

The door at the rear of the courtroom opened and Pamela strode in. She was dressed in a black Dolcé and Gabbana dress with matching Jimmy Choos. Her jewelry consisted of large gold hoops that swung gently in her ears. The hoops were teamed with a heavy gold necklace. Every part of her outfit screamed sophistication, money and success.

She might have been the wife who'd been cheated on, but she looked far from devastated by the harsh blow. Monica couldn't help but admire her courage and willingness to front the jury, the media, the public—and she was beyond grateful her sister-in-law was willing to testify in order to help her husband.

Blake took her through the preliminaries—her name and date of birth and the fact she was the wife of the defendant.

"Mrs Radford, how long have you and your husband been married?"

"Three years."

"And was it a happy marriage?"

"I thought so."

"When did you start having problems?"

"I was pregnant before we got married. Tommy was old fashioned. He wanted us to be married before the baby was born. I was in love with Tommy and I thought he was in love with me. We got married. We were happy. Then, I lost the baby. I miscarried at sixteen weeks."

"I'm sorry. That must have been very hard for you."

Pamela nodded. "It was."

"How did you cope?"

"I went to counseling. I wanted Tommy to come, too. It was his baby as much as mine and he was grieving, too."

"Did he go to counseling?"

"No, at least, not when we lost the baby. He made a paltry attempt to go to therapy when we started having marital problems, but not when the baby died."

"Do you think he properly dealt with the loss of your child?"

"No."

Monica listened to the exchange and silently applauded Blake's tactics. He was helping the jury to see her brother as a flesh-and-blood man who had faced tough challenges and had all the strengths and weaknesses of an ordinary person. He wasn't a monster who'd brutally attacked his mistress. In fact, he was no different than any of them.

"Mrs Radford, you referred to you and your husband experiencing problems in your marriage?"

"Yes."

"Was that a recent thing?"

"Yes, fairly recent. In the past six months or so."

"What do you think led to those problems?"

"I think Tommy was carrying residual hurt and pain over our lost baby. I think he lashed out at me because I was the one that was there. I was an easy target. I also think it was one of the reasons he began an affair. It was a way for him to distract himself, to forget."

"Mrs Radford, how did you find out about the affair?"

"My husband told me."

"Was he remorseful?"

"Yes, he was."

"Did you know his mistress was pregnant?"

"No."

"Did you find any letters from Sara Nakamura?"

"No."

Monica sat forward. Tommy had given evidence that Pamela knew about Sara's baby and Pamela had called Monica that night, ranting about a baby. At the time, Monica hadn't known what to make of it—if anything, she'd thought Pamela was talking about the baby she'd lost—but now it made an awful kind of sense. *Why was*

Pamela lying? Disquiet stirred in Monica's belly.

"Mrs Radford, did you and your husband ever discuss divorce?"

"No. Tommy was very remorseful. He was genuinely sorry for what he'd done. He told me he was going to end it. I believed him. I loved him. I wanted him to stay."

"Mrs Radford, do you own a set of Baccarat kitchen knives?" Blake asked.

Pamela nodded. "Yes. They were an engagement present from one of our friends."

"How many knives make up the set?"

"Five."

"And are they stored in a knife block?"

"Yes. It sits on the kitchen counter."

"Are you missing one?"

"No."

Blake started in surprise. Monica could only suppose it was feigned. There was no way a lawyer such as Blake would ask a question he didn't know the answer to. "No?"

"No."

"Are you sure? Because earlier the police gave evidence that during their search of your home, they discovered one of the knives was missing from your knife block."

Pamela's expression didn't change. "They were mistaken."

Blake nodded and turned back toward the bar table. He picked up an object and had the court officer take it to the witness.

"Mrs Radford, is this one of the knives from your knife block."

Pamela spared it a glance and then nodded. "Yes, it is."

"And how is it that I come to have it?"

"I gave it to you."

"And where did you find it?"

"It was in the dishwasher."

Monica eased out a breath she hadn't realized she was holding. *The missing knife had been in the dishwasher.* It wasn't the same one the police had found in the dumpster not far from the scene. The tiniest frisson of hope trickled through her veins.

"Your Honor, I seek to tender the kitchen knife."

The judge looked over toward Colby. "Do you have any objection, Mr Shearer?"

Colby got to his feet. "Yes, Your Honor. We only have the word of the witness that this is where she found this knife. There is no chain of evidence, no evidence at all that this is how the knife's whereabouts became known."

"That might be so, Mr Shearer," the judge replied, "but that goes for anything this witness says. It's up to the jury to determine whether or not they believe her."

Colby compressed his lips. "Yes, Your Honor."

"I'm going to allow it."

Colby returned to his seat. Blake stood and continued. "Mrs Radford, where were you on the night of the murder?"

"Tommy and I were at home. We got into a silly argument and Tommy left for a while." She shrugged. "It wasn't the first time something like that had happened."

"Did Tommy come back that night?"

"Yes."

"What time did he get back?"

"I'm not sure exactly, but I think it was after two. I'd dozed off on the couch in the living room. I woke when he came in."

"Did you speak with him?"

"No. He went straight into the den. I waited awhile to see if he'd come looking for me, but he didn't. When I found him, he was asleep on the couch in the den."

"What did you do?"

"I covered him with a blanket and then went upstairs to bed. There was no point in discussing things any further that night."

"That sounds very domesticated and very loving for a spouse who'd earlier been in an argument with her husband," Blake observed.

Pamela shrugged. "He's still my husband and I still love him. The nights had turned colder. I didn't want him to catch a chill."

Once again, Monica came alert. She remembered the night in question very clearly. Pamela had called and woken her from a deep sleep. It had been close to three in the morning. Monica could still hear Pamela shouting hysterically down the other end of the phone about Tommy, his lover and a baby. It had all come out so garbled, Monica hadn't known what to believe. It sounded like Pamela had been drinking and she'd admitted as much when Monica asked her.

At the time, Monica hadn't been sure what to make of the conversation. But now, Pamela was giving sworn testimony that she'd calmly and lovingly tucked Tommy in upon his return home after a nasty fight and had then gone to bed. There was no mention of the anguish and torment she'd been suffering that had been quite obvious to Monica over the phone. Pamela's testimony revealed nothing of that.

Pamela was lying. The question was, why? Did she know something Monica didn't? Did she know Tommy needed an alibi and she was his only hope? Icy dread crept into Monica's heart. She glanced again at Colby. His posture remained relaxed, He didn't know about the late night phone call made after Tommy returned.

Should she tell Colby what she knew? That not only had Pamela made a drunken, late night phone call, but she'd also told Monica about Tommy's unborn child—proving that she knew about the pregnancy? But that would blow a hole in Pamela's story and put her credibility at risk. It would cast a shadow of doubt over Tommy's alibi and could result in sending him to jail. *Could she even bear the thought?* Could she reveal the truth at the expense of her brother, the brother she loved with all her heart? She shivered.

Natalie shot her a look of concern. "Are you all right?" she whispered.

Monica barely managed to nod. Unmindful of her broken arm, she held the sides of the seat in a death grip. Oblivious to the turmoil that twisted and turned Monica up inside, Blake nodded, content with Pamela's answer.

"Thank you, Mrs Radford. I have no further questions."

The judge looked across at Colby. "Mr Shearer, are you ready to cross examine?"

Colby jumped to his feet. "Yes, Your Honor." He turned his attention to the witness. "Mrs Radford, you love your husband, don't you?"

"Yes, although I'm not sure I love him the same way as I did before."

"Right. But you don't want to see him go to jail?"

"No."

Colby started in surprise. "No?"

Pamela glared in Tommy's direction. "No. I think he's a lying, cheating disgusting asshole who dishonored me and our marriage. I wish you went to jail for being a lying, cheating disgusting asshole, but the fact is, you don't. You go to jail for being a murderer, but he isn't that." She turned and stared directly at the jury. "He didn't murder that girl. He couldn't have. He was at home with me."

"But not for the entire night, was he?" Colby replied. "Both you and your husband gave evidence that he went to his lover's apartment that night and didn't return home until late. The forensic pathologist gave evidence that the time of death was somewhere between the hours of one and three. You say your husband arrived home at two. He had ample time to commit the murder and return home."

"I guess he did, but the thing is, he didn't do it. He arrived home like you said and went straight to the den. There is no shower there, nowhere to clean up. He was in there less than ten minutes before I went in to check on him. I'm sure I would have noticed if he'd been covered in blood."

Colby looked dissatisfied, but it was obvious Pamela was sticking by her story. There was nothing he could do but return to his seat. Blake stood and addressed the witness.

"Mrs Radford, when you found your husband asleep in the den, was he still wearing the same clothes he'd worn earlier that evening?"

"Yes."

"Thank you. I have no further questions."

Monica shook her head as she watched Pamela leave the witness box. Tommy's wife walked past all of them with her head held high, looking neither left nor right. Monica thought about what Pamela had said, and the implications, and her belly once again twisted with dread.

Why would her sister-in-law lie? If Tommy had told the truth about his movements, there was no need for Pamela to play things down. She could have still admitted they'd fought so hard that she'd been beside herself with anger. That she hadn't even been able to look at him the rest of the night. There was no doubt her testimony strengthened the doubt against Tommy being the murderer, but why had she lied about parts of it? *What had she hoped to gain?*

Monica thought back to the pain and awful anger in Pamela's voice the night she'd called her, railing against her brother. Tommy had testified that the house was dark and still upon his return. *Where was Pamela? Had she taken herself off to bed, like she'd said?* Yet she'd called Monica after Tommy said he arrived home and she'd been beyond distraught. *Had the call come from home...or somewhere else?* Monica snuck a glance toward Blake, then in Colby's direction and wondered what to do. Filled with indecision, she gnawed at a fingernail.

"Are you all right, Mon?"

Natalie's worried face registered in Monica's mind. Once again, she managed to reassure her friend. She looked at Tommy and then back to Colby. She chewed on her nail again. He already knew she was capable of awful deception. He'd accused her of being a lying, conniving witch of the highest order. *What could she possibly say to make him believe that this time she was telling the truth? And with a murder charge and looking at years in prison, the stakes seemed much higher this time round.*

The last time, she'd justified her decision with her desperate need to have a child—a justification he'd disregarded out of hand. But this time, it was truth, and Tommy's freedom on the line. *Would Colby realize the sacrifice she was making by telling him the truth?* She was sure he'd understand that her evidence could quite possibly mean the difference between her brother regaining his liberty and being sent to jail, but would he care?

She didn't know, but with growing certainty, she came to a decision. She'd lied once for her own selfish gain. She couldn't sit by and let it happen again, not even for Tommy. She had to tell Colby the truth.

The judge called a recess and Colby used the time to glance over his closing address. The way things looked now, it was quite possible Tommy would walk. There was a possibility the jury would wonder about the slight window of opportunity Tommy had to commit the crime, but the fact was, there was no way the murderer could have escaped without getting at least some of the blood on them and the defendant had not only returned home afterwards, but had done so in the same clothes he'd left in, the ones he was wearing at his arrest.

It was an obstacle for which Colby had no answer and it might very well mean the result would go against the prosecution. Still, he'd done all he could with the evidence he had. There wasn't anything else he could do. Pamela Radford had been the defense team's last witness. It was now up to the lawyers to offer a few words in summary of their case in a final effort to convince the jury to their side. From the corner of his eye, he spied Monica. She stood a short distance away, obviously waiting for him to notice her. Determined to ignore her, he continued to concentrate on his notes.

"Colby. Do you have a minute?"

Forced to acknowledge her, he looked up briefly. "What is it?"

"I... I need to talk to you."

"I think we've said everything that needs to be said."

"No, this isn't about that. It's about...the trial."

That got his interest. They'd agreed it was a

topic best avoided. What had happened to make her change her mind?

"What about the trial?" His tone was little less brusque.

She came a little closer. "Is there somewhere we can go that's a little more private?"

He looked around them. Most of the people had departed, taking advantage of the opportunity to stretch their legs. "No. This is fine. Say what you have to say and go."

She bit her lip and looked away, as if struggling to find the right words. Impatience surged through him.

"For Pete's sake, Monica. Spit it out."

"Pamela Radford wasn't completely honest in her testimony."

He started in surprise. "I beg your pardon?"

"I said, Pamela was lying about part of Tommy's alibi, especially when she said she tucked him in and left him to sleep it off on the couch."

"What makes you think that?"

"Because she called me at three that morning, an hour after Tommy returned home. She sounded far from being in the state of mind required to do such a thing."

"How did she sound?"

"She was drunk and hysterical with anger. She said all sorts of awful things. At the time, I didn't know what to make of it, but I can tell you one thing, there's no way with her feeling like that about my brother that she could have possibly calmly and lovingly tucked him in."

Colby shook his head and tried to come to terms

with what she'd said. If she was telling the truth, her brother's alibi had some serious dents. All of a sudden, it wasn't so certain that he'd returned home and if he had, that he'd gone straight to bed on the couch. It changed everything.

"What do you think it means?" he asked.

She shrugged. "I don't know, but I can't help wondering why Pamela would lie about something like that. I guess it helps Tommy's case, but what else did she hope to achieve? Don't get me wrong, I'm grateful for whatever it is that made her do it, but they've barely been talking these past months. It just seems…strange."

Suddenly suspicious of Monica's motives, he narrowed his eyes at her. "Why are you telling me this? You must know what it means. Besides, it's not like you're a stranger to deception."

She winced and he felt a stab of guilt. Still, when she spoke again, she held his gaze. "It wasn't an easy decision, but I wanted you to know the truth. I'm sorry. About everything. Telling you about this was just the right thing to do."

"Ha!" he scoffed. "I'm surprised you even recognize the right thing."

She winced again and he took satisfaction knowing he'd hit his mark. The next moment, though, he felt like a shit. He needed to get away from her. He needed time to think. With a muttered word of thanks, he turned his back on her and looked around for Collette. She was gone.

He cursed under his breath and strode toward the exit. He left through the rear door. He immediately pulled out his phone and dialed his junior counsel. He breathed a sigh of relief when she picked up right away.

"Colby, what's the matter?"

Ignoring the preliminaries, he answered her question with one of his own. "Where are you?"

"I'm in the bathroom. Is that okay?"

Ignoring her sarcasm, he rushed on. "I need you to get in touch with the phone company. Call them and get a copy of Pamela Radford's phone records for the night of the murder."

"Why...?"

"It doesn't matter. Just do it." He ended the call with a stab of his finger and in frustration ran a hand through his hair. The judge was about to call on him to make his closing arguments. He had to put her off. Spinning on his heel, he went back into the courtroom.

Monica was nowhere in sight. In the back of his mind, he accepted that he owed her an apology for being so short with her and he also owed her a thank you for coming forward when she had. He was still furious about her earlier betrayal, but she'd gone some way to redeeming herself that day.

Locating the judge's clerk, he asked the man to give the judge a message.

Monica searched in the foyer off the courtroom for her sister-in-law, but couldn't see her anywhere. She needed to talk to her, to ask her about her evidence. Spinning on her heel, she headed toward the bathroom and sighed in relief when she spied Pamela's shiny Jimmy Choos under the door of one of the stalls. There was no one else in the bathroom. In silence, she waited for the woman to finish.

Pamela flushed the toilet and came out of the stall. She spied Monica near the sink and her step faltered. "Monica, what are you doing here?"

Monica stared at her. "You lied in there."

Pamela blanched, but recovered quickly and busied herself washing her hands. "I don't know what you're talking about."

"Of course you do. You called me that night. Surely you remember?"

"I called you? No, I don't think so. You must be mistaken."

"I'm not mistaken, Pamela. You called me and you were hysterical. You told me that you and Tommy had fought. You were furious with him."

Pamela's laugh sounded forced. "Like I said, Monica. You're mistaken. Besides, why would I lie for that piece of shit?"

Monica continued to stare at her as realization grew. Pamela *had* called her that night and not from home. She'd lied in her testimony. If it wasn't to save Tommy, there was only one other reason she'd do that: to save herself.

"Oh, My God!" she said slowly, as the pieces started falling into place. "It was *you*. You weren't Tommy's alibi. He was *yours*."

CHAPTER 22

Pamela's cackle of laughter and the wild unfocused look in her eyes sent a shiver of fear arcing down Monica's spine. It was like watching a person who was well-known and familiar morph into some terrifying being she no longer recognized.

"Aren't you little Miss Smarty Pants," Pamela crooned, the craziness now clear on her face. She took a threatening step toward Monica, evil intent in her eyes. "But you won't tell. It could send your precious brother to jail." Pamela advanced another step.

Monica moved backwards and came up hard against the sink. She forced some air between her parched lips and tried to think. Pamela stood between her and the door. She'd have to duck around her and move fast enough to reach the exit before her sister-in-law attacked. And attack she would. Of that, Monica had no doubt.

With her injured arm, Monica was at a distinct disadvantage and she didn't want to move too quickly across the polished tiles in case she slipped. The last thing she needed was another fall that could do even more damage.

No, she needed to keep Pamela talking, distract her enough that she could make it out the door. With that thought in mind, she asked another question, making an effort to keep her tone casual and sincere.

"I understand how stressful your life must have been, Pamela. My brother's treated you abominably. He should have gone with you to counseling more often. He should have worked harder on his marriage. He took the easy way out and that wasn't fair to you."

Pamela's face twisted into an ugly grimace. "Too right, it wasn't fair! I begged him to seek help and when he told me about the little slut he was fucking, I broke down and cried. I sobbed my heart out, I pleaded with him not to destroy us. He promised to end it, to leave the stupid bitch."

"And he went back on his word," Monica murmured soothingly. "You must have been devastated. He treated you very badly."

"Of course I was devastated! And yes, he treated me like shit! He promised to stop seeing her! He *promised!*"

Her shriek of anguish filled the room and bounced off the tiled walls. Monica wanted to cover her ears, to run and hide, to escape this mad woman who was coming apart at the seams.

And then she realized she had an opportunity to find out the truth of what had happened that night. As much as she wanted to get out of there, she also wanted to clear her brother's name. The key to that lay with his wife. Monica was sure of it. She drew in a breath and eased it out, all the while silently praying for the courage to see it through.

"What happened that night, Pamela?"

Pamela blinked, as if startled from her thoughts and then her face broke into a wide smile. "You want to know what happened the night that little slut was murdered, do you?"

Monica bravely held her gaze. "Yes."

"Are you sure?" Pamela cackled. "Because as soon as I tell you, I'm going to have to kill you. That's how it works, you know."

She followed the announcement with another wild cackle. The craziness was still in her eyes. Monica glanced with longing toward the exit and then steeled herself for what was to come. She eyeballed her sister-in-law. "Tell me."

Pamela stared at her in silence for a moment longer. Eventually, she moved closer, into Monica's personal space. With the sink at her back, there was nowhere Monica could go. With a courage she was far from feeling, she held her ground.

"I suspected, of course, that your precious brother hadn't kept his word," Pamela began. "He promised to end the affair, but see, I didn't trust him anymore. That's the thing about trust: Once it's broken, it's almost impossible to restore. And even if it is, it's never the same again. Tommy deceived me in the worst possible way. He slept with another woman. And though he promised not to do it again, I didn't believe he wouldn't do it again."

"What did you do?"

"I followed him one afternoon, when he left his office. Three days a week, he was home by six. Two days, he arrived home much later. He always said they were the nights he had faculty meetings. For a long time, I believed him.

"After I found out about the affair, he came home earlier on those nights, but then gradually one night, then two, he'd be late coming home again. At first, I assumed he was still attending his meetings. Then I got to thinking. What if he wasn't at the college at all? What if he was with *her*?"

Pamela's lip curled up in a sneer. Her eyes looked distant. Then she blinked and it was as if she'd stepped back into the present again.

"So, one day you followed him?" Monica encouraged, needing to hear it all.

"Yes. It was one of his meeting days. Or so he said. The bastard left his office right on the dot of five. He hopped on a train and went to *her* place. I followed him. I was careful to keep my distance. At first, I didn't know where he was going, though I had my suspicions. They were confirmed when she greeted him with a very friendly kiss at the door."

"Oh, Pamela, I'm so sorry!" Monica cried and right at that moment, she felt ashamed of her brother and the hurt he'd inflicted on his wife. No one deserved that.

Pamela compressed her lips on a mirthless smile. "Yes, well, I should have seen it coming. I should have known he'd go back on his word. He'd lied to me once. What was stopping him from lying to me again?"

"What did you do?"

"I went home, of course. I pretended there was nothing wrong. This went on for weeks. I kept getting madder and madder. Every time he'd come home late, I knew he'd been with *her*. And then I found the letter."

"What letter?"

"The one in his office. I'd stopped by on the pretext of asking him to lunch. At least, that's what I told his colleagues. They let me wait for him in his office. I went through every drawer, every cabinet."

"What were you looking for?"

"Evidence. I had to have something concrete to prove he was still seeing her. I couldn't tell him I'd followed him. He would have laughed in my face, called me crazy. He'd already begun saying things like that. But I wasn't crazy. I knew what I saw. Anyway, I went to his office to find proof he was still involved in the affair."

"So, you found a letter. Was that how you found out Sara was pregnant?"

Pamela looked at her in surprise. "Yes. How did you know that?"

Monica sighed. "Tommy gave evidence to that effect during his testimony and of course, you mentioned the baby that night, when you called."

"Oh."

"Yes, oh. You lied on the witness stand. You

were asked whether you knew about the baby and you said no. That was when I realized something was wrong."

Pamela shrugged, as if it were of no consequence. "Anyway, I found the proof I needed. Sara wrote Tommy and told him she was six weeks pregnant. It had been three months since he'd told me he ended the affair. It was obvious he'd lied to me again."

"So, you confronted him about it," Monica guessed.

Pamela's answering smile was pure evil. "Oh, yes. I confronted him all right."

"What happened?"

"I waited for him to come home. He arrived at his usual time. I had left the letter on the kitchen counter, right where he'd drop his keys and phone. He spied the letter moments after arriving, like I knew he would. He just kind of froze. He knew exactly what it meant."

"Did he try and deny it?"

"No. It was almost like he was done with lying. He confessed that he'd tried, but hadn't ended the affair. He was in love with her and they were going to have a baby. You can imagine how I felt. Of all the ways to hurt me... I'd been desperate for a baby and he'd kept putting me off. Now he wanted to play happy family with his mistress! It was too much!"

Monica nodded, feigning sympathy. "He hurt you terribly. He needed to be punished."

"Of course he needed to be punished!" Pamela cried. "And I was the best person to do it!"

"You and Tommy got into a fight. You called me afterwards and told me about it."

"I screamed and shouted and threw a glass. He just stood there and took it. I think that made me feel even worse, that he was through fighting back, as if I didn't matter anymore, as if I wasn't worth fighting with or for."

Her voice cracked on a sob and then her shoulders began to shake. Monica wanted to offer comfort, but she was scared to get too close. This was a Pamela she'd never seen before. She was angry, irrational, unpredictable, frightening and Monica had her baby to think of. She stayed where she was.

"I *hated* him!" Pamela spat. "In that moment, I hated him more than I ever thought possible!" She fisted her hand and drove it into the tiled wall. Monica winced, but Pamela didn't seem to notice the pain.

"When he walked out that night, I knew our marriage was over. I wandered through the darkened rooms of the house, crying, drinking, screaming with anger and pain. And then I knew I had to do something. I wasn't going to be a victim again."

"You didn't fall asleep on the couch in the living room, did you, Pamela?"

Pamela's lip curled up in disgust. "Of course I didn't fall asleep! *Are you mad?* My husband walked out on me. I knew he'd gone to *her*. It was the perfect opportunity to make him pay."

"You followed him again, didn't you?" Monica said quietly.

"Yes. I followed him in my car all the way to his girlfriend's place. I got there just after he arrived. He didn't even notice me in the dark. His mind was probably on other things."

"You followed him into Sara's apartment?"

"Yes. It was easy. Her front door didn't quite close. In his haste to be with her, he didn't even notice. I slipped into her place without a word. He went straight to the bedroom. I heard them. I heard them fucking. And then they were laughing. I guessed he must have told her he was leaving me."

She paused and her breath came fast. Once again, her eyes took on a wild and unfocused look.

"I wanted to hurt him so badly. I'd brought a knife with me."

"Where did you get the knife from, Pamela?"

"The knife block in the kitchen."

Monica's heart was pounding, but she forced herself to ask the next question. "What did you do?"

"I intended to stab Tommy, to inflict upon him the kind of pain he'd inflicted on me. But before I could put my plan into action, he got up and left. It took me by surprise. I expected him to stay with her all night. He passed within a whisker of where I was hiding in the room across the hall."

"You were so angry, so hurt," Monica soothed.

"Yes, I was burning up with pain. My head was full of noise. I could barely see past my rage. Tommy left and I just charged in there, to where his little slut lay. I started yelling at her, calling her names. She was shocked to see me and I could tell she was scared. She tried to argue back with me, but I was beyond listening to anything she had to say. I screamed my anger as I lifted my arm and brought down hard. The last thing she saw was my knife."

"You stabbed her."

"Yes. Over and over and over. When it was finished, I came to my senses. I saw the blood. It was everywhere. I panicked. I didn't know what to do. I took off. All I could think of was returning home and climbing into bed and pretending I knew nothing about what happened."

"You tossed the knife in the dumpster?"

"Yes, along with a kitchen glove. I've watched enough crime shows to know I needed one."

"What about the knife you gave Blake? He just produced it in the court as evidence."

"I bought another one to match the set we had."

"So it wasn't in the dishwasher. You lied again."

"Go to the top of the class," Pamela crooned sarcastically.

"How did you get home?" Monica asked.

"I stripped off my clothes beside my car and put them in a garbage bag. I drove home in my underwear. The fire was still going in the den. I threw the clothes in and burned them. That's when I spied Tommy. He was asleep on the couch."

"He'd come home," Monica said simply.

"Yes. I still don't know why."

"What did you do next?"

"I went upstairs and took a shower and then I called you. Yes, after all that had happened, I was still upset. I called you and you told me to go to bed, that everything would be all right. You didn't believe me, did you?"

Monica didn't know what to say. Pamela spoke the truth. The night she called, Monica could tell Pamela was drunk. She'd known her brother and his wife had been having marital problems. She just assumed Pamela was exaggerating when she rambled on about Tommy and one of his students.

"I'm sorry, Pamela. You called me in the middle of the night. I was half asleep."

Pamela stared at Monica, accusation burning in her eyes. "You always took his side."

Monica shook her head, feeling helpless. "I tried to stay out of it, Pamela. I didn't want to take anyone's side."

"Yeah, right," Pamela sneered. "He's your older brother. Your hero. The golden boy. You thought he could do no wrong."

Monica refrained from replying. It was true. She idolized her older brother. It had been a shock to discover he'd been involved in an affair. Still, she never believed him capable of murder and she was sadly relieved to discover her faith in him in that regard had been well placed.

"Anyway," Pamela continued, "it's of little consequence now. I showered and changed and eventually collapsed on my bed. I was still there the next morning when the police arrived and arrested Tommy."

Monica stared at her sister-in-law and could

hardly believe what had happened. Her sister-in-law had murdered Tommy's mistress and had very nearly gotten away with it. Monica glanced toward the exit and took the tiniest step forward.

"Stop right there! Where are you going?" Pamela shouted, her eyes wild.

Monica froze. "I...I need to get going. The closing statements are about to commence."

"Ha!" Pamela cried. "As if you care about that! You're going straight out there to tell somebody what I just told you. Admit it!"

"No, Pamela!" Monica lied, desperate to say anything to appease her. "I promise! I won't say a word. But I've been there for every minute of Tommy's trial. I want to be there right to the end."

"Bullshit!" Pamela cried. "You Radfords are both the same! As if I'm going to believe you when you tell me you're going to march on out of here and not say a word about what I've just told you! Do you think I'm *stupid*?"

The last words were spat in Monica's face. She cringed and shrunk back against the sink. Fury poured off Pamela in waves and the craziness was back on her face. Fear held Monica frozen as she tried desperately to think of a way to escape. The exit door was only a few yards away, yet it could have been miles.

And then Pamela took off her shoes. She brandished one of her five-inch Jimmy Choos. Monica had never thought of the shoes as weapons, but all of a sudden, with the heel inches from her face, it looked lethal.

"Pamela, please. Don't do this."

Pamela cackled. "I've already stabbed a woman to death. Do you think I don't have the stomach for it?"

Desperation warred with panic. She had to stay calm. Any moment, the crazy woman in front of her could put her eye out—or worse.

"Please, Pamela. Think about this. I've done nothing to hurt you. You need to let me go."

"Like hell!" And with that, Pamela lunged toward her, her stiletto at the ready.

Monica screamed.

CHAPTER 23

"Colby! There you are! I've been looking for you everywhere."

Colby turned at the sound of his assistant as Collette hurried toward him. "Do you have the phone records?" he asked.

"Yes." She handed him a sheaf of papers. "I've checked the night in question. Pamela Radford called someone at two-forty-three in the morning from her home."

Colby flicked through the pages and found the call Collette had highlighted. He looked at the cell phone number and immediately recognized it as belonging to Monica. His gut tightened.

"This is Monica Radford's number. She was telling the truth. Pamela called her the night of the murder."

"What did Monica tell you?" Collette asked, her expression somber.

"She told me that Pamela lied about the defendant's alibi. The fight Pamela and Tommy had was vicious. Monica didn't believe the woman would have tucked him in later that night. Something's off."

Shock widened Collette's eyes. "That means he's once again in the spotlight. We're going to win this! We can put the guy away." She grinned.

"Not so fast. See, Monica's convinced there's something odd about Pamela's testimony and her motivation for lying on the stand. It got me to thinking about who else might have had a reason to see Sara Nakamura dead."

Collette shrugged dismissively. "Who cares? We have our man. The police are convinced he did it. Besides, it's in Monica Radford's best interests to try and convince you someone else did the killing. The defendant's her brother."

Colby thought about the way she'd lied and deceived him about their baby. He wanted to dismiss anything she said as unreliable, but his gut was telling him different. "I think there might be more to it than that. I think she might be onto something."

"What exactly did she tell you?"

"She was in the courtroom when Pamela testified. She came up to me after and told me Pamela had lied. When I asked her how she knew that, she said her sister-in-law had called her late that night. Pamela Radford was hysterical and this was after her husband had returned home. According to Monica, there was no way the woman would have been tucking him in that night."

Collette's expression turned thoughtful. "That's interesting."

"Yes. And there's something else: Both Thomas and Pamela Radford testified that they'd had a fight. Why would they fight if he was going to give up the mistress?"

"*Hmmm*," Collette replied. "Where's Monica now?"

Colby looked around the waiting area where they stood outside the courtroom. "I don't know. I haven't seen her for a while."

"I saw Pamela go into the bathroom earlier," Collette offered.

A sudden feeling of dread flooded through Colby's veins and settled in an icy lump in his gut. He remembered something about pregnant women needing frequent restroom stops. Could Monica have run into Pamela in the bathroom and had it out with her? If so, where was she now?

As if reading his mind, Collette frowned. "Do you think they might be together? That Monica would confront her about this?"

"Yes, I think that's exactly what she'd do. She was sure there was something off about Pamela's testimony." He paused and was filled with a sudden sense of urgency. "We have to find them."

They spread out, each heading off in a different direction. Small groups of people huddled in conversation. Plastic chairs that lined the walls outside the courtroom were filled with people. Some of them were witnesses, some of them, police. A few were defendants waiting to be called to go in. Colby scanned their faces. None of them were Monica.

He cursed silently under his breath. He was

becoming more and more convinced she was in danger. If she confronted Pamela about her lies, who knew how the woman might react? If Monica had told him the truth, Pamela was likely the murderer.

The thought that Monica could be in jeopardy sent his heart rate skyrocketing. He had no proof that this was the case, but his gut was churning and he'd learned from past experience to listen to it. He wished he'd been kinder to her when they'd last spoken. He'd still been angry and upset about her deception, but despite that, he couldn't deny he was still in love with her. Love wasn't something that could be switched on and off when things turned bad. It didn't work like that. She'd wounded him terribly, but his feelings for her hadn't just disappeared. She was carrying his baby. She would forever be the mother of his child and despite everything, he still wanted to be part of their lives.

He saw Blake and Natalie and went up to them, his breath coming fast. "Have you seen Monica?"

They frowned in unison. "No," Blake replied.

"Is something wrong?" Natalie asked, her brow furrowed with concern.

"I'm not sure. I need to find her."

"Have you tried the bathroom? She's pregnant. Pregnant women have to pee a lot." Natalie smiled.

Colby nodded. His first instinct might be on the mark. Collette had seen Pamela in the bathroom. It was possible Monica had run into her there. He forced a smile in Natalie's direction. "Would you mind checking for me?"

She shrugged. "Sure."

She took off in the direction of the restrooms. Colby followed her. He wanted to make certain Monica was all right. Natalie put her shoulder to the door that led into the women's bathroom. A moment later, she let out a fearful scream.

Colby pushed her aside and raced into the restroom. Monica was pinned against the sink, looking terrified. Pamela held a lethal-looking stiletto in her hand, just inches from Monica's cheek.

"Drop it!" Colby shouted. At the same time, he hurled himself toward Pamela.

She screamed in outrage and lashed out at Monica, but it was too late. Colby plowed into her and the two of them went flying. He twisted his body at the last minute and took the brunt of the fall. They fell hard against the floor tiles.

"Let go of me, you bastard! Let go of me before I kill you!"

Colby ignored Pamela's wild screams. Pinning her hands out of the way, he rolled until he was straddling her hips. Even then, she wriggled and kicked and did her best to escape his hold. The restroom door flew open and Blake and two security guards stood there, taking in the scene.

"Stay where you are!" one of the guards yelled, brandishing a gun.

At the sight of it, Pamela went limp beneath him. All the fight went out of her. She screamed her frustration to the heavens. Colby wished he could block his ears.

He looked across at Monica who was huddled against the far wall. "Are you all right?" he shouted over the din.

She nodded, her eyes huge and scared. His heart tripped over. With a gruff request to the guards to take care of Pamela, he stood and went to Monica. Without hesitation, he took her in his arms.

Unmindful of her injury, she threw herself against him, crying out in relief. "Thank goodness you found us! She murdered Sara! She was going to hurt me! Oh, Colby! Thank goodness you arrived in time."

He stroked her hair and held her close, murmuring words of comfort in her ear. Gradually, her trembling stopped. She pulled slightly away and stared up at him.

"You saved me."

A thousand thoughts went through his mind, but his overwhelming feeling was one of gratitude. "Thank God you're okay. I don't know what I would have done if I'd lost you."

"What made you come looking for me?"

"Collette returned with the phone records. They proved you were telling the truth. Pamela phoned you late on the night of the murder. I remembered what you said about sensing there was something strange about Pamela's testimony and began to wonder what else she might have been concealing. I went looking for you. I wanted to make sure you were all right. I couldn't find you or Pamela anywhere. Natalie suggested you might be in here."

He stared down at her. "You confronted Pamela, didn't you? You confronted her with the truth."

Monica shuddered. "Yes."

Colby wrapped her in his arms once again. "My brave, brave girl. I nearly lost you! What would I have done without you? Don't ever scare me like that again!"

She lifted her head to look at him and tears glinted in her eyes. "Are you still mad at me?"

"Yes, but that doesn't mean I don't love you."

Her eyes widened and filled with hope. "You... love me?"

Emotion formed a lump in his throat. He nodded. "Yes."

The tears that filled her eyes now spilled over and trickled down her cheeks. Her smile was soft and tremulous. "You *love* me."

"God help me, but I do! I didn't want to, especially after everything that happened, but I can't help it. I love you and I love our baby. I want to be with you, always."

Her tears were flowing freely, now. She swiped at them with the back of her hand. "I'm so sorry, Colby. I should never have deceived you! I should have been honest with you from the start. It was a stupid plan. I look back now and wonder what I was thinking."

He nodded. "You and me, both." He paused and cleared his throat. "I'm beyond relieved you're all right, but... You owe me an explanation."

She tensed and then sighed. "You're right."

He hugged her gently again and pressed a kiss against her hair. "Let's not do this here. I need to go back into the courtroom and inform the judge about the latest developments."

"And set Tommy free," she added with a soft smile.

"Yes. And set Tommy free."

In the end, it only took a few minutes with the judge in her chambers to explain what had happened and she was more than willing to return to the court and dismiss the charges against Monica's brother. Tommy looked just as stunned as any of them when he became aware of what had happened. Blake came over and shook Colby's hand and congratulated him on a job well done. Colby returned the sentiment.

The two men agreed to catch up for a drink in the near future. This was loudly seconded by Natalie and Monica. There were hugs and kisses and a few tears from the women as the realization sunk in. The trial was over. Tommy was free.

Colby opened the door to his apartment and stood back to allow Monica to enter. She'd been quiet on the walk home, after bidding farewell to Natalie and Blake and Tommy outside the courtroom. He understood her somber mood. He might have expressed his love for her, but the truth was, they still had plenty to sort out. To his relief, they'd barely cleared the hallway on their way into the kitchen before she tackled the subject.

"I want to say again how sorry I am that I deceived you that way. It was unforgivable."

He took a slow, deep breath, determined to hold on to his temper this time. "Let's start with your crazy baby plan. I just don't understand why you'd do it like that. You're a beautiful woman. You could have your pick of men. Why wouldn't you find someone, date for a while, become a couple and go from there. People do it all the time. Why not you?"

She compressed her lips and frowned in thought. "I look back now and wonder what I was thinking," she admitted quietly. "I guess I didn't want the complication of a relationship. My parents had divorced when I was young; a lot of my friends have gone through broken marriages. I was happy with where I was in life. I had a good job, a nice apartment. I was confident I didn't need a man."

"But what about love, companionship, support? Someone to have your back? There's so much more to a relationship that you haven't mentioned."

She nodded. "You're right. After I met you and started to get to know you, I realized how much I was missing out on, how much I was shortchanging myself by not letting you into my life. By that time, I was already pregnant and I was terrified if I told you the truth about the way our baby had been conceived, you'd hate me. I didn't want the father of my baby feeling like that about me. Besides, I hadn't had a father, not in any real sense and I never felt like I'd missed out because of that. I guess I selfishly thought my baby would feel the same way."

He cupped her face between his hands in an effort to make her see. "My parents divorced, too. Okay, I was a bit older than you when it happened, but it still affected me. I wouldn't wish it on anyone and I never once wished I didn't have a dad. My father's an important part of my life. I couldn't imagine him not being there."

Fresh tears glinted in her eyes. "I'm so sorry. I can't believe I ever thought going it alone was the best way to do this."

He pulled her close and pressed a kiss against her hair. "*Shh*, honey. Don't cry. It's okay. Let's put all this behind us. What's done is done. From here on in, we're going to love each other, care for each other and be honest with each other—no matter what. Agreed?"

She smiled. "Agreed."

His arms tightened about her. He loved the feeling of her in his arms, in his life. This was how it was supposed to be. The two of them together, forever.

It was a long time later, with Monica snuggled up in Colby's arms that he told her what the police had found when they conducted a second search of Tommy's home.

"The first time, they were only looking at your

brother," Colby explained. "He and Pamela no longer shared a bedroom. The police went through Tommy's room, his closet, his bathroom. They turned it upside down looking for evidence and came up empty. Pamela wasn't on their radar. They didn't go near her end of the house."

"This time they did," she guessed.

"Yes. They found a pair of shoes hidden in a box in the back of her closet. They were covered in blood spatter. They've sent them away for testing. I'm sure the blood will come back belonging to Sara Nakamura."

"Pamela told me she changed out of her clothes before she left Sara's apartment. She burned them in the fireplace in her house."

"Perhaps she forgot to take off her shoes? Or maybe she decided to keep a reminder of what she'd done," Colby mused. "Who knows? But if the blood belongs to Sara, coupled with what Pamela told you, we should have enough to put her away for a considerable amount of time."

Monica sighed quietly. "I'm so glad we discovered all this before it was too late. Tommy was so shocked when I told him, but also so relieved."

"Yes, he called while you were in the shower. He wanted to thank you once again. He had no idea that Pamela had murdered Sara. He's sad and confused."

"It makes *me* so sad. He's lost everything."

"Yes. I guess he'll have time to come to terms with it. At least he's no longer looking at a decade or two in jail."

Monica heard the anger in Colby's voice and knew it was directed at himself. She squeezed his arm reassuringly. "It's not your fault you were convinced Tommy was guilty. You were only going on the evidence you had."

He nodded, but looked unconvinced. "Yeah."

She sat up on one elbow and stared down at him. "Listen to me, Colby Shearer! You are an excellent prosecutor. You were only doing your job. Do you hear me?"

A reluctant smile turned up his lips. "Yes, ma'am. I hear you. You're practically yelling at me."

She poked out her tongue, but settled herself back against him. "You're a good man, Colby Shearer. And I love you."

Colby rolled her over and pressed a gentle kiss against her lips. His hand rested on her rounded belly. "I love you, too, Monica Radford. I love you to the moon and back. Today, tomorrow, forever."

"Amen," she whispered and smiled.

NOTE TO READERS

I do hope you have enjoyed reading Colby and Monica's story. If you've enjoyed this book, please feel free to leave a review for Lies and Deception at Goodreads and your favorite digital retailer. Every review is very much appreciated.

Receive a free book when you sign up for my newsletter if you would like to receive news on upcoming stories, release dates, book launches and other snippets. I love to receive feedback from my readers. Please feel free to contact me at chris@christaylorauthor.com.au

Ordinary Evil is the next book in The Sydney Legal Series.

Here's a sneak peek:

Excerpt from

Ordinary EVIL

BOOK FIVE OF THE SYDNEY LEGAL SERIES

CHRIS TAYLOR

When a nine-year-old girl fails to arrive home after hopping off the school bus, a community is galvanized into action. Daisy Green, a lawyer at Sydney Legal, has a daughter, Emma, who travels on the same bus. She's beyond grateful her daughter is safe, but feels for the mother of the girl who has disappeared.

Christian Grayson is also a lawyer at Sydney Legal and he's closer to the awful incident than anyone might think. His uncle is the bus driver and Christian is currently staying in his uncle's house. Christian and Daisy bond over their combined efforts to find the missing girl.

Then Emma disappears on her way home from school and the community is put on high alert. Daisy is beyond herself with terror. What has happened to Emma and where is she? Daisy will have to rely on Christian to find out...

Chapter 1

Daisy Green pulled her cell phone from the pocket of her suit jacket and checked the time. She grimaced. If she didn't get a move on, she'd be late collecting her daughter from the bus stop. Again.

Emma had barely spoken to her during the short walk to their house the last time she'd been late and Daisy didn't blame her. It seemed more and more often, Daisy was held up at work and her seven-year-old was forced to walk the hundred yards from the bus stop to their home on her own.

It wasn't like Daisy planned it that way. She tried really hard to leave work in time to meet Emma's bus. It was just that her work as a lawyer at the prestigious Sydney Legal didn't always run on time and it seemed like the day was barely beginning when three o'clock rolled around. Often she was meeting with clients or on the phone and it was difficult to cut either activity short, particularly when the client was a juvenile who was in trouble with the law.

As a child advocate, Daisy loved her work, but it was quite often demanding and stressful and upsetting and she found it hard to leave her young clients in the middle of a serious conversation so that she could collect her daughter from the bus stop. It would be easier if she had someone she could rely on to meet Emma every day, but the fact was, there was no one.

Daisy closed her eyes on a quiet sigh. Peter had been gone five years. It should have been long enough for her to have adjusted to living life on her own. Even before his death, he'd barely spent more than a month or two at a time at home. As an officer in the Australian army, he'd often been sent on deployment. He'd done three tours of Afghanistan before he was killed by an IED. The vehicle he'd been traveling in had run right over the improvised explosive device. The driver had also been killed.

It saddened her to know her daughter would never know her father. Emma had been two when Peter died. All she knew of the man who'd adored her was what Daisy told her and the photos and pictures that filled nearly every room of their house. Some days, Daisy wondered if it was healthy to have so many reminders of Peter, but she couldn't bring herself to remove any of them. He'd been the love and light of her life, even if it had been for such a short time.

The sound of the phone ringing at her elbow interrupted her morose thoughts. She leaned over to answer it and then paused. If she didn't leave now, she'd be late and Emma would give her the silent treatment again. It wasn't that her daughter meant to be rude. She was merely expressing her disappointment that her mother hadn't made it to the bus in time.

Daisy understood Emma's need to keep her close. She was the only parent Emma had. Daisy could well understand her daughter's insecurity and tried hard not to exacerbate it by being late.

Ignoring the phone, she pushed away from her desk and gathered her handbag and coat from the wooden locker that stood in one corner of the room. The phone continued to ring, but she forced the ever-present guilt aside and strode to the door. With a brief wave of farewell to her secretary on her way past the reception desk, she headed toward the elevators.

"Momma! Momma! You made it!"

At the sight of Emma running toward her, Daisy smiled. A moment later, her daughter threw herself at her. Daisy laughed and hugged Emma close, pressing a kiss against her blond hair.

"Of course I made it, honey!"

"Last Friday you were late," her daughter muttered, her tone faintly accusatory.

Daisy nodded. "You're right. And I'm still sorry about that. Sometimes things come up at work and it's hard to get away. I—"

"I know. You're a very important person with a very important job," Emma interrupted.

Daisy frowned and wondered where Emma had gained her insight. Had she been talking to some of her friends, the daughters of two other lawyers Daisy worked with? The three of them often bemoaned their workload and the difficulty they had leaving the office on time. At least the other two had husbands to help share the burden. Sometimes Daisy wished her parents lived closer.

"We got to do art today at school, Momma. I painted a picture of my Dad."

Daisy's heart skipped and she swallowed the lump that had formed in her throat. "Did you, honey? That's nice."

"Yes, he was as tall as a giant and as strong as a bear and he had curly blond hair and brown eyes, just like mine. And the nicest smile you've ever seen. You always tell me how much you loved his smile."

Daisy stared in shock at her daughter, a little taken aback. Emma looked back at her, her face a picture of innocence. She looked so much like her father, a father she'd never know... Daisy blinked back tears and pulled her daughter close.

"You're right, honey. Your daddy did have a lovely smile."

Emma pulled back gently and regarded her mother intently. "Do you still miss him?"

A surge of emotion tightened Daisy's chest, blocking off her air supply, but she forced herself to reply. "Yes, sweetheart. I miss him very much."

"Do you think I'll ever have another daddy?"

Daisy started in surprise. "Why would you ask something like that?"

Emma shrugged and stared at the ground. "I don't know. Annie Walker said she's getting a new daddy. Her momma met him at the hardware store a few months ago. He's moving in with them over the weekend."

Daisy's mind spun as she tried to think of something to say. The thought of dating again filled her with panic. Despite the gentle urging of her colleagues and the recent marriage of her best friend, Sally-Ann Li, she'd resisted their attempts at matchmaking. She was happy on her own. She didn't need a man in her life. Most of the time, she even believed it.

Giving Emma another quick hug, she took the coward's way out and avoided the question. "Let's go inside. It's getting cold out."

As if on cue, a gust of wind blew across the path in front of them and sent dry leaves and grass clippings spinning in the air. Daisy walked beside Emma in companionable silence. It was broken by the ringing of her phone. Tugging it out of pocket, she glanced at the screen and answered it.

"Hi, Marcie. How are you?"

"Daisy! Thank goodness you answered! Did you meet Emma today at the bus stop?"

Daisy frowned at the fear in the woman's voice. "Yes, of course. She's here with me now. Is there something wrong?"

"Lila hasn't made it home. I called the bus driver and he said he dropped her off at her usual stop. She should have been home by now. I got caught up in traffic and arrived home a little late.

I've already walked her bus route. She's nowhere to be found. Can you ask Emma if she talked to Lila-Jane on the bus? Perhaps she said something to her about her plans?"

Misgivings swirled in Daisy's stomach, filling her with dread. Her grip tightened on Emma's hand. "Of course. Hang on." Covering the mouthpiece, Daisy tugged at Emma's hand to gain her attention. "Honey, did you see Lila-Jane on the bus this afternoon?"

"Yes. She was sitting a few rows behind me."

"Did you speak with her?"

"No."

Daisy nodded and returned her attention to the phone. "I'm sorry, Marcie. Emma didn't speak with Lila this afternoon."

The woman on the other end of the phone cried out in a voice that was tinged with panic. "Where *is* she? She knows better than to go wandering off. She knows the rules. She's to come straight home after she gets off the bus. No detours. I knew I shouldn't have started letting her walk home by herself. It's just that, she's nearly nine and she kept bugging me, telling me she was old enough to do it. After all, it's only half a block. Oh, God! What if something's happened to her? What if someone saw her get off the bus and has driven away with her?"

Marcie's tone rose to a strident cry filled with fear and panic and Daisy immediately understood. At the same time, she made an effort to comfort the woman.

"I'm sure she'll turn up, Marcie. It's been less

than ten minutes. Perhaps she got distracted on the way home. There's a park right by your place. Did you check there?"

"Yes! I've checked everywhere! I can't find her!"

"Are you sure she got off the bus?"

"Yes! I already told you. I called the driver. He said he dropped her at her usual stop."

Daisy fell silent and tried to ignore the increasing dread that filled her veins. Unconsciously, she drew Emma close. "Is there anything I can do to help? Perhaps I can come over and look for her with you?"

"Would you? All I want to do is call the police, but then I feel foolish. She's only been gone ten minutes."

"Of course I'm happy to help and Emma can help, too. We'll come right away."

The woman's relief was palpable. "Thank you, Daisy! I really appreciate it. I'm sure I'm over reacting, but she's my baby and she's never been late before. I just want her home."

"We'll find her, I'm certain," Daisy reassured the woman and prayed silently that her words would prove true.

Ending the call, she tossed her phone into her handbag and once again took Emma's hand. Walking quickly, she headed toward their house.

"Is anything the matter?" Emma asked.

Daisy shot her daughter a quick look and forced a smile. "I don't think so, honey. Lila-Jane Morrissey hasn't arrived home from school. Her mother's a little concerned."

Emma frowned. "Did she miss her stop?"

"No. Lila-Jane's mom called the bus driver. He said he dropped her off."

"Maybe one of her neighbors has puppies, like the Owens family do. I love stopping by their place to pat the puppies."

Daisy stared down at her daughter in surprise. "Do you stop there on the days when I've been late meeting you at the bus stop?"

Emma kept her gaze focused on her feet. She scuffed the pavement with her shoe. "Yes. Sometimes. But I never stay more than a few moments."

Daisy opened her mouth to reprimand her daughter and then closed it again. It wasn't Emma's fault that sometimes her mother was late meeting her off the bus. Coming to a halt, she bent down until she and her daughter were on eye level.

"I know how much you love puppies, Em, but it's important you listen to me. I don't want you stopping on your way home for anything. I'll try even harder to make sure I'm here on time, but if I'm not and you start walking home, I want you to promise me you'll go straight home. No stopping for puppies or anything else. Do you understand?"

"But, Mom—"

"No 'buts', Emma." Taking her daughter by the arms, Daisy maintained stern eye contact. "This is important, Emma. I need to know that you'll do as I say."

A stubborn expression crossed her young daughter's face and Daisy's heart clenched at the sight. She looked so much like her father... Still, this was important and Daisy wasn't about to give in.

"Emma..." Her voice held a warning.

The little girl's shoulders slumped on a sigh and she slowly lowered her gaze. "It's not like I go into their yard. It's only if the puppies are close enough to the fence. I—"

"If you want to pat the puppies, honey, we can do it when I get home. Even on the few occasions I haven't been here to meet you off the bus, I haven't been far away. Now, I need you to tell me you're on board with this and that you're going to do as I say."

The girl remained silent. "Em? Look at me." Daisy's tone brooked no argument. With another sigh, Emma looked up at her.

"No stopping for the puppies, okay?"

"Okay." The words came reluctantly, but were issued just the same.

"Promise?"

"Promise."

Daisy hugged her daughter close and then just as swiftly set her away. "We need to hurry. I promised Lila-Jane's mom we'd help look for her. Come on."

"Do you think Lila-Jane ran away?" Emma asked.

Daisy frowned. "No, honey. Why would you say that? Did Lila-Jane mention something to you?"

"No, but I'm reading a book about a boy who lives with his evil step-mother and he decides to run away."

"Lila-Jane's mom is lovely. I'm sure her daughter hasn't run away."

Emma shrugged as if the issue was of no concern. "Whatever."

At the thought of Marcie's desperation, Daisy took hold of Emma's hand and together they picked up their pace. In no time at all, the two of them had climbed the steps to Marcie's house. Daisy pressed the doorbell. Almost instantly, the door was opened and Marcie's worried face appeared.

"Oh, thank goodness you're here! Just knowing I have someone else looking for her is such a relief."

Daisy offered a smile of reassurance. "We'll find her, Marcie."

Ignoring her comment, Marcie bent low and spoke to Emma. "Are you sure you didn't talk to Lila-Jane on the bus?"

"Yes, I'm sure. She was behind me, sitting next to Jonathon Cleaver. Maybe you should ask him."

Marcie immediately stood and looked hopefully at Daisy. "Do you have Mary Cleaver's number? Perhaps Lila-Jane said something to him?"

Daisy shook her head. "I'm sorry, I don't. Why don't you call the school? They probably won't give you her number, but they might call her for you."

"Yes, yes. That's a good idea." Marcie patted her pockets in search of her phone. "Oh, dear! Where did I leave my phone? I thought I put it in my pocket. I must have left it inside. I—"

"Here. Use mine." Daisy unlocked her phone and handed it to Lila-Jane's mom. She moved a short distance away to give Marcie some privacy while she made the call. A few moments later, Marcie was finished.

"What did they say?" Daisy asked.

"They're going to call her and get back to me." Her voice faded away and she stared off in the distance. The trees stood stark and naked in the winter breeze. All of a sudden, she shivered and rubbed her hands up and down her arms. Daisy moved closer. She didn't know the woman well, but no one should be forced to endure such a thing alone.

Words of reassurance formed in her mind. They seemed so ineffectual, but she said them just the same. "It's going to be all right, Marcie."

Marcie merely offered her a quick nod, as if beyond words at that time. The two of them stood there in silence. Emma scuffed the toe of her shoe along the porch. A blue wren darted among the bushes that formed a hedge along the front fence. The stillness was broken by the sound of Daisy's phone. Both women sighed in relief.

Daisy checked the screen. "It's the school."

Chapter 2

Christian Grayson reached for a beer from inside the door of his uncle's fridge. Kicking the door closed with his foot, he twisted the top off the bottle and tilted it to his lips. Swallowing greedily, he relished the cold yeasty taste. Thank God it was Friday. It had been a long week.

Padding in his socks across the living room, he pushed open the sliding doors that led out onto the back deck. Making himself comfortable on one of the loungers that filled the small space, he sighed quietly in relief. He'd survived another week.

Almost immediately, he was beset with a barrage of memories of Justine. He wondered if she was even now enjoying a glass of wine, relishing the idea of the weekend that lay ahead. Had she stopped by for pizza on her way home from work, like she used to do when they were together? Perhaps the new man in her life had other ideas? Was she even now making memories with someone else? Memories that should have belonged to him?

Cursing under his breath, Christian took another gulp of beer. *What did he care what Justine was doing anymore?* She'd broken up with him more than three months ago and God knows she'd withdrawn from him emotionally weeks before that. He should have guessed there was something going on with her, but the truth was, he'd been so immersed in yet another court case, he hadn't realized anything was wrong. When she came to him with her suitcase in hand and told him she was leaving, he'd been taken completely by surprise. Which just went to show how out of touch he was, just like she'd said.

She needed to be with someone who appreciated her, she told him. Someone who'd be there for her. *Really* there, not just a man who made all the right noises, but who spent more time with his clients or buried knee deep in cases than he did with his live-in girlfriend.

Shocked that the woman he thought he would marry was walking out on him, Christian had made a desperate plea to keep her. He promised to be more attentive, to make time for the two of them. He told her he'd take her to Sydney that very weekend. They could take in a live show, visit the markets, wander along the beach. All the things they didn't get to do living in the country.

"It's too late, Christian. I've found someone else."

And with those words, she tore his heart in two.

The sound of the front door opening snagged his attention. He forced the memories aside and took another sip from his beer. "I'm out here,

Uncle. Grab a drink and come and join me."

A few moments later, the sliding door opened and Frank Grayson stepped out onto the deck. His uncle was still dressed in his bus driver's uniform. Christian smiled at him in greeting and saluted him with his bottle.

"Good to see you, Uncle Frank. I bet you're just as glad as I am to see the end of the working week."

His uncle grimaced. "Yes. I just wish it hadn't ended in such a distressing way."

Christian's smile faded. "What do you mean?"

"A little girl from my bus run hasn't arrived home. Her mother's frantic."

Christian sat up in the lounger and leaned forward. "What do you mean she hasn't arrived home?"

"Just what I said. I dropped her off at her usual stop and continued on my way. Her mother called me a short time later to say she didn't come home." Frank shook his head. "I don't know where she went."

"Did any of the other kids see anything?"

"She's the last child on the bus. There was no one else. I was already on my way home when I took the call from her mother."

Christian shook his head. He didn't have any children, but he could imagine how concerned the mother of the missing child must be. "Did you see anyone strange hanging around the bus stop? Anyone you don't normally see?"

"No. The police have already asked me that question. There was no one. At least, not that I saw. I only pulled up for a moment. Just long enough to let her off the bus." Frank ran a hand through his sparse gray hair and dropped into the nearest chair with a heavy sigh.

"It's not your fault, Uncle. Besides, kids go missing in the city all the time. She's probably gone to the shops or something and is taking longer than usual to get home. I'm sure she'll turn up."

His uncle looked at him, the lines on his weathered face creasing in concern. "She's been missing for more than two hours. Where could she be?"

"Did anyone try to call her?"

"She's nine, Christian. She doesn't have a phone."

He shrugged. He couldn't keep up with kids these days. It seemed everywhere he looked they were plugged into one device or another. He remembered the days when he was at school when all the entertainment to be had was a book or a pack of playing cards. *How times had changed.*

His uncle stood and headed toward the door.

"Where are you going?"

"I'm going out to look for her. I can't sit here while a little girl is missing. I was the last person to see her. I have to find out if she's all right."

"It's not your fault she's gone missing," Christian said.

His uncle regarded him grimly. "I know, but I feel responsible just the same. I shouldn't have let her off the bus without her mother being there."

"Does she normally get off the bus alone?"

"Yes, but—"

"But, nothing. You weren't to know she was going to turn up missing, Uncle Frank. I think it's wonderful you care about the kids who ride your bus, but once they climb off it, they're no longer your responsibility, no matter how you feel."

"I get it, Christian. I do. But it doesn't change anything. I'm going out to join the search party. I'm not sure what time I'll be back."

His uncle disappeared the way he'd come and Christian didn't hold back a sigh. There was no way he was going to be able to enjoy his Friday evening knowing a little girl in his neighborhood was missing. Finishing the last of his drink, he stood and followed his uncle back inside.

Frank was in the process of pulling on a coat. The sun had long since set and the air held the chill of winter. Compared to many cities around the world, Sydney experienced a mild winter with temperatures rarely falling anywhere near freezing, but still, July wasn't the time to be outdoors without boots and a warm jacket. Stifling another sigh, Christian followed suit and proceeded out the door behind his uncle.

"Do we have any idea where this child might have gone?" he asked as he climbed into the passenger side of his uncle's pickup.

"No. The mother has spoken to some of her daughter's friends. No one has a clue where she might have gone."

"Have the police organized a search party?"

"I'm not sure. They hadn't at the time I spoke to

them. That was about an hour ago. I'm guessing that they might have done something about it now."

Frank checked over his shoulder before reversing the truck out of the drive. Christian's thoughts once again turned to the mother of the missing girl. A wave of sympathy swept over him and he sent a silent prayer heavenward that the child was found unharmed. Night had well and truly settled in and with it a drop in temperature.

"What was she wearing?" he asked.

"A pair of jeans and a red sweater."

"What's her name?"

"Lila-Jane Morrissey. She's a third grader at Chatswood Elementary. She's been catching my bus for the past year. Such a sweet thing. And so polite. She never fails to say hello and good-bye. Not like a lot of kids these days who walk past me like I don't exist."

Christian didn't respond. He knew exactly what his uncle met. He came across kids every day in the course of his job who'd failed to master the simple art of good manners. He didn't like to think he'd become immune to the rudeness. Rather, he chose to ignore it in the pursuit of gaining the young offender's trust and getting to the truth of what might have happened to cause them to be in his office in the first place.

His uncle continued to drive in silence. They were barely half a dozen blocks away when Frank pulled into the driveway of a modest two-story bungalow. The place was aglow with lights and several other vehicles lined both sides of the street.

Frank pulled the car to a halt and switched off the ignition.

"This is Lila-Jane's place. Her mom's been doing it tough since the divorce. I can't imagine how she feels right now."

Christian acknowledged his uncle's comments with a nod. Frank opened the door and climbed out of his truck and Christian followed suit. The number of cars surrounding them indicated at least half a dozen or more people had come out to show their support. He could only guess that they were inside the house. Frank walked up the three steps that led to the front door and rapped sharply on the wooden panel.

Christian waited off to one side, not sure what he was doing there. Before he could formulate an answer to his unspoken question, the door opened. His breath caught in his throat at the sight of the woman who stood on the other side. Her dark hair gleamed in the porch light like thick, rich molten chocolate. The silken threads curled around her ear and kissed the very top of her neck. Her eyes, large and round, matched almost exactly the color of her hair. And then it hit him. He'd seen her before.

In fact, he'd seen her only a few hours earlier. Her name was Daisy Green. She was a lawyer who worked on his floor. Or rather, *he* worked on hers. He was the newcomer, the one who'd only been in town a few months, escaping his life in the country. He'd come to Sydney in an effort to surround himself with the anonymity of the city; licking his wounds in private and mending his broken heart. Still, he'd managed to notice Daisy Green, even if he had yet to utter a word in her hearing.

She pushed the door open. A frown marred the smooth skin of her forehead. "Mr Grayson? What are you doing here?"

Frank nodded in greeting. "Hello, Mrs Green. I heard Lila-Jane was still missing. I wanted to stop by and see if I could help."

Christian's heart sank.

Mrs Green.

She was married.

Ordinary Evil will be released on
27 February, 2018 and is available for pre-order
from your favorite digital retailer.

ABOUT THE AUTHOR

Chris Taylor grew up on a farm in north-west New South Wales, Australia. She always had a thirst for stories and recalls writing her first book at the ripe old age of eight. Always a lover of romance and happily-ever-afters, a career in criminal law sparked her interest in intrigue and suspense. For Chris to be able to combine romance with suspense in her books is a dream come true.

Chris is married to Linden and is the mother of five children. If not behind her computer, you can find her doing the school run, taxiing children to swimming lessons, football, ballet and cricket. In her spare time, Chris loves to read her favorite authors who include Richard North Patterson, Sandra Brown, Kathleen E Woodiwiss and Jude Devereaux.

You can find out more about Chris and sign up for her newsletter at her website:

http://www.christaylorauthor.com.au